I AM

NOT A

MONSTER

I AM NOT A MONSTER

CARME CHAPARRO

TRANSLATED BY DICK CLUSTER

Previously published as *No soy un monstruo* by Planeta in 2017 in Spain. Translated from Spanish by Dick Cluster. First published in English by AmazonCrossing in 2018.

Published by AmazonCrossing, Seattle

www.apub.com

Amazon, the Amazon logo, and AmazonCrossing are trademarks of Amazon.com, Inc., or its affiliates.

ISBN-13: 9781503905375
ISBN-10: 1503905373

Cover design by Caroline Teagle Johnson

Printed in the United States of America

For Berna, Laia, and Emma, for anchoring me to happiness.
For Mama, for everything.

For my father.

I want to dig in the earth with my teeth,
I want to clear away the earth bit by bit
in dry and fiery mouthfuls.

I want to mine the earth until I find you
and kiss your righteous skull,
untie the gag, and bring you back.

—Miguel Hernández, "Elegy for Ramón Sijé"

Time to try again.

Not just any child will do.

It has to be a careful choice. Otherwise so many months of waiting, so much work, and so much thinking and rethinking won't be worth a damn.

Nor will what comes after. Success or failure. Everything depends on this choice, this afternoon.

That's why not just any child will do.

So the thing is to pay close attention. This is the key moment, and failure would be intolerable. Now more than ever.

What about that boy over there? Five years old, maybe six. Could he be the one? It's a nerve-wracking thing, making this choice.

No. He won't do.

He's old enough, but he seems a tad clingy. Dependent. He's gripping his mother's hand too tightly, and he keeps looking up to make sure she's still there. As long as she is, his world is in order.

Maybe he won't stop crying. Maybe he'll spend the whole day curled up in a ball, paralyzed by fear.

He won't do.

It'll take more looking.

Maybe a girl? Too risky. Too many little princesses. The thing is to find someone brave—a boy who thinks he's a superhero.

There's another one. What do his clothes say? Shoes offer a lot of clues. He's not very tall, probably four years old. He just let go of his mother's hand. What did he see? What caught his attention?

Maybe he'll do. Maybe.

Maybe today will be the day.

Just thinking that sends the heart racing.

The body quaking with an odd kind of fear.

Look at him again. There's a spark.

That boy means salvation.

The game begins.

This time, for real.

The point of no return.

1

INÉS

In American movies, there are always donuts. Right off the bat. The donuts reveal that this is a meeting of addicts—alcoholics, cheaters, failures, something. When the camera pans around the room and shows pathetic faces, sad fluorescent lighting, and a smell of stale urine (not that the odor percolates off the screen, but you can tell it's there, acrid and nauseating, as if you were sticking your nose in a public urinal), you know that someone is going to confess to a big, hidden shame.

But we're not in America. We're in Spain, where group therapy doesn't come with donuts, and we avoid the risk of having to create a Diabetics Anonymous before we're through. Here, if you end up in a self-help group, the tragedy plaguing you most likely looms so large that these meetings are your last-ditch alternative to suicide. This is the last thing you'll try before locking yourself in with a good bottle of whiskey and a fistful of pills your doctor says are going to help you overcome the trauma—but they don't.

Everybody here today would rather be dead. Better dead than in this room. Better off even in hell, which is what some think they deserve, than here and now.

Something has brought them here. A strange blend of guilt, pain, rage, and a will to survive. This is their only lease on life, because they all know they'd be better off dead. Just like me. But I don't know that yet. Not at this stage of the story.

Let's look around. That man, for instance—that rotund, bald man wearing a sweatshirt meant for a teenager and pants for a retiree, as if he were made of remnants of different people. He can't even open his eyes. How long since he stopped looking at things? How long has he been unable to put one foot in front of the other to get him somewhere he really wants to go, as opposed to letting the current carry him? How long since he took hold of anything—a glass of water, even—because he truly wanted it, his brain saying, *You're thirsty. Reach out your arm, arc your fingers toward your thumb, pick up the glass, bring it to your mouth, and drink.* If we could get inside his head, we'd see that it's completely occupied, or unoccupied, by an immense emptiness. A chasm of sloshing waves, one after another. Sometimes a thought hangs suspended, like the eye of a hurricane—he doesn't know, he doesn't remember, nothing is pulling at him. But that's just an illusion, those gentle winds and clear skies. The storm in which he's living never lets up. *It was your fault. Your fault. You don't deserve to live.*

Or that girl over there with the greasy hair and the oversized pants. How long since she thought of herself as a human being? I see how she's gripping her purse so tightly that the blood stops flowing to her hands, as if this object were her only link to life, and if she let go of it, she'd fall irredeemably into the black hole she's trying to get out of. What could have happened to her? She's barely past childhood. I ought to feel bad for her.

What am I doing here, then? What am I doing among these tormented souls, when I don't need to be yet? My editor—yes, *sigh,* I have an editor—thinks a session like this is the ideal place for me to find inspiration for my next book. After the worldwide success of my debut novel, *A Dense Wood,* all he does is pressure me to get back to the task.

Sometimes I get so paranoid that I think he's bribed people around me. Like the cleaning women, who shoot me hostile looks while pushing their carts full of toxic products around the studio. *Write another book. Write another bestseller. Write another moneymaking machine.* Fortunately, human beings haven't yet developed the capacity for telepathic thought. At first, my editor was gentle, subtle, courteous. Now I have the feeling that he'd resort to almost anything, as long as it gave me an idea for a new big hit. Sometimes I wonder just how far he'd go to offer me the thread of a plot. And no matter how often I repeat that I only had one book inside me and I'll never be able to write another, he—echoed by the entire publishing house—says that I can do it, that I just need to find the proper *click* to transform my MacBook into a word processor with diarrhea. But I don't have any ideas. I had one, and it's done. It turned into a book, and that's that.

In short, that's how I've ended up here. I'm at this meeting so my editor will leave me alone for a while. If he thinks I'm working on something, he'll calm down.

But it's tough doing things like this. Someone might recognize me, and I don't want that. If they find out who I am, they won't let me stay. For certain assignments in the past, I've tried wigs and disguises. Today I'm wearing sunglasses and a short blond wig. With a base of yellow makeup and purple shadow under my eyes, I, too, can look fragile, as if sadness were oozing out of my skin.

However much I try to pass for someone else, though, there's always one thing that gives me away: my voice. It's so characteristic that I can't disguise it. The *s*'s at the ends of my words have a special sound, as if I don't know how to stop the phoneme in time, and it slides through my teeth. *Trees-z-z. Things-s-z-z.* No speech therapist has ever been able to help. My current one says it's my special trait, the one that gives me "personality." So here, I have to keep quiet. At least for today.

Fortunately, there's no table covered with donuts around which to strike up conversations, and today's session leader is on time and gets right to the point. Or maybe he doesn't really want to be here either. He wants to get things over with as quickly as possible, to get away from these souls chained to hell before they pull him down too.

"Could everyone take a seat, please?" the psychologist says in a honeyed voice.

I checked him out on his Facebook page before coming. There's nothing but photos of meals, Madrid streets, and a book or two. A real lone wolf. A sad guy. It shouldn't be hard to get information out of him if I need to.

"Please, everyone, let's find a seat."

We do. Without meeting each other's eyes. Ashamed of ourselves. Or maybe, ashamed of what we're going to hear, as if we were old gossips leaning our ears against the confessional. Blushing, and dripping with pleasure.

"I think Lucía would like to tell us something today, wouldn't you?"

The girl gripping the purse looks up and starts to talk.

I wish I'd never heard the story she's about to tell.

2

ANA

"What's her name again?"

"Arén. Ana Arén. The old-timers call her 'the head of the class.'"

"Because of all the head she gives?"

Luis Arcos laughed. "*Shh*, lower your voice. Nobody here has gotten anywhere with her, as far as I know. The nickname is from her initials, A. A. It's like the highest score on a test. And the rating she deserves." Arcos's eyes went wide as his hands traced the outline of the chief inspector's curvy body.

"A ten? I'd give her a fifteen. She's got an ass to write home about," responded José Barriga. His own body suggested that once he hit his thirties he'd have a gut to match his last name, *belly*, so he might not be the best person to comment on the looks of others.

"You're the new guy, right?" The voice came from behind him, where Detective Charo Domínguez had heard the whole exchange. "Do you want some advice? Keep your eyes off her ass and take a peek at her feet. Do they look small to you? Because when she kicks you, you'll wish you were back on the receiving end of your hick-town donkey instead. Arén's short temper about those kinds of comments is legendary. Don't tempt fate, buddy."

"Shoot, for a piece of her, I'd take a kick in the balls," Detective Barriga said with a smile. He'd been recently assigned to the unit and clearly didn't hear a thing the detective had said. "You don't know the effect a female boss in uniform has on me."

"Ladies, could you quit laughing like hyenas?" Another voice cut in, startling them all. Too many people were overhearing the conversation. "Who are you, anyway? The new guy?"

"Um," Barriga sputtered, taken aback by the stripes on the uniform of the man who'd appeared out of nowhere. "Um, yes, sir, Commander. Yes, sir."

"Cat got your tongue all of a sudden?"

"No, sir, I didn't mean—"

"Get to work," said Major Bermúdez. "I don't want to start bawling anybody out this early in the morning. Doctor's orders, it's bad for my health. And if it's bad for mine, it's bad for yours. Get to the briefing room now, both of you. And you"—he looked scornfully at the new addition—"make sure the chief inspector doesn't hear you, or you won't have enough skin left on your ass to wipe it with a Q-tip. You got me?"

The briefing room smelled rotten. So did the whole building. For decades, the sweat and bodily fluids of tens of thousands of detectives and suspects who passed through had been adhering bit by bit to its walls. They say all police stations smell alike, but that's not true. It depends on the nose. For example, a police station didn't smell the same to the dictator Franco's torturer Melitón Manzanas as to the terrorist who fell into his clutches. Nor to the new cop sweating with fear versus the veteran who's had it up to his neck. No, each station has its own smell. Some have the nauseating stench of tobacco and feet that no Odor-Eaters can fully eliminate. Others give off whiffs of cologne their personnel used for so many decades, like the Varon Dandy that some old-timers still keep stashed in their lockers. Others smell of the sweat accumulated since the time they were built.

But all of them smell, to a greater or lesser degree, of fear.

Ana Arén's station smelled, on top of all this, of perversion. The walls of the Provincial Brigade of the Judicial Police in Madrid had the whiff of old men who'd been caught jerking off outside school buildings. The station was located in a residential area—although when it was built, sixty years before, it had been surrounded by shacks—with lots of schools and bushes to hide behind. *Psst, psst,* the exhibitionists would whisper to the children when just watching them go by wasn't exciting enough and they needed to get the kids to look at them. The more the little ones were scared, the harder the men would get. *Uh-huh, uh-huh, uh-huh.*

In the seventies, Spain had bigger things to worry about than pigs like that, but for Luis Bermúdez, it was personal. Since he joined the force, Bermúdez had seen a lot of perverts, and they disgusted him more than anything. He could have strangled them with his bare hands. They often hid behind innocent-looking faces with the eyes of a dead octopus. In more recent years, Major Bermúdez had led a technological campaign. He was one of the first to realize that sex criminals who preyed on children were no longer crouching behind bushes or inside cars; instead they worked through computer programs that obscured their IP addresses, the online ID that would otherwise allow them to be found. Even before all the manual Olivetti typewriters had disappeared from the police stations of Spain, Bermúdez recruited the best IT specialists within the ranks to serve under his command in the Judicial Police, the country's main detective force. He fought to create a group of agents who would sniff through the web in search of sick operators, even in the days of dial-up modems when subscribers paid by the minute for connection.

Turnover in that unit was high. Few staffers could handle going home every night with images of children suffering terrible sexual abuse, difficult for any but the sickest of minds to even imagine. These were images you could never get out of your head. Never forget. Agents devoted to fighting internet pedophilia were tainted forever, their brains never able to completely reset.

It had been years now since Bermúdez's superiors had taken control of this task force of IT savants, moved it out of his command to the national police headquarters in Canillas, and ostentatiously renamed it the Technological Investigation Brigade, recently renamed again as the Technological Investigation Unit (TIU). The personnel assigned there devoted themselves not only to unmasking pedophiles but also to uncovering their origins. By this time, all the world's lawlessness circulated through the web. All the rottenness, cruelty, and deprivation of the planet was compressed into zeroes and ones that transmitted evil at the speed of light.

Ana Arén—the chief inspector in charge of the children's unit of the Servicio de Atención a la Familia for Madrid, which fell within the provincial Judicial Police division commanded by Bermúdez—sat on the edge of one of the tables at the back of the room. Her pose was informal, arms and legs crossed. She didn't like to sit up front. From the back, you could see everything better. If you could open your perspective and focus your gaze in the other direction, you could observe life in more detail. Sometimes the reaction of an eye gave you more information than the object in its view.

"Hi, Chief Inspector." Charo Domínguez took a seat beside her.

"Hi, Charo. How are you adjusting to the new job?"

"Not so new, Ana, I've been here for months now," the policewoman replied, taking a sip from the small thermos she brought to the station every morning, a strange mix of milk and honey. "Wait till you meet the new guy. I caught him talking about your ass."

Ana decided to change the topic. She was in no mood to get angry either.

"How can you drink that crap every morning?" Ana asked.

"Look who's talking. The woman who drinks Coca-Cola for breakfast. Surely good for the digestive system," someone joked from behind her.

Sub-Inspector Javier Nori García had hurried in late. His cheeks looked flushed from exertion. Surely he'd come from one of his daily jogs. Ana figured his mind had been wandering and he'd lost track of time. That was how he was.

"If you say the same thing enough times, Nori, even Shazam can recognize it," Ana said by way of greeting. "When you get pulled away from your computers to go running, Azotón, everything seems strange to you."

That nickname—el Azotón, the Scourge—had been conferred on Sub-Inspector Javier Nori by his colleagues at his first post, a precinct in Zone II of Barcelona, just off Las Ramblas. He'd been given the nickname because he was the whip scourging the motorcycle-mounted thieves of the narrow streets that traversed the historic part of the city. He set up the first digital registry of two-wheeled crime in Barcelona and always carried it with him, in one of the first PDAs on the market, which in the mid-nineties cost almost as much as a computer does today.

"I swear, Ana, if anyone in this unit ever hears you call me that, my vengeance will know no bounds." Nori swept his finger across his neck, implying that he'd cut off his boss's head.

"*Azotón?* That's what they called you?" Charo laughed, almost dropping her thermos.

"And you—keep quiet, or I'll find you a nickname soon. Another of my pleasures. Man does not live by jogging and computers alone. Señorita Castillos, let's say."

Ana had rescued Charo from the drudgery of guarding embassies and consulates, or "castles" as they were called within the police department. She had been rotting away on guard duty, protecting foreign diplomats and their families in long and boring watches out on the street, observing the official residents and the whole ecosystem of luxury within which they moved. She and Ana had met at a conference about security, and Ana saw right away that the young woman had a brain, ambition, and a work ethic, all of which she was now demonstrating in the SAF. Within a few months, she'd become one of the best investigators of the unit under Ana's command. She had an astounding ability to connect one idea with another.

"Nori, do you miss your jihadis?" Charo responded. "I don't miss my diplomats. Not in the slightest. And their children, even less. They kept us out at night too often and too late."

"All right, pipe down, everyone," the commander said from the other side of the room. "This is important. I just came from a meeting with the top brass."

While her colleagues took seats where they could find them, Ana closed her eyes and smelled the fear that had adhered to the walls over the years. That reminded her of where she was and what her job implied. She needed to get back to basics, to the origins of her vocation, to what really mattered, because sometimes she lost track of it among the bullshit of routine.

"Okay, shut up, everybody," Bermúdez repeated. "You're going to hear about some changes that are coming down the pike."

That produced a wave of silence. *Changes.* That magic word was a fusillade that made everyone open their ears and shut their mouths in the hope that no such bullet would hit them. Some even, instinctively, leaned slightly to the left or the right so the missile would whiz by without grazing them. But the commander had no time to fire. Cell phones went off, several at the same time, which in a police station always means bad news.

Every time.

3

INÉS

"In my case, the number is thirty," the girl grasping the purse began to explain with surprising self-possession. "Thirty seconds separated my life now from the one I used to have and will never have again. Sometimes those thirty seconds are just enough time for a glance. You're staring at a spiderweb as if someone hit the pause button on your brain, or you're checking out a pair of boots in a shop window to decide whether you deserve them or not, and you don't realize that he's not there anymore. Then you bang your head against the wall, because you want to smash your skull against the stucco and scatter your brains, leave everything covered in blood. Because you didn't notice. How could you not? How could you not notice that absence? How could you not notice that he got away from you, he slid away, he's gone, you don't have him with you anymore? Your son's hand is warm, soft, small. Your son's hand is wrapped around your own, holding on to the only thing in the world he knows is safe—his mother's love. And suddenly he's not there, and you haven't noticed."

As she went on telling her story, the girl gripping the purse seemed to disconnect from the world, unplug herself from reality. She didn't look at anything, as if her eyes turned inward, toward her soul, toward the endless loop of despair she was living, searched for all her pain so as not to have to chew on it ever again, so as to vomit it up once and for all, so it would never come back. Please.

"But that wasn't how it went," she said. "If it did, I'd at least have an excuse. A moment of inattention, like so many parents have every day. Who hasn't gone through a scare like that with her kids? Losing sight of them, not knowing where they are, feeling your heart jump in your throat, having the world go blank. Until they show up. Because they always do. Well, almost always. But in my case, it was worse. It wasn't a moment of inattention. I was the one who let him go. I purposely let go of Bruno's hand so he would die. I killed him."

How was she holding back the tears? I couldn't stop looking at her. Her body was like a magnet. Her voice pierced my soul. I tried to remember every possible detail. How her jaw went slack, as if she were about to faint, and left a grotesque grimace on her face. How her ankles were so strangely twisted, her feet turned outward. How the five liters of blood in her body flowed into her hands, converted them to claws, holding on to this world.

"If only I'd left my mother's house thirty seconds earlier, none of it would have happened. A Wednesday like this, right now, I'd be fighting with Bruno because he'd left the whole kitchen covered in baby food from his snack. Because he was independent almost from the minute he was born, he wouldn't have tolerated my trying to feed him his purees. At only three months, he already held his bottle by himself. I remember the motion of his little hand trying to grab it, beating at the air, reaching for the bottle. He was . . ."

Captivated, hooked on her story like junkies on heroin, the addicts gawked at her. They closed their eyes out of courtesy, but also to better enjoy it, concentrating only on the motion of the drug through their veins. I did, too, in all honesty. Maybe that's why these kinds of meetings are always well attended, because we all need our daily fix of other people's misfortunes. We're addicted to the pain of others. Was I that way too? Did I need other people's pain to feel good myself? Or to do my work? One of my cell phones went off in my bag. I ignored it.

"Lucía is very brave to tell her story here," the session leader said, I suppose to make us think he was serving some purpose there. "You've all suffered a lot, every one of you. But with each pain, yours and that of others, you're learning how to heal yourselves."

The pain of others helps us heal ourselves? Maybe this guy was more of jerk than I'd first thought. Or maybe he was right. Maybe the misfortunes of others *do* make us think our own shitty life isn't so bad. Anyway, pity always goes well with arrogance.

"I was at my mother's house," the girl went on. "She had to pick up the kids from school because I'd gotten a job for three hours a day cleaning an office, and they didn't let us come in until everybody left, at three p.m., so we wouldn't bother them. You know, cleaners don't have enough class to mix in certain environments. This was during the time we were teaching Lucas, my middle one, to pee and poop in the toilet, and we always tried to take off his diaper inside so he'd get used to asking to pee. 'It's okay if he pees on the floor or wets his pants,' my mother said. 'He's at home, we'll change him, and that's that, because that way he'll notice when it happens and learn to control himself.' And that's what we were doing, with Lucas learning to go to the bathroom. So I had to pay attention to him when, with his coat and cap already on and the four of us about to leave Grandma's house for our own, he said, 'Peepee, Mama, peepee.' 'But you've got a diaper,' I said. 'We just put it on you, so you can go ahead.' 'Nooo, Mama, that's icky,' he screamed. So what are you supposed to say? You have to wait. I gave my mother the baby and told Edu to watch both of them, Grandma and Bruno (and he already felt so much older and more responsible that he put on his proudest face), and I took Lucas's coat off. How many times have I thought of that moment, the pee that turned out to be the difference between life and death? I confess I've often been tempted to blame Lucas for his brother's death. After all, if he'd only peed in his diaper, Bruno would be alive now. For a while I couldn't look at Lucas's face, and I started to hate him. I needed to hate him so I wouldn't kill myself—so I wouldn't kill everyone."

The iPhone went off again in my purse. I wasn't going to answer, not at this most touching moment of the story. But exactly three seconds after it stopped, the other cell started to vibrate, my personal one. Not many people had that number, so whoever was calling knew me well, or at least I'd trusted them enough to give them my private number. Maybe it was something important. The number on the screen was a long one, a switchboard. I didn't recognize it. Trying to make as little noise as possible and crouching down to be less visible, I discreetly left the room.

"Where is that idiot now?" On the other end of the line, Manuel was seething, having gotten more and more pissed off with every ring without realizing that I'd picked up and was listening. He was a professional bumbler. "I called both her cell phones. What the fuck is she doing?"

"Manuel?" I said, neither loudly nor softly, pretending I hadn't heard his outburst.

"Is something wrong with your voice? You sound weird."

"No, no," I said, stepping outside the building to find an isolated place. "I was quiet for a long time, and my throat must have gone dry."

"You? Quiet for a long time? Tell me who performed that miracle, and I'll build them an altar."

"You ought to like it when I'm quiet. It means I'm stirring up less trouble for you, boss. Especially at certain times," I said, restraining my desire to hang up on him. "What's so urgent? I'm in the middle of . . . something."

"I need to get in touch with that hacker you know. Right away."

Really? Why? Why on earth did he need to talk with him?

"I'll call him if you want," I said, lying.

I'd always given out that my acquaintance was an IT genius who lived physically cut off from the world. Someone who never answered calls and whose real identity even I didn't know. Someone with whom you had to communicate by leaving code words on a voice mail and then waiting until he felt like answering.

"I can call him right now and leave the code for him to call me back. But you know he answers when he feels like it. And he'll only talk to me, because he doesn't trust anybody."

"Try it, Inés, try it."

"What should I tell him is going on?"

"An issue."

"An issue. I admire your capacity for synthesis. Do you think 'an issue' is a good enough reason for him to contact you?"

"A personal issue. I can't go into details now. But I need to get out of a situation, is what it is."

Well, how interesting. Things must be pretty bad for Manuel Grana to call me to solve a personal problem. My neurons began to enthusiastically applaud.

"Okay, boss. I'll leave the code on his voice mail and see whether he calls back."

I hung up, wondering what Manuel needed to hide that made him seek out the help of a computer whiz like Joan Arderiu, my friend in Barcelona, a man who could, it seemed, hack into anything, anywhere. Then I remembered where I was and why. I hurried back to the room where the therapy session was going on. I was just in time to hear the end of the story from the girl with the purse.

"Finally, I managed to get the three of them into the car: Bruno next to me in his car seat, Edu behind me because he was the oldest and didn't need so much watching, and Lucas behind the passenger seat so I could see him in the rearview mirror. By now it was night, and the few drops of rain were turning into a downpour. In March, the dark comes on quickly, you know? And the temperature drops, too, which is why

I didn't take off their coats when I buckled them in. I know, I know, that wasn't right, because it's very dangerous to buckle in the kids with their coats on, especially bulky ones like they had on that day. The belts don't tighten around their chests the way they should, and if there's a crash, their little bodies can lurch forward so hard the belts can cut off their heads. But it was late, and we were in a big hurry. They still needed their baths, their dinner—Bruno needed to be nursed—their pajamas, stories, and everything else that the two older ones dreamed up to prolong the time it took to get them to bed.

"So I put them in the car and we left. From my mother's town to where we lived was only five kilometers. The road was narrow—it had curves and no lights—but I knew it like the back of my hand. All those late nights I'd gone this route, even on foot when I was a teenager coming home after a night out. I could drive it with my eyes closed, even in the rain. To the right, fifty meters, change of grade, a little to the left, and again a little to the right. The windshield wipers weren't doing much good, and I could hardly see anything, but no cars were coming the other way, so no headlights shone on the asphalt, and I could drive slowly down the middle of the road without concern. Suddenly the wheels stopped gripping the road. It happened subtly and smoothly, but the car lost its purchase, slid a little, and got stuck on something. It wouldn't move. I put on the hand brake, turned on the hazard lights, and rolled down my window to see what was going on. Maybe a heap of gravel had fallen on the road and we were stuck in it. I couldn't see anything, and the only noise was the water pouring down from the sky. I looked in the back. Edu and Lucas were asleep. Only Bruno, in the seat next to me, was still awake. He was hungry. Soon he'd start to howl, wanting to nurse. I had to hurry."

Lucía squirmed in her chair. Though she hadn't lost her composure and still seemed far away, you could see how her pain was growing and her soul was showing through, like her body was getting turned inside out. I glanced around the room. Everyone was looking at the floor.

They were ashamed of hearing something so intimate and painful, as if they were old village gossips indeed. But they couldn't help it. They were hooked on the tragedy.

"I didn't know it, but that was the last time I was going to see Bruno. He was right there, my son, in the passenger seat, lit up by the little dome light of the Peugeot. That's my last image of him, and I mean, goddamn, it's a really shitty one. I can't even see the little dimple in his chin or those long eyelashes that made everybody fall in love with him. The last time I saw him, Bruno was an orange face full of shadows, and I could only guess at the hollows of his eyes. Suddenly, something hit the car hard on the driver's side, and we started to slide to the right. *We're going off the road,* I thought. *My god, we're going off the road.*"

Now Lucía was paralyzed, holding her breath. If you don't breathe, it hurts less. If you don't breathe, you can squeeze the pain until it explodes, like pus from a pimple. The trick is to hold your breath a long time and just let it go little by little while you press tighter and tighter. That's what Lucía's body was doing, instinctively, getting ready for the intensity of pain that was about to hit her. Again.

"I tried to open my door, but I couldn't. The rushing water had blocked it. I lowered the window and twisted my way out. I knew where we were, on a stretch of road that crossed a dry riverbed, but somewhere upstream the clouds had let loose so much rain that it had become a river again. I kicked off my heels. They weren't very high, but I couldn't get anywhere with them on. When my foot touched the ground (I couldn't tell whether it was pavement or not) I realized how strong the flow of the water was. We were lucky the car had run aground on some-thing, because otherwise it would have floated out of control. I had to hurry. I tried to open Edu's door, the one behind mine, but I couldn't get it open either. The water was blocking it too. *Shit, shit, I should have unbuckle them while I was still inside.* I banged on the window to wake him up. 'Unbuckle,' I said. 'Unbuckle quickly, honey. We're home, and I don't want you to get wet.' But he didn't listen. My voice bounced uselessly between the rain and the glass, throwing my own desperation back in my face. I had to try the other door if I wanted to get my kids out of there. Getting around the car was a nightmare; I couldn't see a thing, and I'd made the mistake of shutting off the engine, so we were completely in the dark. And the roar of the water was terrible—both from the sky and in the riverbed. In that kind of noise, it's impossible to think. But maybe that was better. *Don't think, just act.* Grabbing on to whatever handhold I could, even just the car body with my fingernails, I made my way around the Peugeot. When I got to the passenger side, I had a moment of calm. The car blocked the force of the water so I could get the rear door open without much trouble. Feeling my way, I unbuckled Lucas—'Honey, come on, grab hold of Mama'—and tried not to sound hysterical while I told Edu to unbuckle himself, that it was very important, and to scoot out his brother's door. I settled Lucas on my left hip. I breathed. 'Edu, honey, get out. There's water. Don't be scared. Grab on to Mama,' I told him. Edu was six, and he could get out of there if he held tight to the belt of my jeans. There was no other solution. The hardest thing was to get Bruno out while I held on to Lucas with my left arm and protected Edu with my body, but I managed to do that. In a delicate balance, the four of us started to move away, step by step. 'Edu, you're performing like a champ,' I yelled above the sound of the storm. 'Hold on tight, tight, tight to Mama's belt. Very tight, honey, like on the zip line, you know? You'll see how quickly we can get across the river.' I don't remember the kids saying anything. They didn't cry. Or maybe they did. Maybe all three were bawling, or all four of us were, but I wasn't aware of anything, because all my senses were focused on getting us out of there. I thought we were going to do it, I really thought so, until we left the protection of the car and the water smashed into us with all its force. I was about to fall over. It was up to the middle of my thigh. I was slipping. I sank. It was hitting me harder and harder, and four or five steps later, I fell. Instinctively I let go of Lucas and Bruno to try to stop the blow with my hands. Lucas managed to grab on to my sweater, and Edu, by some miracle, kept holding on to my pants, but Bruno, who was only three months old, slipped, and I lost him. I think I've never screamed so loud. I felt around desperately under the water with my right hand, in a panic, until I found his head, and I grabbed his hair and pulled him out. *We're not going to make it,* I thought, *we're not going to make it.* I tried one more step when suddenly there was no more footing under me and all four of us sank. I had hold of all of them, trying to get us out of there, trying to pull their heads from the water so they wouldn't drown, when I realized the truth. And the truth—the damn, fucked-up, horrible truth—was that we could survive, but not all of us. All four of us could never do it. I had to choose who would live and who would die. I could have thought about a lot of things. Edu was the oldest, my first son, the one who changed my life forever. Lucas, the middle one, was the most affectionate, always giving me hugs. And Bruno, Bruno still smelled like a baby, I still wanted to eat up his chubby cheeks. For a long time, I thought all those things about my kids as I decided which one I would send to his death. But I've realized I projected all that back into my mind later on. In the real moment, my mind went blank, and my body decided. 'I'm sorry, Bruno, I'm sorry,' I told him in tears. 'I love you, Bruno, but I've got to let you go. I've got to let you go to save your brothers. Goodbye, Bruno, goodbye. Forgive me, please. I love you.'

"And I let go of him.

"'Goodbye, baby, goodbye.'"

Lucía couldn't continue. All the pain she'd been holding in overflowed like the flash flood that had taken her son. Mixed in with the sobs were two words that she repeated in a loop: "Thirty seconds, thirty seconds." The air in the room had become electric. Just breathing it in brought cramps. For the first time, I really understood the pain of a mother when one of her children dies.

And I couldn't stand it.

I got out of there without looking back and without caring who saw or recognized me.

After that, I couldn't wait. There was no putting it off till I got home. As soon as I was in the car, I searched on my phone for the rest of the story. And there it was, in an article from a local paper two years back. "After leaving the baby, the mother fought to bring her other two sons to safety. One of them, the oldest, grabbed a tree branch and saved his life. She and the middle one, two years old, were carried by the water but managed to escape the fierce current thirty meters downstream. 'Edu, save Edu, please. He's in a tree,' the police said that the woman screamed before losing consciousness. A man who'd been able to stop his car just in time on the other side of the road and escape the torrent heard the screams and alerted the Guardia Civil. The three survivors are recovering from hypothermia in the hospital. They are receiving psychological treatment. The police have declared that the torrent formed in barely half a minute, that the huge flash flood came down uncontrollably like a tsunami, sweeping everything away. The baby's body was found yesterday, Sunday, forty-eight hours after the tragedy, fifteen kilometers below the accident, caught among the remnants of trees the water had swept away. His funeral will be held tomorrow."

Without giving me time to digest what I'd just read, the phone vibrated in my hands—an incoming call. I didn't answer until the sixth or seventh ring, by which time the caller had hung up, but they tried a second time. It was my boss, Manuel, again. Such a pain in the butt.

"Inés. Another boy. Another boy just disappeared from the same shopping center as two years ago. Remember?"

Did I remember? Did I remember? My stomach lurched.

"Get over there right away. I'll send you a backpack so you can plug right in to the evening news. We'll lead with the story. Call me as soon as you get there."

"Look, Manuel—"

"Look what?"

"You know that . . ." And what was I going to say? How could I explain to my boss that I didn't want to go? "You know I don't like stories about missing kids."

"Will you listen to yourself? 'You know I don't like stories about missing kids,'" he mimicked, in the voice of a whiny child. "Get right over there, Inés. Call me for more details when you're on your way. I'm waiting for them to confirm we've got an exclusive. If what my source says is true, this is going to be big. Very big."

4

ANA

When Chief Inspector Ana Arén reached the mall, she wanted to hang whoever was in charge of security up by his balls. Not a single door was closed, and nobody was watching any of them. If someone had really just kidnapped a child—if it wasn't a false alarm—the kid and the abductor would already be long gone. Not to mention any possible evidence they might have left on their way out, which by now could be stuck to the shoes of any of the hundreds of people who had swarmed in and out, now irretrievably lost in some housing development here in the suburbs surrounding Madrid. Hadn't the mall security staff learned anything from what had happened two years before? Hadn't that been enough of a lesson for Spanish society as a whole?

"Chief Inspector, Chief Inspector," she heard someone call behind her. "Over here."

With so many people wandering around, it was hard to know where the voice was coming from. Ana had always been astonished by the behavior of human beings in a mall. The living mass flowed along the passages in apparent disorder, wandered with no particular destination, one foot in front of the other—right, left, right, left—as if they were only there to kill time. The mall offered everything the visitors required:

air-conditioning in summer, heat in winter, bathrooms, benches, water fountains, and a smooth surface to walk on without fear of stumbling.

"Here."

Ana had expected a uniform, but a woman in civilian clothes was talking to her. Did that mean the technical team was already here? Only members of the detective squads went without uniforms, and this officer wasn't wearing one. Normally in a crime scene—and God grant that this wasn't one—the underling sent looking for her was some poor scholarship student fresh out of the Police Academy in Ávila.

"Chief Inspector, hi, welcome. Thanks for coming so quickly," the woman continued. "Sorry for the bad manners. It must be my nerves. You're an institution within the force, you know. Oh, sorry again. I haven't introduced myself. I'm Sonia Calero, from the Madrid West station. We've been expecting you."

"When did you get here?"

"A patrol car got here ten minutes after a call from a witness who said there was a woman screaming that someone had taken her kid. Right away, it was clear this wasn't a false alarm, so they called us. They caught me off duty. I was shopping right next door, and I came."

This was the same mall from which Nicolás had disappeared two years ago. It seemed like a bad dream.

"What can you tell me about the case?" Ana asked while the two of them hurried toward the spot where the boy had disappeared.

"We're in the process of questioning the mother and trying to find the father. She's hysterical, very flustered, can't put two words together. We've called a doctor for her."

"How long has the boy been gone?"

"Two hours. They called us right away, and we got here quickly, but so far, there's no trace of him in the mall or its surroundings. He's four years old, named Manuel. The mother was holding his hand. The boy stopped at the window of a toy store, charmed by some action figures from something called *Paw Patrol*."

Sonia spoke very quickly, which made her hard to understand. She was stringing together words as she walked jerkily, almost without stopping for breath, like someone competing in a speed-walking race.

"What's that? A cartoon show?" Ana asked.

"That's it. I can tell you don't have kids. Oh—sorry for getting personal. Forgive me, please. From what I can tell, they're the hit of the season. My nephews love them. Police in the form of dogs."

"Dog police? Just what we need. They'd never think of having a monkey judge, would they?" Ana's tone was bitter, but Sonia laughed.

"Well, you know, our uniforms look good, even on a dog. Over there, in the store, is where we've set up emergency operations."

It was the toy store that Sonia had already referred to, the one whose window the boy was looking in when he disappeared. Good place for business, bad place to disappear—right next to one of the doorways that led to a lobby with elevators and emergency stairs. If someone had snatched the kid, it would have been easy for them to grab him and get out of there in a few seconds.

Inside the store, the owner was patiently answering the questions of the police, but by now he must have been sorry to have offered up his shop for their base camp. Surely he'd done so not just out of good will but also feeling a bit guilty because the little one had disappeared right in front of his window.

Ana and Sonia went past the group questioning the store owner and headed for the back. Beyond a half-open door, in a small storeroom without windows or ventilation, the mother was sitting on some toy boxes with a blood pressure cuff on her arm. The doctor looked at Ana and held up a hand for her to wait.

"One hundred fifty-two over 91, pretty high."

The mother didn't answer. She had to be sweating pure adrenaline if her son had disappeared two hours ago. Ana needed to be in possession of her wits. Or at least, as much as possible under the circumstances.

"What's the mother's name?" she whispered to Sonia.

"Lola. And her son is Manuel."

"Tell the doctor to give her something to relax her, but nothing very strong. I need her thinking clearly."

"Okay."

"But don't let her hear you."

"Sure, sure," Sonia agreed. "I'll tell him, but she won't know."

"Lola, hi, Lola, I'm Ana. Chief Inspector Arén." Ana spoke gently while stroking the mother's arm.

Ana liked to lightly touch the victims. The skin was the largest and most sensitive organ of the body, two square meters of pure receptivity, the best way to get in contact with the feelings of other people and let them know, *I'm here, at your side, to help.* Although sometimes you had to be careful. With some people, when the pain was too great, skin-to-skin contact produced a painful electric shock. When the suffering is extreme, victims fold into themselves, in the fetal position, to protect the vital organs. And any external contact is felt and understood as life-threatening aggression, stabbing to the center of physical and emotional pain.

"Lola, I'm here to find your son."

The woman looked at Ana as if she didn't know what those words were supposed to mean. *Here? Find? Son?* She gave the impression of searching for the meaning in some corner of her brain.

"You have to help me, Lola. Every minute that passes is vital. If we want to find Manuel, I need your help."

"I . . . I . . . I've already told it all to the police," she answered at last, stammering as if coming out of a dream. "I don't know any more than that. Where's my baby? Where?" Lola started to shake and cry. Her body rocked rhythmically in time with her sobs.

"Lola, Lola, honey," Ana kept it up. "Look me in the eyes. We're going to find Manuel."

"He's called Manu. If he's lost and somebody calls out 'Manuel,' he won't answer. Manu, that's what you've got to call him, Manu."

"Good, Lola. Good. Manu. So you and I are going to find Manu."

Ana addressed her in the familiar way, as *tú*. She didn't like *usted* in these situations, because she thought the polite form put up a kind of wall—me, the cop, over here, and you, the victim, over there. So she always used *tú*, though it sounded strange to some people.

"We're going to find Manu, but I need you to focus. Okay? I need you to concentrate. We're in this together, honey. Let's start from the beginning. What happened?"

"I . . . I . . . we were walking. I'd promised that we'd go to the play space, here in the mall, if he didn't cry when I dropped him at school. He changed schools this year, you know? I'm separated now, and we couldn't pay for the private one anymore. Manu's having a hard time adjusting to everything—the new house, the separation, the school. So I promised him we'd go to the playground, the play area in the mall, with the bounce house and all. So he wouldn't cry."

"What do you remember about the moment he disappeared?"

"Well, Manu . . ." She sighed and swallowed the mucus accumulating in her nose. "One of the few things that calms him down these days is *Paw Patrol*. Do you know it? That cartoon on TV with dogs who are firefighters and police. He loves it. We get to school late every day because he wants to see one episode, then the next. So when he saw the *Paw Patrol* figures in the window, we stopped. You should have seen his face, eyes as big as saucers. He let go of my hand to take a good look. He was right there, with his hands and face pressed up against the glass. If he could have reached right through, he would have. I . . . I . . . lost track. My phone buzzed. It was a WhatsApp message, and I answered it."

"Who messaged you?"

"My husband. I mean, my ex-husband. He wanted to take Manu this weekend. It wasn't on the schedule, though, and I got mad."

"Could I see your phone, please?"

Sure enough, there it was. The ex-husband's message. Ricardo, according to the screen. Ana turned around. "Is the ex-husband here yet? Have you located him?" she asked Sonia.

"No. Not that I've heard. I'll go ask. Be right back, Chief Inspector."

The message had come in at 5:15: *Lola, I'll take Manu tomorrow to spend the weekend together. Don't pick him up at school on Friday. Pack his suitcase, and leave it in the secretary's office. I'll pick it up on our way out.* Lola's answer was a long paragraph in which she told Ricardo she was so fed up, and what was he thinking, because she had no intention of letting him take the boy. If she had to change the lock and call the police, that's what she'd do. The husband had messaged her at 5:15 and she'd answered at 5:19.

"Lola, did you answer this message right way?"

"Yes. As soon as the WhatsApp beeped, I picked up and answered him."

"But it says you waited four minutes to answer."

"I . . . I . . . I answered right away, I swear."

The husband's message seemed to have been written purposefully to anger his wife. To provoke a reaction from her. Four minutes to write a five-line message was too long. But, who knows? Maybe she wrote and erased and wrote and erased more than once until she got it the way she wanted. If he often provoked her, it wouldn't be unusual for her to take so long to compose the right response.

"Chief Inspector, can you come here a minute?" Sonia called from the doorway that connected the storeroom to the shop. "We can't find the husband," she whispered, leading her to a far corner of the store. "His phone is shut off or out of the coverage area. And, you know."

"Yes, I know that in most disappearances of a minor, someone in the family or the inner circle is involved. But he could also be at the movies or in bed with the younger woman he left his wife for. Or in a meeting at work."

"At his job, they say he left after lunch."

29

"We can't just assume it's the husband, Sonia. Maybe so, maybe not. Right now, we can't reject any possibility. If we want to save Manu, we have to keep our minds completely open."

How many times had she repeated that same speech to every novice who joined her unit? Keep an open mind. Don't reject anything. Sometimes we eliminate the first solution that comes to mind because we think it's too easy. Or too impossible.

"We've requested a list of all the employees in the mall. Security and cleaning are subcontracted out. We have a group of officers going store to store, locating the owners to ask them for all the info on their workers. Also whether they've fired anyone recently."

"Have you notified the TIU?"

"The internet guys?"

"Yes, please call them on my behalf. And call my unit, too, and ask them to connect you with Sub-Inspector Javier Nori. Tell Nori to check the list of known pedophile sex offenders to see whether there's anything unusual going on with any of them."

"Oh, and one other thing, Chief Inspector," Sonia said.

"What's that?"

"There's been a leak. Someone has been talking, and the press are already outside. A TV crew, I mean. One of the police officers securing the perimeter saw a technician setting up a live feed."

"Keep them out of the mall. Send a patrol car to watch them discreetly, and tamp down the panic among the people when they hear what happened. When that reporter goes live, phones will ring all over the building. I don't want a panic. We've still got some time before the eight o'clock news. As soon as it's on TV, social media will start to smoke, and this will turn into a living hell."

"Right, Chief Inspector."

Ana snorted. How had the media found out so fast? If it was Inés Grau out there, Ana was going to have problems. Shit. Inés.

She went back into the storeroom.

"Lola, do you have a photo of your son?"

"Yes, of course. Here." She showed Ana the phone again. "I took it just minutes before he disappeared."

Lola started shaking. *Disappeared.* Saying the word out loud had made it real, that her son was not with her anymore. That she'd lost him. Or that someone had taken him.

But Ana Arén saw something else. Something that froze the blood in her veins. The photo of Manu. Four years old. Dark hair, straight, in a bowl cut. Big brown eyes. The spitting image of Nicolás!

This couldn't be.

Not Nicolás again.

Not The Taker.

Not again.

5

INÉS

Everything was so serene. It looked like any other afternoon in one of the boring—yet surprisingly full, as always—malls on the outskirts of the capital. Only a few people knew what had just happened there.

And even fewer knew something worse: it seemed to have happened in a way that was identical to two years before.

The Taker.

Too many bad memories. I'd felt the knot tightening and rising up my esophagus as soon as Manuel gave me the news.

"Are you on your way yet?"

"Relax, boss. I'm calling from the car. I'll be there in ten minutes," I told him, while I pulled off the blond wig I'd worn to the therapy session and tried to clean away the yellow makeup and the fake shadows under my eyes with a baby wipe that had gone dry after sitting for months in a half-open packet in the glove compartment. "Is a mobile unit coming for the live feed?"

"We don't want to attract attention with a mobile unit. Once people start tweeting that they saw a giant Channel Eleven truck full of antennas, the competition will start calling their police contacts, and our scoop will be all over. We want to be the only ones carrying the story at eight. They'll shit their pants."

"Backpack, then?"

"Yes."

"If it doesn't work, you'll be the one shitting your pants. Don't blame me, you hear?"

"Quit sniveling, Inés, for Christ's sake," he huffed. "You don't think there's perfect 4G coverage in one of the most important shopping centers in Madrid? You think the phone companies want to lose the volume of business represented by those thousands of bored people wandering through a mall? What can they do to entertain themselves but keep looking at their phones? Anyway, I don't think the police will be jamming anything, not in a missing-child case."

The mobile units for live television feeds send their signals by satellite. Once stabilized, it's practically impossible for them to suffer interference or crash—except in the case of very unusual solar flares or somebody pushing the button that should never be pushed. However, the fashion lately has been live feeds from backpacks, so called because a small transmitter stuck in a backpack worn by the camera operator sends the signal to the studio through a cell phone line. An outage of cell reception, and goodbye live feed. Sometimes, in front of the eyes of millions of viewers.

I was driving more than 140 kilometers per hour, risking any number of traffic tickets to try to get to the mall in time to talk with any police officer who could give me more information about the missing child before I went live. If my connection crashed because of the goddamn backpack, I was going to throw a fit when I got back to the studio.

"I don't want to look foolish in front of the viewers," I said. "Need I remind you of our blooper reels from past backpack adventures? Just go search on YouTube, if you've forgotten somehow. I told you I didn't want to do more live feeds with those pieces of junk, because I'm the one whose smiling face is on the air. Not you. The people think it's all my fault, even the technical stuff. I'm out in public, and they say, 'Hey, what happened to you yesterday? How come we saw you all cut up in little strips?' Do you have to deal with that, boss? No, you don't! They don't do it to you, because you've never been on TV!"

"Those are exceptions, Inés. How many times have I told you that? I don't want anybody to scoop our exclusive. There are only two days left in the month. We need to come out on top in the ratings."

"I'm not going to argue anymore. I'm going 140 on the M-40, and I'll get in a wreck. Which reminds me, if I get a ticket, the station's paying. So listen, tell me what you know about the case."

"A four-year-old boy disappeared. He was with his mother. The parents separated a few months ago. Nobody can find the father. They were on their way to the kiddie park when the mother got distracted looking at her phone. The boy let go of her hand, and then he was gone."

"That's all? Where's the big news? A missing kid? He got lost. Or his father took him. Didn't you say they just broke up?"

"Inés, listen. The police think it could be the same guy who took Nicolás two years ago. The Taker. Do you think he could be back in action again?"

The Taker. Fear stormed my body from the depths of my reptile brain, the oldest part of our consciousness. The shock was so great that I almost lost control of the car. I squeezed the steering wheel tightly. Tensely. It was impossible. It couldn't be The Taker.

"How can they know that so soon? Who told you this?" I tried not to stammer, though the questions were flooding in. "One of those cops you hang out with, going to those 'intellectual' shows?" Oh shit. Why had I said that?

"Watch your tongue, Inés. You're close to being over the line."

"Sorry, boss. But you know how those cops drive me crazy, the ones who only leak stories to the reporters who go out drinking and who-knows-what with them. I'm not saying you're the one doing the inviting, okay?"

"You're seeing ghosts, Inés. Sometimes I think you're losing it. We're not in the eighties anymore. That stuff doesn't happen these days."

"So you say."

"Let it go, all right? We don't have time for this. How much longer till you get there?"

"Turning in to the parking lot now. Who's coming with the backpack?"

"Wait, let me ask Production. Carmennnn!" He was calling the producer of the eight o'clock news who'd be sitting five desks away from him. "Who'd you send with the backpack for the live feed from the mall? Adrian," he answered, talking to me again. "Adri will be there in ten minutes. He'll call you when he arrives. You'll be in the teasers, and then the first segment will open with you."

Inside, everything looked normal. Nothing strange. So far, the police had managed to squelch the news of the disappearance, so it was just an afternoon in the mall, like any other. But the calm wouldn't last for long.

I went through the first floor and began to think my boss had gotten a false tip until I saw two cops inside a small knickknack shop, talking with the owner. They were questioning her, and one of the police officers was taking notes. I couldn't hear them, but I could imagine the dialogue: "Did you see anything suspicious? Do you recognize this boy? Have you seen him around here? Have you seen anyone prowling around? Can you give us a list of your employees?"

But what was worrying me was something else. Nicolás? If The Taker was involved, that meant Nicolás might be too. What leads could the police have that made them think the two cases were related? What made them think the same person had taken the two kids? The boy had just barely gone missing. It was impossible.

But I had to concentrate on getting more information. Where would the command post be? They must have taken the mother somewhere for questioning. And somewhere else the technical crew would be looking for clues. I had to find them to get the information I needed.

"Is that you? Is that *really* you?" Oh shit, not now. "Oh, wow, I can't believe this. It's like a dream come true. What are you doing here? I'm such a big fan of yours . . ."

Why do people have to screech so sharply when they recognize someone from TV? Can't they maintain a normal tone? They sound like overworked divas from a third-rate opera. It's emotion that does that to the voice. Maybe aggravated by gender. Although I preferred not to imagine this woman with a deep voice.

"Yes, ma'am, it's really me," I answered, trying not to lose my cool. "Sorry, but I'm working and kind of in a hurry."

"What's your name?"

Ah, the usual. People throw themselves at you because they think they've seen you on the tube, but they don't remember your name. Sometimes not even what program you're on.

"Oh! Really? Wow, I loved your book." Well there, things are looking up, at least she knew who I was and didn't confuse me with some actress. "But, it gave me such nightmares! I mean, I was so terrified. Don't write anything else like that, okay? Beautiful as you are, how can you think up such tragic, frightening stories?"

So people will read them, ma'am, so people will read them. It appeals to readers' morbid curiosity when these things happen to somebody else. That's what I was about to say. But I didn't have time for explanations.

"Could I take a picture with you? Really, I can? If not, my friend Conchita, who goes to painting class with me, she'll never believe it, you know?" While she was talking, she opened her purse and began digging away. "Oh, I can't find it. I must have left it at home. Because nobody ever calls me, you know? So why should I bring my phone? Then my kids scold me because they can't get in touch." She reminded me so much of my mother. "You're even prettier than on TV. Has anybody said that to you before?"

Yes, hundreds of times. Prettier, younger, thinner. Television makes almost everybody look bad.

"Ma'am, I'm in a big hurry. The news is about to go on, and I have to do a story, live."

"Ah. Of course. You've come to talk about the police action, right?"

"Have you seen them?" Maybe I'd get something out of this conversation after all.

"On the second floor. In the toy store, across from the coffee shop, the one with the newest brand? I'm sorry, I can't remember the name right now. The one where they charge you three Euros for a coffee just because they give them weird names and serve them in fancy cups. Maybe there was a robbery, because the police have been going in and out of that store for a while. But I saw some doctors, too, and a stretcher. Maybe it was a murder. Do you think?"

"Turn on the Channel Eleven news at eight, and I'll tell you then."

"A murder? That's why you're here? Oh god, now you're scaring me. Who could have been killed?" So she went on, while I rushed up the escalator to the second floor.

I wasn't at the top yet when my phone rang.

"Are you here? I'm just parking. Right next to the supermarket entrance." It was Adri.

"I'm inside, looking for the police, to see if I can find out anything."

"You realize we've only got ten minutes before we go live, right? Transmission moved up the time for our feed, to 7:54. And the director wants us ready now. They're a little nervous. We're the opening segment tonight."

"They're always nervous," I said, and sighed. "Look for a good spot outside, a little bit away so the mall shows up well on the screen. I think they light it up at night, so we won't look like we're in a cave or something. There's a Chinese restaurant across the street. The sidewalk in front of there ought to offer a good shot. I'll see you in five"—I looked at my watch—"four minutes."

If I wanted to get there on time, I'd better run. My phones went off again, one in my hand and the other in my purse. Surely the boss asking me where the hell I was. Sorry. If I answered the phone, I'd never be on time for the feed. I pictured him yelling from his desk in the editing room. Manuel would have to wait. Either I answered, or I went on TV. But not both.

"Three, two, one, theme music, up on channel A, voice." I could hear the instructions coming from Bea, the director, through the hidden earpiece that was my umbilical cord to the room full of machines where the director ruled.

"Inés, you're going on now. They'll cut to you right away. Good luck," said Cris, Bea's assistant.

"He's four years old, and they've been looking for him for more than three hours. Manuel Jiménez disappeared this afternoon in a mall in Madrid." The powerful and deep live voice of the anchorman mixed with the headline theme echoing in my ear. We were on the air. No going back now.

"Camera two, studio," ordered Bea from the control room.

"Good evening. We can tell you, in this exclusive report, that sources within the investigation assure Channel Eleven News that the case could be related to the disappearance two years ago of Nicolás Acosta. We're going live to Shopping West, in Majadahonda. Inés Grau, good evening. Could this be another kidnapping by The Taker?"

"Duplex up," commanded Bea.

Breathe, I told myself. *All under control. Poker face. Automatic pilot. Look at the camera as if it were the most important thing in the world to you. You can do it. The topic does not distress you.*

This topic does not distress you. Go.

"Good evening. We're going to tell you, in this exclusive report, exactly what we know so far about the disappearance of this four-year-old boy. According to police sources to which Channel Eleven has had access, some of the clues point to the possibility that The Taker could be at work again."

6

ANA

The Taker? Had Inés Grau really said that the case of Manu's disappearance could be related to The Taker? *That would trigger quite the shitstorm,* Ana thought. She'd been hoping to keep the investigation secret a bit longer, to have more room for maneuvers, because it was clear by now that this wasn't a case of a lost child. What they were facing was a kidnapping.

Or maybe something worse.

The boy had been gone for five hours. Was this going to be the same thing, all over again? In spite of all her training and years of experience, Ana didn't know whether she could face this all again.

Not The Taker.

But the case was too much like Nicolás's. The same type of kid, the same age, physically identical, and taken from the same place. The only thing that didn't fit was that The Taker had been dormant for almost two years. Could he have kept Nicolás alive all this time? Ana didn't want to cling to that hope. Or had he managed to control his impulses until they grew stronger than his willpower?

Because there had been no sign of The Taker for the past two years, her unit was convinced that something had happened to him. Either he was in jail for some other crime, or he had died, or he was living in some other part of the world. The sexual compulsion of this type of psychopath was so strong that they were incapable of stopping until someone stopped them.

Or some thing.

"Aren't you going home, Ana?"

"Nori! I didn't see you. I didn't know the commander had sent you."

"He didn't send me," Nori said, "until Inés decided to announce on Channel Eleven News that this could be related to The Taker. You couldn't hear him yelling all the way over here?"

"A lot of crap falling from above?"

"A lot is an understatement. A tsunami of crap." Javier Nori sighed. "A tsunami flowing at supersonic speed, rolling directly toward us from the doors of the Ministry of the Interior itself."

"The Minister in person?"

"The Minister. In person."

"Well," said Ana, trying to lessen the tension, "let's look at the positives. Now you know we have Divine Providence on our side, because the ministry thinks highly of pinning medals on statues of the Virgin. Maybe the Minister has called on his forerunners to plead for the intercession of Our Lady of Sorrows to help us find the boy. Maybe we can solve the case through divine intervention."

"Ana, one day, one day you're going to get caught. Somebody who shouldn't hear you is going to be listening, and that'll be the end of you," Nori warned. "And then no amount of investigative success is going to save that head of blond hair dyed black. That'll be the end of the meteoric police career of Ana Arén. Goodbye. Ciao. The end."

"Unfortunately for you," Ana joked, "we have a ways to go before that day comes. And, anyway, how can we get through all this without a dose of black humor, huh? We'd go crazy, sweetie, if we haven't already. Who can stand to see so much depravity, perversity, evil? We're not made of any special stuff, just a bit more accustomed to this shit than the rest of the world. By the way, did someone named Sonia call you on my recommendation?"

"Yeah, when I was already on my way."

"Listen, Nori, I'm getting an idea."

"Don't scare me, boss." It wasn't good when one of your friends on the force called you *boss* in that way. Not good at all.

"That computer program, the Parkinson's detector that Joan and you adapted a few months back, to find suicide bombers—do you think it would work to find pedophiles?"

"Hell, I don't know." For a few seconds Nori's face went blank. "Don't start in with your crazy ideas."

"Why don't you give him a call? Maybe there's something? Call him and see what he thinks."

While they were talking, they reached the parking lot. "My car's here. Call me, whatever you've got. As soon as you know something, Javi, tell me."

"Will do. What about the father? Have you ruled him out already?"

"No way. He was off the grid, with his cell shut down, until nine p.m. Impossible to trace where he'd been. They've taken him to the station. That's where I'm going now, to see if the commander has gotten anything out of him."

"Keep me informed. I'm going home to see whether I can come up with a way to convert a program that finds terrorists about to launch a suicide attack into one that finds pedophiles who just kidnapped a child. A breeze, as you can see."

There weren't many situations in which Ana could think as freely as when she was driving at night. Her mind would be set at ease, and she'd manage to tie together ideas that could seem absurd but shaped themselves into a new logic that was perfectly valid. She disconnected so much that sometimes she had no idea how she'd gotten where she was going, and sometimes it seemed as if the trip never happened at all—as if it was nothing but neurons randomly firing in her brain.

But not tonight. Tonight her brain was being asphyxiated by the possibility that everything that happened two years ago was going to repeat itself.

"They've got him in room three," said Mara, the policewoman on guard at the entrance to the provincial headquarters.

"Has he said anything?"

"No idea. I've been stuck out here since they brought him in. I passed all those tests at the academy, just to end up behind a counter watching a door."

"We've all been there—or worse. I'll let you know how it goes with the father, okay?"

"Sure, yeah."

"I'm headed there now. See you soon."

The interrogation rooms were in the basement, between the jail cells and the meeting room. Most were so old they didn't even have one-way mirrors, but Manu's father had been put in one of the modern ones. "Modern" in a manner of speaking, of course: a room with another alongside it (which originally had also been an interrogation room) from which to watch what happened. Plus, it had a video recording system that any officer with the proper authorization could see from his or her computer.

"How's it going, Commander?" Ana asked.

"Going nowhere. We didn't get a thing out of him."

"Where did he say he'd been?"

"Around. Here and there. That he was exhausted, that the separation has hit him hard, that his head was whirling and he had to leave work early. Says he parked his car at the north entrance to the Pilar

Woods, about ten kilometers from the mall where his son disappeared, and that he was aimlessly wandering through the forest."

"With his cell phone off, of course," noted Ana ironically.

"Says he was getting too many messages, and he wanted to shut everything out. We lost track of his signal on the M-503. That's where he turned it off."

"That's the road to the mall."

"True, but also to the Woods. He could easily have gone both places."

"Did he know that his son and ex-wife were going to be at Shopping West?"

"He claims he didn't, but he could have followed them. He could have waited outside the school to see where they went. There's no way to know."

"What does your instinct tell you, Luis?"

"I don't even want to venture a guess, Ana. If he's the one, then this isn't something that just occurred to him. If we've got him here now, it means he already had a plan for what to do with the kid, had it all mapped out."

"Are you going to keep holding him?"

"As long as we can. The full seventy-two hours."

"And if it's not the father? If it's The Taker?"

"Yeah, I heard about what that reporter said on the news. Which means someone tipped her off. Internal Affairs is looking into it. I'm so fucking fed up with leaks."

"Nori tells me that Interior has been after you."

"The Minister himself called the director general of the police. The Minister! A case that requires discretion is flying all over the ether because a reporter not only spilled the news but also linked it to the story that traumatized all of Spain. You don't have anything to do with that, right?"

"Fuck, Luis, what do you think? That I tipped her off?"

"Don't get like that. It's just that you're friends. Internal Affairs has already asked about you."

"I knew it. I knew it! As if I didn't have enough to deal with, having to relive all that!" Ana pounded her hand against the wall for emphasis. "Fuck all of them, Luis, fuck all of them."

7

ANA

She tried to take the boy's hand. She squeezed it tightly, but it slid out from her grip. She looked at him to urge him, silently, to make an effort to help himself. To keep holding on to her so he wouldn't fall. But suddenly, instead of a face, the boy had a black hole, and in the middle of the hole, an enormous crimson mouth twisted into an expression of disgust that soon changed to mockery. Shocked, Ana opened her hand and let him go. The creature fell into the void. Far, far away.

The nightmare had come back. The same dream that had tormented her for months after the disappearance of Nicolás. The same agonizing dream that had come to her when, at the age of just twenty-two, she found her father's body decomposing and full of worms in his modest apartment in Barcelona. Only then, the dream didn't have a child falling into the void. It was her father.

Ana had not always been blond. She was born blond, yes, to her mother's amazement and her father's suspicions. Both of them were so dark. How could they have produced this little ball of nearly transparent hair, skin, and eyes?

Fortunately, the two maiden aunts of the family, Aunt Antonia and Aunt Ursula, hadn't wanted to miss the moment the new baby would be born. Who better than two sixty-something virgins to tell a mother

how to birth a child? Antonia and Ursula thought only *they* were quali-
fied to accompany and guide their niece during the process of expelling
the fetus, so they showed up on the maternity floor with all the necessary paraphernalia as soon as the tightly knit neighborhood network
of friends, associates, and nodding acquaintances spread the word that
Carmen's water had broken.

Antonia and Ursula were the reigning gossips of the family. To
their amazement, the doctor didn't let them into the birthing room, so
they had to stay on guard, almost in the doorway, while the nervous
first-time father bit his nails in the waiting room. Thus they were the
first to receive the news from the nurse, who exuded moral supremacy:
"Señoras, something very strange has happened, as you'll soon see. Tell
me it isn't the work of the devil, that this couple, such dark brunettes,
has produced a blond angel! God have mercy on the little one." The
nurse was wound up, convinced that the father was going to disown
the daughter as a bastard.

Aunts Antonia and Ursula bore the shock with dignity, because this
was no moment to embarrass the family. Their poor nephew, saddled
with a daughter who wasn't his! So blond, so impossible to hide, everyone would know! A policeman who couldn't keep order even in his
own house would be the laughingstock of his neighbors and colleagues.

While Antonia and Ursula mulled over how to manage the situation, the nurse, as if inflicting her interpretation on the maiden aunts
had not been enough, went looking for the father in the waiting room.
"Just look at how dark you are, sir," she blurted as soon as she saw him.

He lifted his head to look at her, not understanding a thing. What
was this white-clad woman telling him?

"Look," she said. "You've got hair blacker than charcoal. And your
wife too. Skin as dark as a gypsy. I don't mean to offend you, of course.
Anyone can tell you're not gypsies, from a mile away. But your daughter—
it's a girl, did they tell you that?—your daughter is almost transparent. I'm
telling you all this so you don't think we've switched babies on you. That

girl was already blond in her mother's belly. Something happened there, inside. Or before. Because you know how these things are. You know how some"—she stressed the *some* to erect a wall between such women and her dignified self—"women are." And with her head held high and a satisfied smile, the nurse swiveled and walked off, her heels beating the rhythm of her contempt all the way down the hall.

When at last the family was allowed to visit mother and daughter, no one knew how to act or what to say. Rodolfo held the baby as if taking advantage of every second before they made him give her back because she wasn't his.

But Aunt Ursula let out a shriek. "I know, I know, I know, I know, I know," she declared. "She's Paulina—that's who she is—she's Paulina. Can't you see?"

Carmen, the mother, didn't understand a thing. Who was this Paulina they were talking about? But Rodolfo smiled, tightening his arms around his daughter, cradling her against his chest. Now he knew the girl was his. The illegitimate daughter of a Dutch sailor had been reincarnated in this baby who still didn't have a name. Great-Grandma Paulina, Great-Grandpa Tomás's wife, had come back more than a century later to defeat the genes of the Aréns at last.

Blond Paulina had come into the Arén family a century before out of pure stubbornness, because in fact she had never loved her husband, Great-Grandpa Tomás. Not, at least, the way they said love ought to be, the kind of love that the rest of the maids in the household where she worked had told her about, the love she believed had to bring a ravishing passion that turned your stomach inside out. For Paulina, the earth didn't stop spinning when she saw Tomás. Her heart didn't ache out of a need to see him, and she didn't vomit from nerves waiting for the next glance from the man. From *her* man.

No, Paulina knew she didn't love Tomás. But he was her best card. The only good card that life had dealt her. Bet or pass? She bet. Tired of watching her mother wait in vain for the return of the Dutch sailor who'd left her pregnant, Paulina sought that absent paternal figure by marrying a man who would give her stability and a kind of armor against the barbs of a hypocritical society. When she decided to marry, there was only one eligible man, reasonably good-looking, and available—the man who brought the boxes of recently caught sardines to the service door, the boxes of the cheap and nutritious food that kept the domestic staff of the house alive.

His name was Tomás. He was twenty-five years older than she. A widower. Childless. The only card available. The only decent one that life put in front of her. And she bet everything on it.

He was a sailor, like the father Paulina never knew, but Tomás's little rowboat could barely take him a few kilometers from the port of Barcelona, just far enough to eke out a living catching sardines to sell to the city's poor. Thus Paulina could be sure that her husband would always come home. A sailor, but practically a freshwater one. A man not tempted by other ports.

Paulina turned out not to be very fertile, or maybe it was that her sailor got bored with always catching the same sardine in the same sea. In any case, they had only two children. True, those children gave them nine grandchildren who gave them twenty-three great-grandchildren. But in spite of all those descendants, the genes Paulina had inherited from the Dutch sailor vanished under the overwhelming power of the black eyes, cinnamon skin, and deep-blue-black hair of the Aréns.

Not a trace of blond porcelain in the biological legacy of the family. No eyes even a little bit lighter. No hair with a slight chestnut tint. No skin any closer to white.

Paulina's genes disappeared, forgotten like the sin of an ancestor, that of the great-grandfather who married a woman born outside of holy matrimony. A bastard, in short.

They disappeared, until Ana was born. Then it turned out Paulina hadn't vanished, had never surrendered; she was merely crouching in expectancy, waiting for the right moment and the proper woman. Four generations later, the bastard daughter of the Dutch sailor was reborn in the beautiful blond girl. Paulina took her revenge by reincarnating herself in a woman who, in the early twenty-first century, could aspire to a world of opportunities that Paulina herself never had.

Resurfacing in Ana, Paulina also avenged all the humiliation that Elisa, her mother, had suffered for getting pregnant as she did. Elisa had always hoped to meet the man of her dreams on one of those foreign ships that came to the port of L'Escala from the rich countries of northern Europe in search of the wine, sardines, anchovies, and coral that were the town's only wealth. Elisa had never liked what the Catalán tongue called the *nois* of the town—the boys, the lads, so uncultured, provincial, unlettered. They grew into practical men whose only dreams were to survive. Elisa wanted something more. Dreamed of something more. And her parents were getting very tired of that.

Every Sunday brought the same family fight. Elisa never wanted to go to the great weekly occasion for encounters between the single men and single women of L'Escala at the carousel on the pedestrian promenade of the village after the noon mass. Men and women, in separate groups, strutted up and down the *rambla*, showing themselves off, like stallions and mares at an auction, trying to attract someone of the opposite sex. Not Elisa. Elisa always escaped to go down to the port and dream about Jules Verne, about a voyage in a submarine, or travel from the earth to the moon, or a journey to the center of the earth.

"Damn the hour that girl learned to read!" her father always shouted at her mother. "Damn the hour you talked me into letting her go to school. Now her head is full of nonsense. Either you talk it out of her, or I'm going to have to beat it out."

Elisa was a virgin when she fell into the arms of Hendrijk Wersteeg, so blond and strong, so drenched in the odors of the sea that the mixture of salt and sweat on his skin stuck in the girl's throat like a fishbone, leaving an eternal scar. The only time in her life she made love was among the rocks at the far end of the town beach, with pieces of broken shells in the sand digging into her skin. Elisa didn't know how to describe what she'd felt on the night that changed her fate. She wouldn't have known how to say whether it felt good or whether it hurt. Whether it was long or short. Whether she felt that this was love. Years later, when she tried to evoke that moment, she could only remember the smell of the skin of the Dutch sailor she never saw again. Sweat and salt. Desire.

The future intended for her—a fisherman husband, or a small-scale smuggler, a house in the town, and many kids—evaporated while Paulina was growing in her belly. In spite of her mother's tears and protests—*If you throw her out, I'll kill myself; I swear I'm going to take my life*—her father disowned her without a second thought, banishing her from the house. *You've stained the family name. We're poor, but we have our dignity. I never want to see you again. Damned be you and your descendants.*

He gave Elisa time to toss a few clothes into an old bag, along with a few Jules Verne books she hadn't returned to the library.

Swallowing her tears, she walked off toward a new fate. If she survived the first months until the birth of her daughter, it was thanks to her younger brother, Xavier, who pulled out from under a floor tile in his room—the tile in the corner under which he had painstakingly dug out a secret place—all the money he'd saved from smuggling. Smuggling a bit of coral pulled from the sea floor by the beach. A few sacks of salt on which no tax had been paid. Preserved anchovies for the refined tastes of the rich of Can Fanga, as the townspeople, in those days, called both the city of Barcelona and its inhabitants. While a few residents of L'Escala grew rich off the contraband trade, those who took the greatest risks got only the crumbs. Still, those crumbs added up to more bread than Xavier ever made from an honest job.

"Take it, Elisa. Take it, sister. It's just a few pesetas, but it's all I have. When I make more, when I get rich, I'll come find you and take care of you both, you and the child. I love you, sister," Xavier had said, wrapping his arms around her. "If anything happens to you, send me word."

Xavier's money was enough for her to rent a squalid shared room in a pension in La Barceloneta, the sailors' quarter of Barcelona. There she met Amparo, another village girl who cleaned house for a bourgeois family growing wealthy off the construction of the new parts of the city.

"The Duràs," Amparo told her one day, "are looking for a nursemaid for their child who will be born in three months, they expect. Are you interested? You'll live in their new house, the one that's almost finished now, in the Passeig de Gràcia. With stables for their horses, even. Can you believe it? You'll live in a palace. I told them you're a widow and you know how to read, that you're clever and educated. Go, let them meet you. While you're nursing the child, they'll feed you well, and you'll have your own room that's warm and sunny. Much more than women like us can hope for in life."

And so Elisa raised two children—her daughter Paulina and a spoiled petit bourgeois who, once he turned six, grew ashamed of this provincial nursemaid who wasn't on the level of his divine, rich mother nor his divine, rich social circle, ashamed of the fake mother who was so different from the ladies who visited his parents' mansion.

"You're old and ugly. You're all used up," the boy cried one day to the woman who had fed, cared for, taught, and petted him for six years of his life.

Until that moment, Pau had always sought consolation and affection from his *tata* Elisa, who had been a real mother to him—the one who cleaned his wounds, who played hide-and-seek with him, who told him bedtime stories, who came to his bedside when he woke from a nightmare. Pau's universe was Tata Elisa and her daughter, Paulina. For the boy, his parents' world was something phony and annoying he had to pass through once in a while. Clean and stiff and starched, and he found it so hard to stay quiet and calm the way Papa and Mama always told him he had to be. He was the *hereu*. He had to learn how to behave. Pau withstood those moments by thinking of how good it would be when he went back to Paulina, how he would tell her about all the pounds that friend of his mother's had put on, the one who always wore those ridiculous ruffles over her breasts, or how they would laugh about the bad breath of the Marquesa del Puig.

But one day, while Elisa was stroking Pau's head because he was crying with rage because he couldn't climb the tree from which Paulina was sticking her tongue out at him as she sat on one of the branches, the child looked at his tata and spit out new words: *You're old, you're used up, you're ugly.* These words hurt Elisa more than her abandonment by the Dutch sailor, because she believed something about this boy that she had never believed about Hendrijk Wersteeg: that he was hers. But he wasn't. He never had been. Pau was just a dream, a temporary loan, an ersatz love who, the more he grew up, paid her back with the most absolute disdain. *You're old and ugly, your clothes are ugly, your hair is ugly, your hands are ugly, you're not like my mama at all.*

And although Elisa kept quiet, blinking back her tears and swallowing the hurt, Pau did not. And so, spurred on by the six-year-old dictator who had suddenly appeared, the Durà family found a *nanny* instead of a *tata* to raise Pau—a French nanny, a quality girl who wanted to learn Spanish and came with good references from Señora Durà's cousin, the Spanish ambassador in Paris, to whom they had written in haste with the request to send them a girl of quality who could take care of their son and teach him French.

When Charlotte arrived, they gave Elisa a choice: you can live on the street, or you can be a housemaid somewhere else. Repressing her anger and thinking of Paulina, Elisa chose the second option. And so the Durà family passed her along, like a piece of old furniture, to the corrupt assistant to the head of city planning for Barcelona, in return for construction permits in the city's new districts that would make them even richer than they already were. This assistant would never have the money or prestige or social position to build a mansion and fill it with servants, but this way, with a single servant, he managed to climb one small step on the social ladder. Elisa moved and spent the rest of her life wearing the skin off her knees, cleaning floors in return for a little food—just enough not to die of hunger—for herself and her daughter, and a bed in a moldy, windowless basement room. There, little blond Paulina grew up.

A century after her years in that basement and her marriage to the man who came selling sardines, Paulina was reincarnated in the blond girl whom her parents named Ana. There was no previous Ana in the family, and Aunts Antonia and Ursula complained without end, but her father didn't yield. *We're naming her Ana because that's what my wife wants.*

"But there's no Virgin with such a name," the aunts protested. "Saints, yes, but no Virgin. We have to name her after a Virgin, or the curse of the bastard daughter will be repeated."

"What goddamn curse?" Rodolfo shot back in a burst of masculine authority that shut them right up.

Ana was born blond like Paulina, but she didn't stay that way forever. After she entered the Police Academy in Ávila, she became a dark brunette. Because Spain, in 1990, had not yet completely shaken off the spell of *landismo*, as it was called. All those films starring Alfredo Landa, and others like him, served to lift the spirits of the iconic Iberian male—short, dark, and hairy—by making him the symbol of sexual potency at whose feet Swedish female tourists would swoon, when such tourists started to appear in the country in the late seventies after Franco was gone. So being blond was all well and good as far as being a Swede strolling down the beach in a tiny bikini, but not for steamrollering your way into the masculine turf of the National Police Academy. Because that was how Ana lived her life: everything to the limit in everything she did. Yet in the academy, it didn't matter what physical tests she passed or what exams she aced with the highest scores. To her classmates, she was still La Nancy, that other icon of the period, the doll with the blond hair that had taken little Spanish girls by storm.

She dyed her hair black the day her father died. To be exact, not the day he died but the day she found his body. In the worst of coincidences, Rodolfo Arén suffered a stroke during the week of an unprecedented heat wave in Barcelona. The forensic examiner said he must have been in the bathroom, just stepping out of the shower, when he had the stroke. He crawled to the living room to try and pick up the phone and call for help. That was where Ana found him, a week later. Naked. Dead. Rotting. "Papa, Papa!" she yelled while she turned the key in the door of the family apartment, already guessing what had happened before she stepped inside.

Mondays, Wednesdays, and Fridays were the days that his little Ana called him from the academy to tell him how she was doing. *I'm going to be a police officer like you, Papa. I'm going to make it.* But one Friday he didn't answer. Ana tried to brush it off. It was unusual, but she didn't want to worry. Worrying was a feminine trait. A trait of Las Nancys. She forced herself not to do it. She put all her willpower into not thinking about him.

And she succeeded, cursed be her soul.

But on Monday, again, he didn't answer. Now worry formed a lump in her throat, but she didn't dare reveal it to her superior, or even her classmates. La Nancy couldn't say anything. She couldn't complain or ask for favors. If she did, it would show she wasn't man enough to join the force.

Then Wednesday, on the eighth ring, Ana knew without a doubt that her father was dead. So dead that she could smell his corpse at the other end of the copper wire, and the smell grew stronger with every unanswered ring. Ana called Laura and Genaro, who lived in the apartment across the hall from him. "Wait, I'll go ring the bell," Laura had said. "Maybe his phone's broken. I'll go see whether he's home. Don't hang up."

But nobody answered the door. And Ana said, *Enough. Enough about Las Nancys, enough about being a woman, enough neurosis. No more.* She went to talk to her superior, told him what was happening, and headed for Barcelona at the risk of being expelled. She'd fix that up when she returned. Or not. Right then, it didn't matter.

She got to the small apartment in the Ciutat Vella without having slept, after an awful night in a bus that stopped in every village and town in between. The longest night of her life.

The scene was very hard for a twenty-two-year-old, even one studying at the Police Academy, even a tough girl. The smell hit her like a punch. Ana, always so sensitive to odors as a child, smelled death before she opened the door. Then she saw the maggots on the hallway floor, wriggling in something she later realized was the fluid draining from her father's corpse, a small river that began at his body and flowed almost to the entryway.

On tiptoes, so as not to step on anything, with her back pinned to the wall and her fingernails seeking purchase on the stippled paint, Ana made it to the living room. There was what was left of her father. Five days in a suffocating heat wave had converted Rodolfo's body into a hunk of meat that nearly disintegrated at the touch. When Ana stroked his cheek—*Papa, I love you, Papa*—the skin dissolved under her fingers. From dust we come, and to dust we return.

Ana never forgave herself for the fact that her father had died alone because she, feeling guilty about being a woman in a man's world, hadn't dared ask permission to go to Barcelona and find out what was going on. Rodolfo must have lain there flat on the floor, the examiner told her, agonizing by the telephone, for days. It took him forty-eight hours to die, naked on the floor tiles. If on Friday, when he didn't answer her call, Ana had listened to her intuition and jumped on a bus, maybe she would have gotten there in time to save him. Even if he'd been disabled, even if La Nancy had to push a wheelchair for the rest of his life. But no. La Nancy didn't ask for permission, and she would have to live with that decision forever.

Ana took revenge on her body. She cut her hair, dyed it black, and let go of the woman she had been up to that point. She had always tried so hard, but being a woman wouldn't do, just as it hadn't for her great-grandmother Paulina, so she proposed to do things differently. She began to attune her body and attitude to the male capacities she associated with survival and success. Without her even realizing it, her voice got a little deeper, her stride less graceful, her smile sourer. Her mind changed too.

When she got her first posting, at the age of just twenty-six, it was to coordinate a shift of six policemen at the front desk of the station of one of the toughest neighborhoods in Madrid. Every shift, they logged at least a hundred crime reports and a dozen arrestees brought in by the motorized patrols and beat cops of the barrio. And Ana had to assert her authority over them all.

On her first day at her new job, with the laurel-leaf insignia designating the rank of inspector on her sleeve, Ana made the acquaintance of one of her subordinates.

"Hi, sweetie, you're the new one, right? Lucky you're so good-looking," the policeman said with a wink.

"Do I know you?" she answered, swallowing to cover her nerves. "Either my memory fails me, or you and I have never even had a cup of coffee together. So here's how it is, and let me make it completely clear. From today forward, I'm your boss, and that's how you address me. Get it?"

Months later, one of the cops on her shift confessed to Ana that this moment had set them all straight. It had told them that the newbie had guts and needed to be respected.

Goodbye, Nancy. Hello, Chief Inspector Arén.

That was how it had been until Nicolás disappeared and she didn't measure up to the challenge of finding him. After a few weeks of national trauma, the country seemed to have forgotten the boy, but Chief Inspector Arén never did. Her failure made her reconsider her career. And now it had happened again.

Another boy. And the specter of The Taker again.

The morning after Manu disappeared, Ana turned on the news while downing her first daily dose of caffeine, always cold and carbonated—the only way it would wake her up. Lola, the mother of the boy, was on the television. Ana turned up the sound.

"Please," the woman said, trying to hold back her tears in front of the horde of reporters who'd been camping outside her door. "I know you're a good person, and Manu is very little. Look, here he is at his birthday party. See how cute and happy he is? Nothing will happen to you. You still have time, so just give him back. Leave him wherever you want, but let him come home to his mother, please. I forgive you. I know you're good."

The transmission cut from the mother's distress to a series of photos. In voice-over, the reporter explained that the woman had taken these pictures minutes before the boy disappeared. Ana had already seen them. They were the photos she'd used in the opening hours of the search. The boy wore tight black pants and white sneakers, but what was most striking was a Superman T-shirt on which someone had imprinted *SuperManu*. Anyone could see how much like Nicolás he looked.

Ana muted the TV. More pressure to solve the case. Having the mother crying on every news channel, over the radio waves, and on every web page didn't usually help an investigation, although in a case like this, to show such a clear image of how the boy was dressed when he disappeared could help possible witnesses remember him. But it would also flood the phone lines with false reports.

The memory of Nicolás paralyzed Ana. What if she failed again? What if this child, too, went up in a puff of smoke and was never heard of again?

Then she got a call from Inés, fishing for a tip, which only ratcheted up her anxiety. Ana called Major Bermúdez. It was 7:00 a.m., but he'd be up already—if he'd ever gone to sleep.

"Anything new, Luis?" Ana put the phone on speaker while she rifled through her dresser for something to wear.

"No, unfortunately. No idea, no clues."

"Still holding the father?"

"Right here, still. He keeps saying he went for a walk in the Woods, worn-out and disoriented. He said he was even thinking about taking his own life. But nothing to corroborate any of that. And his phone, as you know, was off. So far, he's our best lead. I'll tell you more when you get here."

"The Minister? Have you seen the mother on TV? They'll be after us from all sides."

"It's seven a.m., Ana. The Minister's sleeping or taking his first piss. The shitstorm hasn't even started. But I'm not very optimistic. You know that politicians have their own logic that has nothing to do with ours. So I'd recommend a heavy raincoat, just in case."

"Yeah, and it's too early for puns. I'll hop in the shower and get right over."

And Ana, dark-haired Ana, took a long, hot shower. A shower of the kind that could exorcise all your inner demons, but now it didn't even wash away the sadness and fear that had accumulated over the past few hours.

What Ana didn't know was that the anger she was feeling—and what would happen in the next few days—would forever change her. Again.

8

INÉS

Choosing a career in journalism means giving up on regular hours. If you don't know that already, you learn it the hard way. When you're a crime reporter, all the more so. The bad guys don't sleep or respect holidays. In truth, they don't have much consideration for us. Well, for humanity in general, really.

A case like the recent kidnapping kept us working around the clock. That Thursday, I had to get up at five to go live for the morning news. A marathon. However much you value your colleagues on the night shift and sympathize with their schedules and how shorthanded they are when putting together such a long show, still, getting up so early to hop on the merry-go-round of another live feed every half hour, from seven to nine, leaves you wiped.

But our theory about The Taker had stirred up such a tornado—rumor had it that the Minister of the Interior had personally called the news director at my channel, and not for purposes of congratulation—that I didn't have any choice but to get up before the crack of dawn. Four hours of sleep, then a few minutes to put myself together to look young and fresh and glowing. Television is all image. It doesn't matter how many hours you've worked and how few you've slept. All the viewer cares about are the forty seconds you appear on-screen. If you've got bags under your eyes or a lock of hair out of place or your jacket is twisted or you slip in your pronunciation of the slightest syllable, that's what they'll remember. That's what can ruin all your work.

The big problem we confront when we have to do the morning show, apart from sleepiness and faces from hell, is what to do with our kids. My four-year-old son Pablo was already in preschool, but it didn't start till nine. Fortunately, we had an English kid living with us for the year, an au pair who could cover for me. That way, Pablo got to practice his father's tongue and had a kind of temporary older brother too.

But the morning shift brought another problem. Was there anything new to say? At 6:30 a.m., there was no new information to speak of. All I could do was make a call I'd been avoiding for twelve hours. I took a deep breath. She answered on the third ring.

"Ana? Hi, baby. How are you doing?" I hoped I hadn't woken her up.

"Dodging shit, thanks to you." Her tone surprised me.

"Thanks to me?" I didn't know what I could have done to provoke that.

"Sometimes you're a space cadet, Inés. They think I'm the one who leaked you the idea about The Taker and all the information on the kid who disappeared."

"You're kidding!" I wasn't expecting that. "Ana, we haven't talked for weeks. Between your crazy life and mine, we hardly see each other."

"Tell that to the Minister, who's got the shit factory running. Who *did* give you the exclusive, in fact?"

"It's not mine, I swear. It didn't come from any of my sources. Somebody told my boss, Manuel. I didn't know a thing until he called me and sent me running to the mall. I was in the middle of something else, and I barely got there in time to go live. Everything I said on-screen came from him. I didn't even have time to make a call."

"Manuel has a source inside the police force? But he hasn't moved his butt from that warm seat in the studio for years! How can he have a source that would leak him something like this? It's too soon for any of us to suspect what might be going on."

"Well, that's what happened. Somebody gave it to him. Now that you say it, though, I can see how strange it is. Another strange thing is that half an hour earlier, he'd called and asked me to put him in contact with Joan."

"What the hell does your boss know about Joan?"

"Take it easy. Don't get upset. He just knows I have a friend who's very good at searching the web and sometimes gets me stuff I can't get any other way." I was trying to calm her down, but having emotional conversations when I'm about to go on camera makes me nervous and disrupts my concentration. "That's all he knows. What kind of idiot do you think I am?"

"Just be careful, Inés. Don't get Joan in trouble."

"Hell no. Just calm down." I didn't like the way this conversation was going.

Ana had to be having a hard time, taking charge of another case so similar to Nicolás's. Nor was it easy for me, though I didn't fully realize that until my adrenaline level dropped and I could rest.

"But listen, that's not why I called. You know I don't like to ask you for info and don't want to get you mixed up in TV stuff, even less so with The Taker, but I need some new little detail for today's show. Something to keep the exclusive going."

"Inés!"

"I wouldn't ask you if it weren't necessary. And I don't want you to tell me anything truly secret. Just something that doesn't compromise you that we can report."

"With friends like you, who needs enemies?" Ana snorted.

"Please," I pleaded, while parking outside the mall. It was close enough to home that I could have gotten there quicker by walking. The traffic, even at this hour, had been getting worse and worse. "Something that will come out today but that's not public yet."

I waited for an answer. Silence.

"Something that doesn't point to you. Something a lot of cops know by now. That anybody could have leaked to us."

"Well, the father," Ana said grudgingly.

"Whose father? The boy's?"

"Manu's father, yes. He's been detained. We have him in a cell at our unit."

"Did he do it?" I screeched, so worked up I almost tripped on my heels.

"We don't have any evidence against him, but he can't prove where he was between three thirty and when we picked him up last night."

"Holy fuck!" I tend to curse a lot—what can I do? "There's a piece of news! That undercuts The Taker hypothesis," I added, relieved.

"Don't jump to conclusions, Grau; you're getting ahead of yourself. All lines of investigation are open. Including The Taker. We're working on several hypotheses, including the dad. So far, we can't reject anything. But I haven't told you anything. You haven't called me or seen me for days. I'm not your source, and you're not trying to get me fired. Right?"

"Of course not, sweetie. No way. Leave it to me. Have a good day."

"That's in a manner of speaking, right?" she answered. And hung up.

A working hypothesis that provided an alternative to The Taker. Maybe it was the father, after all. Maybe.

With luck.

I did my live shoot like a queen. That's sarcasm, of course. A queen doesn't do a live feed at seven in the morning on the outskirts of Madrid with a wind chill factor of forty and not even a lousy coffee bar in sight. I rattled off my scoop about the father being held, and I did it again at seven thirty, eight, and eight thirty. Then I went to the studio.

"Good story about the father," some colleagues said when I got to the cafeteria to try to warm up by pouring boiling coffee directly into my gut. "Do the cops think he's the one? What did they tell you? Can we forget about The Taker? Is that all out the window?" Journalists gossip just as much as neighbors, although in our case we have an advantage: there's always a reliable source we can ask. And we ask, of course we do. If only to be able to show off later in front of our friends or the other mothers at our kids' schools.

"They don't know. The cops are still lost. Also, my source isn't connected directly to the case." I lied to protect Ana while taking small sips of coffee. It really was hot. "He's just repeating what he hears. He's not in the middle of the thing, so everything gets to him a little late."

"So it's going to be another long day. Several teams are already working on the story."

"Have they come out of the story meeting yet?" The heads of the different departments and of each newscast were meeting to determine the stories that would be covered that day. Once they emerged, the rush of phone calls would begin.

"Not yet. Don't worry, the phones will start ringing off the hook once the three o'clock team finishes requesting the stories they want by noon. Then we'll be off and running. If we don't come back with footage it's our fault, not theirs, even if they give us our marching orders too late."

The whole day was chaos. But as always, the hurry, the nerves, and the stress all stayed behind closed doors. Closed lenses, let's say. On-screen, everything looked polished and orderly, like a starched white handkerchief. Without a wrinkle. Without a blemish. Our exclusive on the father's detention gave us a leg up on all the other news channels.

When I got home that night, my son was already asleep. For a four-year-old, eleven o'clock is quite late. Once it got past nine, Sam said, Pablo was toast. So he'd put my son to bed. Sam was a treasure. He was a drama student at a university in the southern part of England, but he'd decided to take a year off. A friend had told him about her experience spending a summer in France, and he thought, *Why not?* I'd been thinking of a girl—au pairs are always girls—but Pablo, with many fewer prejudices than I have, asked for a boy. "Mama, that way I can play soccer with him, since you don't like to play."

In his profile, Sam stated that he could cook, although his notion of cooking, we learned later, was putting precooked food in the microwave and adding a personal touch that was almost always based on some strange sauce out of a jar. In his months with us, he'd become a great fan of gazpacho and its relative, *salmorejo*, even recording a couple of video tutorials for his family and friends. "Maybe that way they'll eat more vegetables," he said. Now I was teaching him to make bean and meat stews in the pressure cooker. If he kept on this way, I could see myself sending sausages to him in Plymouth through the mail.

He also loved outdoor sports and anything to do with creativity. I thought he could be a good influence on Pablo. Not just as someone in the house taking care of Pablo and teaching him English so he could understand his father's family, but also as an older brother he could do boy things with. Besides, my unpredictable hours meant I needed to have someone at home who could cover for me if my bosses summoned me at 5:00 a.m. or if a story had me out working till one in the morning. Sam took Spanish classes from 10:00 a.m. to 1:00 p.m. The rest of the day, he was free. I didn't get involved in what he did or where he went, or whom he was with, but we did have an agreement: he had to make himself available if I asked him to look after Pablo outside the usual schedule.

I knocked on the door of his room to tell him good night. Almost always, at that hour, I'd find him with his earphones on, stretched out on the bed, watching some Netflix series he'd gotten hooked on.

"Buenas noches," I said.

"Good night, Inés," he replied in English. "See you tomorrow."

9

LAURA/JOAN

Laura had been living alone for four years now, since poor Genaro died. She'd been living discreetly, just as before—not bothering anyone, not making noise, not standing out. The life Genaro had given her had been a boring one, without peaks or valleys as the saying goes. She'd never gotten along well with her husband, nor badly either. And that's what she'd settled for. Señora Laura, the neighbors called her now, out of respect for age or widowhood or both. Suddenly that's who she was—a poor, respectable old woman who lived in a third-floor walk-up. The neighbors carried her shopping bags if they happened to meet her on the stairs.

Laura could have become obsessed with death. What else did she have to wait for? Everything in her day-to-day existence seemed to lead to the family tomb, a rectangular niche 50 centimeters tall by 50 wide by 210 deep on the third story of block number three on Santa Eulalia in the sprawling, cliffside Montjuïc Cemetery near Barcelona's southern edge. *At least the worms that devour me will have a seaside view,* she thought. *Like the ones eating Genaro now.* Poor thing, always so mannerly, so correct, so devoted to walking the proper path. And for what? To end up in the digestive tracts of worms with a view of the Mediterranean.

The first few months after Genaro died, as she lost contact with the rest of humanity, Laura became increasingly convinced that she wasn't an interesting person. That she was as flat and gray as she'd been during her married life. So she stopped making any effort to socialize. The first alarm was sounded by Conchi, the local hairdresser. Laura had never missed one of her Thursday appointments, even after the operation on her shoulder. Four days after the surgery, with her arm in a sling, there she was. "Wash it and set it, same as always, please, Conchi."

So when Laura missed two Thursdays in a row, Conchi called her. "We miss you, honey. Baby, what's happened to you?" As she listened to the languid response from the other end of the line ("I'm perfectly fine. How else would I be? Just here, alone"), the hairdresser decided to organize a neighbors' patrol to try to liven up Laura's life. Operation Widow Rescue, the neighborhood ladies called it, as excited as if they were going to patrol the surface of Mars, not the streets of Ciutat Vella.

On the wall calendar that a hair-dye company had given to Conchi, they marked the visiting days assigned to each of them. Mondays, Maruja. Tuesdays, Roser. Wednesdays, Carmen. Thursdays, Amparo. Fridays, Conchi. And weekends, whoever could manage. At first, everyone reported for duty with excitement, like students for a class trip. But it was no use. Neither visits, nor coffee, nor even the chocolate *neules* that Roser brought her one time—nothing worked. Laura remained shut up inside herself. Lethargic, languishing. "If she goes on like this, she'll die," they all said. One more they'd lose. A life sentence.

Laura's lack of enthusiasm began to infect the rescue patrol. The first to miss one of the meetings of moral support was Amparo. "I have to take care of my grandchildren," she excused herself. Two weeks later, it was Maruja. And so on. Little by little, the members of the team drifted away. Little by little, they let Laura fall further and further into her lassitude.

Genaro's widow remained wedded to the idea that she was ordinary, anodyne, with nothing to offer to life.

And it would have gone on like that, until the predictable conclusion in the tomb with the worms and the seaside view, if she hadn't crossed paths with Joan one day on the stairs. They'd lived across from each other for a long time. The two apartments shared the third-floor landing, which looked down on the ruins of a forum that soldiers of the Roman Empire had built twenty-two centuries ago. But Laura and Joan hardly knew each other, just meeting on the stairs a few times a year. He had a very strange schedule, and she hardly ever left home.

That afternoon, by some miracle, their paths converged. Laura was coming back from buying hypertension pills, and Joan was on his way to get something to eat.

"My condolences, Señora. I heard your husband passed away."

"Six months ago, dear. Six months ago."

"Sorry, Señora. It's just, we don't see each other much."

"Are you growing a beard?" she asked.

"I've always had a beard. Even before the hipsters made them fashionable."

"The who? Oh, never mind. It doesn't matter, dear. Please call me Laura. I'm not that old," she said, laughing like an embarrassed teenager in the face of the tall, broad-shouldered man looking down on her. "We don't see each other much, as you say, or we just don't pay much attention. It's this modern society where nobody pays attention to anything but those websites, you know, those things they're always talking about on TV. But, young man, you don't look good."

"I'm tired. I've gone days without sleeping. I've had a lot of work, and now I can't get back to a normal rhythm."

As if events had predestined them to meet in that precise moment of the existence of the universe—curving space-time to join two points that were previously millions of light-years apart—that sentence changed Laura's life, and Joan's.

First it was half a blister pack of Orfidal pills. *Take them, honey, take them.* No, no, but thank you. *Yes, yes, take them. I always tell the doctor I can't sleep, and he always prescribes me a few boxes of this. I complain every time, whether I'm sleeping well or not, just in case, you know? Women my age like to hoard things. It must be because of everything we didn't have, after the war. Do you want to see the cupboard where I keep all the pills? I've got a ton of them. Look, come in. Here they are. All kinds. Want something else?*

And so, almost without noticing, Laura Aguilar became an unofficial supplier of pharmaceuticals. First for Joan. Later, and very timidly at first, for some of her neighbor's most intimate friends. Young people like Joan—for her, forty was still young—with strange schedules or too much noise in their heads. It was just a few pills, especially antidepressants and sleeping pills, but it made her more enthusiastic than anything in her life. Finally, she found a will to live. She carefully rehearsed all the arguments she'd give the doctor on her next visit. She had three doctors, two from the private coverage she retained from her husband's job, and one from the national health service—three sources from whom to extract prescriptions, and luckily, they had no connections among them nor any possibility of sharing the old lady's records. None of them would have believed it anyway.

In her late husband's old computer, and thanks to the Wi-Fi access Joan gave her as a present—*supercoolgranny* was the password he assigned her—Laura could find just the right symptoms to fool each doctor. She convinced one she was an insomniac, another that she was depressed, and the third that she was anxious, so she always had a big enough stash to supply her boys. They, in return, gave her something more important—the will to go on.

At first, when the boys came to her house to get the four or five pills they needed, they just exchanged pleasantries in the doorway. But little by little, Laura began inviting them in. First it was "All I have is tea," but later she'd keep a bucket of ice in the freezer to dispense chilled beers at any hour of day or night. Then she bought cured sausages, the expensive ones, to go with the beer and cheese strong enough to raise the dead. She got so enthused that she was almost to the point of shaving her head after binge-watching all the *Breaking Bad* episodes that her new friends had given her on a flash drive. *All I need is a chemistry course or two,* Laura thought, *to feel like a Catalán version of Walter White.* She even bought over the internet—her first online purchase ever—a classy T-shirt with "I Love Heisenberg" printed on the front, in English. She didn't quite dare, yet, to shave her head. She'd gone modern, but not too far. *If only Genaro could see me,* she thought. He wouldn't believe it. He'd die of fright.

"Joan, Joan," she said that Thursday, as she tapped her knuckles against his door. Always softly, avoiding the bell that was so strident and might wake him. "Joan, dear, I'm going to the doctor. Do you need anything?"

"No, thanks, Laura. You know I only take sleeping pills when I really need to," he answered, opening the door in pants and a T-shirt, and taking a look around to see what nosy neighbors might be on their way up or down the stairs. "Only when I've got those peak jobs with crazy hours and my head won't get back to normal."

"Oh, honey, at your age? And when you're looking so handsome?" Laura flashed him a naughty smile. "If only I'd found a guy built like you, and not Genaro, I could've been really happy, don't you think?"

"I don't know, Laura," he said, laughing and opening the door for her to come in. "I almost think you asked the doctor for pills for your libido. And I'm not so young. I'm forty, after all."

She laughed, too, doing her best to wiggle her hips on her way into his apartment.

"If only I could be that age again and have you," Laura said, then winked at him, putting her purse on the floor, a clear sign she was planning to stay awhile. "Listen, by the way, did you hear about the boy who got kidnapped in Madrid? They say it could be that Tooken again."

"The Taker."

"The Tamer?" she asked.

"The Taker. That's what the papers started calling him a few days after Nicolás was kidnapped, remember? Wow, already two years ago."

Joan leaned against the wall and ran his hands through his dark, curly hair. He truly was tired. He'd been up all night working, trying to help Ana and Javier, who'd asked for something crazy: to convert his computer program for detecting suicide bombers into one that could find pedophiles about to commit a crime. He didn't have the slightest idea where to begin.

"The Taker is an abductor. It refers to a legend created on the internet, in a forum where people post doctored photographs made to look supernatural."

"Oh my god, photos of ghosts!" Laura raised her hand dramatically to her forehead as if she were about to faint. You never knew when she was pulling your leg and when she was for real.

"More or less. It was something created for fun, but it got out of control."

It had gotten out of control and turned into myth. A user on a supernatural photos forum posted an image of nineteen kids playing in a park and Photoshopped behind them a tall, ghostly figure, of a thin man in a black suit with long tentacle-like arms. The Taker. The creator of the image, who used the pseudonym Max Pain, came up with the story that the picture had survived a fire at an insane asylum and that, tracing its origin, he'd discovered that the photo and the children in it had all disappeared, decades before, without a trace.

What would have been just one more joke in a small, specialized internet forum went viral instead. Tens of thousands of people throughout the world believed the case was real. They thought The Taker existed, that he was a tall, deformed, half-ghostly man who made children vanish. That was why the Spanish media had nicknamed the unknown kidnapper The Taker. Because the child disappeared without a trace.

"Oh, you're scaring me now. Do you think it's him? Do you think he's at work again?"

"Nobody knows anything yet. So don't worry. And anyway, you don't have any grandchildren to worry about." Joan was trying to put her at ease.

"Worse," she said. "Much worse. For a woman my age who has never had children or grandchildren, all the kids of the world are her grandkids. You don't know how much we suffer for all of them. A grandmother only worries about *her* grandkids. But we, the nongrand-mas, wear ourselves out over every child who falls off a speeding sled or eats too much junk food. It's like endless suffering. But I'm sorry to say, dear, that you really do look terrible today."

"Well, I'm trying to solve this problem, and I don't know what to do."

"If I can help you . . ."

If I can help you, the old woman was saying, but really—you had to know how to interpret her—she wasn't offering or making a suggestion, only expressing a wish. *Please, please, please let me help you. I need something to do.*

"Well, I don't know. I don't know, to tell you the truth, what you could come up with. But stay for a cup of coffee, and I'll tell you about it."

Since she was staying, he ought to be hospitable. Anyway, he needed a cup of coffee himself. He hadn't slept all night, and he was nowhere near getting through his work.

"Well, yes, tell me." Laura marched to the kitchen to fill the Italian stovetop espresso pot that Joan insisted on using, even in a day and age when someone like her had moved on to the modular machines. What a stubborn man he was. "Would you like a cookie or two? I have some at home."

"No, and I don't like you cooking for me here either. I'm a grown-up."

"Oh, honey, allow me my little ways," she said, with an exaggeratedly pleading expression, almost a parody, but charming in its way. "This is the grandma in me, like I was saying. I traffic in pills and know how to use a computer, but I'm still a grandmother."

Laura brought the coffee, cups, and sugar to the living room on a small striped tray.

"So what can I help you with? I've got fifteen minutes," she said, peeking at her small, gold-plated watch, an engagement gift from Genaro that had been on her wrist for fifty-three years. "The doctor is expecting me."

"Okay, how can I explain this? You know what Parkinson's disease is, right?"

"Of course. You know Angelita, Roberto's widow, the one who lives two floors up from us, in number nine, with her hair more puffed up than those women on the celebrity gossip shows? Oh, you don't? Well, she's got Parkinson's. You can see it. Her hands shake so much she can't pick anything up."

Laura sipped her coffee, taking just enough each time to feel the intensity of the taste. She wanted to extend that pleasure to the max. She wasn't allowed to drink much coffee; two of her three doctors had prohibited it because of hypertension or something. Those were real results that had come out in her blood tests and didn't have anything to do with her invented symptoms. Therefore, she fought against her caffeine habit every day, allowing herself just one demitasse cup. She savored each sip as if it were the last.

"A group of Spanish researchers," Joan said, "has developed a computer program that can detect when someone has Parkinson's."

"A computer tells them that?"

"Well, an information technology program, yes."

It was actually an algorithm linked to the neuroQWERTY program, and it could detect when a person was developing Parkinson's even before the first physical symptoms had appeared. With medical advances, it would soon be possible to delay the appearance of the disease. The earlier the detection, the better the prognosis. And Parkinson's was just the beginning.

The secret, Joan said, lay in the way a computer user typed on a keyboard, which is distinct for every user, just like fingerprints. The strength of the impression, the way we hold our fingers, the time we take to let the keys pop back up, the rhythm with which we type, and the mistakes we make—all these add up to unique patterns. In fact, our unique keyboard-prints could make it nearly impossible for anyone to pirate our digital identities, buy with our credit cards, or write a WhatsApp message in our names. Because nobody types just like us.

But if someone suffers brain damage or stress or other factors, that person's keyboard-print will change. All that's needed is to know what each variation indicates, whether it's a case of a neurodegenerative disease, or depression, or if that person is about to go on a suicidal terrorist mission.

Two years before, when Sub-Inspector Javier Nori was working on identifying and surveilling radical Islamists on the internet, Joan had proposed the idea of adapting neuroQWERTY to try to detect when the criminals were going to commit a terrorist act.

Professional assassins have few biometric reactions before they kill. Their blood pressure doesn't rise, their pulse doesn't race, and their mouths don't go dry. But novice killers, like the European sleeper cells of the Islamic State, can't control their bodies that way because they've never killed before. And this influences their keyboard-print. The only thing Nori and Joan had to find—*only*, as if it were a piece of cake—was how their keyboarding pattern changed in the moment when they were getting ready for the massacre.

It was known, for instance, that suicide attackers tend to sweat because of the adrenergic discharge produced by peripheral vasoconstriction. They blanch, get tachycardia, hyperventilate. But how might this influence the way they type? The only thing Joan and Nori had to go on, if they were going to find a way to stop suicide attackers before they struck, was the way their fingers flew over the keys. The question was how to detect when a significant change meant they were going to blow themselves up.

Over the years, Nori had created a multitude of false profiles on the internet, posing as a young sympathizer of radical Islamism, and these false profiles had garnered more than a thousand contacts. So the first step was to infect those contacts' computers with a virus containing his specially modified version of neuroQWERTY. That part was done.

Then came the hardest part: waiting. To see what changed in the keyboard patterns, they had to wait until one of those contacts committed an actual suicide bombing. After several attacks in Syria and Iraq, Nori and Joan had enough elements to create an algorithm that would detect the moment someone was beginning to exhibit the physical symptoms that preceded such an attempt. They hoped to be able to use this to stop the next big jihadist attack in Europe. If that next terrorist was included in their program, they were convinced they'd spot him or her—and, hopefully, be able to intervene.

The problem was that they couldn't go public with any of this. No police force in the world knew the program existed. All the two of them could do was give anonymous tips.

"Hmm. I understand what you're saying, mostly. Not all of it, but I get the idea," Laura said. "What does this have to do with the man who kidnaps children?"

"Well, now Ana has come up with the idea that we could try to find a formula to identify pedophile sex criminals that same way, through their keyboard-prints. Actually, not just to identify them, but to know when they're excited or stressed because they have a child in their hands. But how do you measure such perverse and guilty excitement?"

"Well, dear, something occurs to me. With, you know, the underwear."

"Underwear? What are you talking about?"

"The web page for panties. David and Pep showed it to me the other day when they came for their pills." Joan shot her an astounded look. "Don't you know it? Come here." Laura was already walking toward Joan's work desk, where three computers were powered up and running twenty-four hours a day. "I don't want to touch it, because these are your things. You type, go ahead: the three *w*'s, you know, and then *smellypanties*—all one word—dot-com."

"Smellypanties.com? Are you kidding me?"

"You say you need to detect how that pattern, about the typing, changes when certain people get aroused just by imagining what they're going to do. That's what happens to men who buy from this site. Look. It's a page where women sell used panties—that's what it is."

I'll wear them three days for you, so my scents ooze all over them. Every night, I'll masturbate so the juices of my orgasm soak them through and through, and then I'll put them in a vacuum-sealed bag and send them to you to play with as much as you want. Joan read wide-eyed, under the photo of the body of a girl wearing red cotton undies. "No fucking way!"

"I told you. David and Pep say the craze started in Japan, but now it's come to Spain, and these sites are making piles of money. They have thousands of customers. The women who are selling can't keep up with the demand for them to stain the panties and ship them out. Some customers even want them with a little, you know . . ." Joan waved for her to continue. "You know. Um." Finally, she had to say it. "A little of their poop."

Joan smiled. Laura's idea made sense. Maybe it would work. Maybe if he could gain access to the computers of the customers of that site—get the list by hacking into their servers—and observe their typing when they were ordering a pair of underwear and when the underwear was scheduled to arrive, it would be possible to establish the correlations to create an algorithm to detect excitement similar to that of pedophiles.

"Laura, what a brilliant idea!" Joan wrapped her in a big, tight hug.

"Come on now, dear, your neighbor may be a grandmother, but she's not made of stone. And at my age, there are things I just can't do, that aren't good for my heart." Again, she flashed that wicked look. "So don't be coming on to me. Just let me go. I'm on my way to the doctor now." Laura picked up the purse she'd left on the floor next to the couch. "My supply of Orfidal is running low, and your friend Adolfo told me he needs quite a few."

"Yeah, that poor guy has been working for a week with little sleep, trying to stop a very complicated cyberattack. So don't be late. I've got my work cut out for me, too, trying to see what I can do with this site. Give me a kiss, and off to the doctor."

It could work. Really, it could. When Joan sat down in front of his three computers, he forgot about being tired. The first thing he had to do was hijack the server of smellypanties.com and monitor all the clients and their orders. If there were really several thousand, as Laura had said, he'd soon have an algorithm that could detect the correlation between the patterns of excitement or arousal and the changes in keyboarding patterns. Then he just had to ask Sub-Inspector Nori to pass on the police list of known pedophiles—and, if possible, suspected ones—to infect their computers and apply the filter to them. He just hoped he'd be able to do it in time to save Manu. If his computer skills weren't good for this, then what the hell were they good for? To protect a slew of rich corporations from hackers? Well, yes, that was his bread and butter, but it wasn't what made him a good person, somebody who felt useful. He called Nori.

"Great idea. And you're telling me you got it from a woman over eighty?"

"That's right. A widow who throws caution to the wind. Maybe you can meet her someday."

"Was she Ana's neighbor, too, back in the day?"

"Yes, Laura's lived here more than fifty years. Hasn't Ana ever mentioned her?"

"The pill peddler?"

"Yeah, something like that. Listen, when you can, give me the list of pedophiles."

"Damn it, Joan, are you trying to get me fired?"

"You think I'm not running as big a risk? We're tiptoeing on the edge of legality, Nori. And I've screwed up too many times in the past, so I'm out of chances. Even if I find the magic algorithm, if I don't have anybody to use it on, what good will it be? I need that list."

"And what if they catch me trying to smuggle a flash drive with that data out of the station? Or someone checks my computer registers and sees I've downloaded it to an external drive?"

"You know how to clean your computer without leaving a trail. Don't raise stupid objections. Time is precious, and the clock is running against this kid. Every second counts, Nori."

"And suppose it's the father? He disappeared for a number of hours after the kidnapping. His cell phone went completely dead. We're holding him now. Ana questioned him yesterday but didn't get anything."

"How's she doing?" Joan asked, worried. "How's she holding up? This is Nicolás all over again."

"I don't even want to bring it up with her. I've seen her crying about the Nicolás case. She still hasn't gotten over that. And now the same thing again. A kid who could be Nicolás's twin vanishes into thin air from the same place."

"Like a loop. And she's running the investigation again. She won't sleep until she finds Manu. I'm worried about her, Javi. This could put her over the edge, like the last one nearly did."

"Let's hope the kid shows up soon. And alive. You know Ana can find him if anyone can."

"And our job is to help her, Nori. That's why I need that list. If I can come up with an algorithm, then we have to slip it into the computers of the people who could have done this. The people who could be The Taker."

"Which reminds me, did you know that Inés Grau was the one who came on Wednesday night with the exclusive on her news show?"

"Yes. More shit for Ana to deal with. Although your bosses are more worried about the case, Inés's scoop can't be good news for her."

"Yeah. A few minutes later, the Minister called. The shitstorm was intense."

"The whole police force knows Ana and Inés are friends. So they must think Ana's the one passing her the info. I'll call Inés to see what she can tell me. Have you talked with her?"

"No way. I haven't even had time for my daily one-hour run. I haven't been out there at all for over a day, and I'm climbing the walls. I need to run to think. And to get out of this bad mood. Being so pissed off is dulling my brain. I have to sweat out the bad blood—that's the only way I know to get rid of it."

By ten at night, Joan had gotten the list of the customers of the used-panty website and was sending them fake emails to implant the virus that would allow him to analyze their typing patterns. Then he'd just have to compare that data with the moments when they ordered and received the underwear, to try to extract the formula. The phone rang. His boss.

"Joan, what are you doing? Aren't you monitoring High Pharma?"

"Yeah, I've got it on one of my machines," he lied, "but right now, I'm cleaning the Credit Caja system. There seem to be some worms in there."

"And those alarms you've got—what good are they? Go look at the pharmaceutical one. They're one of our best clients, and we've got a problem. Someone's trying to hack into their central system in Kalamazoo to get into the research data on the new molecules. That's hundreds of billions of dollars. Their engineers don't know where it's coming from or how to stop it. It's serious, Arderiu. Serious."

Just what he needed. Here he was trying to help find a missing kid, and he had to slam on the brakes to deal with a case of industrial cyberespionage at a drug manufacturer. A rival pharma company or some hacker working for a mafioso who wanted to pirate the formula, he supposed. He was tempted to tell his boss to go to hell or to say that right now there was nothing he could do. But he restrained himself. He'd changed. He wasn't the same man as before. And he had to show that, every day. Like an alcoholic in rehab.

"Don't worry. I'll get on it right now. In a few hours, the attack will be history."

And he started to waste precious time that he could have devoted to helping the four-year-old who'd disappeared in the mall, already more than twenty-four hours ago.

10

ANA

Everything was beautiful, and that scared her.

Everything was beautiful when Ana moved into her small apartment on Calle de Amaniel, her new place with exposed beams of burnished wood, on a street that was quiet in spite of being just a short walk from the Gran Vía in central Madrid.

She thought of her father every day. But by then, it had been four years since Rodolfo's death, and the nightmares of his corpse falling apart in her hands had begun to loosen their grip. At first, the dreams were so real that when she woke up she could still feel the dust in the grooves of her fingertips. She would look at her hands and seem to glimpse the remains of what had once been her father's muscles, veins, nails. She'd exhale toward them, lightly, to blow the remnants away. *Off you go,* she'd say. *Time to become something else. Go blend with other atoms of the universe, turn into hopes or grass or a star or the new Shakespeare. You're not my father anymore. Now you can go.*

In her new place on Calle de Amaniel, the nightmares began to fade, and when Ana closed her eyes, seated on her couch that was so white and surrounded by walls so white as well, she felt at last that she had found a home.

Everything was beautiful, but that scared her too.

She was afraid of loneliness, for example. Up till then, Ana had always lived with other people: with her family, or in the Police Academy, or with roommates as a police intern.

She was also afraid of not fitting in. Ana had felt excluded too many times in her life. First the chubby nerd in school, the girl who won all the writing and math contests, at the head of the class though she never set out to be. Later she became the weirdo in college, the only one who didn't cut classes to hit the bars, who didn't play cards or let anyone borrow her lecture notes, the one who had to work afternoons and couldn't ever hang out. And in the Police Academy, she was La Nancy, the blond who'd suddenly slimmed down—and who then had to learn to conduct herself like a man. The doll who was capable of biting, if need be.

There was no way around it. Ana liked to win, even if she also liked to get along. She *needed* to get along. She had a vital need for people to like her, a need that was almost unhealthy.

Only, the two things were incompatible. She learned that through hard knocks. Either you win, or you get along.

But not both at once.

That Thursday morning, Chief Inspector Arén wanted to win. At any cost. To beat the bastard who had taken that child. To defeat him, smash him, stomp him, destroy him.

Manu's father was still being held at the station. Maybe a long, cold night in a cell had forced him to think things over.

"Hello, everyone," she greeted her colleagues. "Anything new?"

"The search teams have gone over the area around the mall with a fine-tooth comb, twice," Luis Arcos said. He looked worse than anyone; at his age, he didn't tolerate sleepless nights very well. "They haven't found anything. Not a trace. Like the kid went up in smoke."

"Don't even think of using that expression in public," Ana warned them all. "Don't even think of saying 'not a trace' or 'up in smoke.' Erase those words from your vocabularies, you hear? We've got enough pressure from the media speculating whether or not this is The Taker all over again."

"But Chief Inspector, suppose it is."

Her team was worried. They'd failed two years ago and didn't want to go through it again. The wound was still open. If it was the same psychopath, many colleagues would feel it deeply. The investigation would suffer. Ana couldn't accept that, but more importantly, neither could Manu.

"For now, all hypotheses are open. We aren't rejecting anything. Who's on the mall employees?"

"Me," said an officer.

"And who are you?"

"José Barriga. I joined the unit yesterday, transferred from the station in Fuencarral."

"Okay, José Barriga. Did you get a good look at my ass yesterday? Enough to tide you over for a while, or should I turn around slowly so you can satisfy any doubts?" Ana challenged him, remembering what Charo had told her the day before. "No? Okay. Then we can go on, without any distractions." She smiled. "Barriga, joined our team at a great time, didn't you?" she said. "I hope you don't jinx the unit. Anyway, what have you found out?"

"I've got the list of all the employees in the mall. So far, none with any record of sex crimes. A few thefts is all. But we're still missing some, because not all the stores have turned in their lists."

"Then hurry up. Go over there and jump over counters if you need to." What the hell was the new guy waiting for? Manu had disappeared more than sixteen hours ago, so they should have checked out all the employees by now. "And get lists of former workers too. Question the current employees, get them at work or go to their homes, and ask whether anyone noticed any suspicious behavior. Take Arcos with you."

"Yes, Chief Inspector."

"Oh, and one more thing! Two years ago, the mall parking lot didn't have cameras. Ask whether they've installed any, and bring me the list of the license plates of cars that went in and out during the past twenty hours."

On her way downstairs to the interrogation rooms, Ana ran into Nori.

"Did you get any sleep?" Nori asked.

"Three hours, enough to run on adrenaline all day today." Worn-out, she rubbed her eyes while leaning against the banister that had been crying for a new coat of paint for decades. "Anyway, I bet I slept more than you. You've been out jogging, haven't you? Giving up sleep for jogging is like a sickness with you."

"Running is like faith, baby. How many times have I told you that? Either you've got it, or you don't. Once you've got the bug, you're the biggest convert in the kingdom." Javier put his palms together, like he was praying. "And you're wrong. I haven't been out this morning. I went last night when I got home, needed to sweat out all the shit from yesterday." He looked up and down the stairwell to make sure no one was around. "Have you talked with the commander?"

"Yeah." Ana looked puzzled. "We spoke a while ago. Is something up?"

"Apparently there are changes in store. Remember when we got the news of the boy's disappearance?" That was just a day ago, though it seemed an eternity. "Luis was about to tell us he's leaving."

"Leaving?!"

"*Shh*, don't shout. Anyway, the director general will freeze all transfers with all this going on."

"We'll see. If Luis goes, that's bad news for the whole division. Well, I need to be heading off for room three," she said. "Manu's father's still in there, right?"

"Yup. Good luck."

Room three was the most modern in the station. Although saying that wasn't the whole truth. It would be more accurate to say that it was the least obsolete. The least decrepit. The one to be least ashamed of. Though, in point of fact, why make the place comfortable if the idea was to extract truths in there? Why paint the walls, or fix the bad legs that made the tables rock, or remove the rust that had eaten into their tops, or replace the worn-out chairs? Why, given the guests in this place, worry about appearances or comfort at all?

As they aged, the interrogation rooms became part of the machinery of fear. The suspects, particularly the first-timers, imagined everything that could have gone on there over the decades. They faced the ghosts of the thousands who had been questioned—and tortured, maybe, in eras past—who had sat on the same chairs surrounded by the same walls.

But what made room three different was a modern audio and video recording system. Modern by police standards, that was. Any member of the Judicial Police who had the proper access credentials could see, on his or her computer, what was happening inside. Obviously, the interrogator had the power to cut the signal at any point, because sometimes it was better for certain things not to leave the room. At least, not right then. And sometimes never.

Before going in, Ana observed Manu's father through the one-way mirror. No matter how many times she'd done this, the chief inspector could never get used to it. She always had the feeling that the suspects on the other side could feel her presence, which was what happened to her when she sat in the interrogator's chair. Ana could perceive the gazes fixed on her mouth, her hands, her movements. She sometimes imagined pairs of eyes passing over her, trying to guess her next move and which way her next question would tilt. Like a chess player, Ana had to think many moves ahead, and each one was only a prelude to the endgame she had in mind. The checkmate. The collapse of the guilty party. The confession.

Ricardo didn't look any different from any other man under arrest who had spent a night sleeping on the hard cement of a police station cell. He was a mixture of exhaustion, cold, fear, despair, and loneliness. A person who urgently needed someone to come into that room, whomever it might be, to question him, to talk, for God's sake, to at least offer him a fucking word.

Twelve hours in a cell made suspects a bit more receptive. *You need to let them ripen, Ana, before you go pressing out the juice.* That was what Major Bermúdez always said to her. Let them stew in the juices of their own conscience. And those who haven't got a conscience, let them stew in their own fear. And those who've got neither conscience nor fear, you've got to stew them yourself.

Manu's father seemed to be sufficiently ripe. A night without sleep is tough. After twenty-four hours without disconnecting, one's brain doesn't see things the same way. It starts to be unable to control itself. The barriers of conscious humanity drop away. Prudence, shame, and control fall apart. For the police, that makes it easier to defeat the accused.

"Good morning, Señor . . . uh"—Ana pretended to consult the folder in her hands—"Señor Jiménez. Are you comfortable? Do you need anything?"

"Manu, Manu. Where is he?"

He was a good actor; that was clear. Ana sat down in the chair across from him at the metal table. *Where is Manu?* She practically believed him.

"That's what we want to know, Señor Jiménez, that's what we want to know. Where's Manu? Tell me, and we can be done with this. You're tired, I'm tired, we're all tired." Ana talked to him and looked at him like a teacher explaining something to a child.

"I didn't do anything! I didn't do anything!"

He was starting to shout. A good sign. If he were guilty, of course. Officially, what was happening in room three of the basement of the station was not an interrogation, because in an interrogation, the accused has the right to a lawyer. Officially, this was a conversation, a talk, an exchange of ideas. Later on, in a trial, when some defense attorney got clever and tried to strike what the defendant had said in these moments, Ana would remind the judge that in no article of the criminal procedure law was it written that the police were not allowed to chat with a person who had been detained.

"Let's start at the beginning. Where were you at 5:15 yesterday—Wednesday—afternoon?"

Ana pretended again to be looking at her paper, as if this questioning were a mere formality, an annoying procedure she wanted to get over with as quickly as possible.

"I've answered that a million times already. I was exhausted. The divorce is hard for me to deal with, okay? It's not easy to have your wife tell you she doesn't love you anymore. That it's over. Goodbye, but you know what . . ."

"Chief Inspector. Chief Inspector Arén."

"You know what, Chief Inspector Arén? You know what was hardest of all? For my wife to tell me that my body revolts her. That she couldn't touch me. That my skin repelled her. Has anyone ever said this to you? Have they?" Manu's father buried his head in his hands, ashamed of his own weakness. "That I disgust her. Do you believe that? My own wife."

"We've all been rejected at one time or another. I can imagine how hard it must be." Ana was feeding him bait, little by little. "You must have been very angry."

"What do you think? Huh? What? That I threw a party?" Now he was getting mad at her. Good. "Of course I got angry. And I tried to argue with her. She loves me—she must love me. All this is something that's gotten into her head," he said, stabbing at his skull several times with his index finger. "Here, in here, this foolishness has gotten into Lola's head."

"I believe you did get angry, very much so. That you lost it, lost control. And did something you didn't want to do."

Patience. Patience. The key to a good interrogator was patience. To act like it didn't really matter, so that the silence of the detainee didn't put you off your stride, so his lies didn't drive you nuts.

"You wrote your wife this WhatsApp message." Ana handed him a photocopy of the screenshot from the mother's phone. "At 5:15 on Wednesday afternoon. Could you read it to me, please?"

"Yeah, I wrote it. 'Lola, I'll take Manu tomorrow to spend the weekend together. Don't pick him up at school on Friday. Pack his suitcase, and leave it in the secretary's office. I'll pick it up on our way out.'" Ricardo raised his eyes, as if remembering only then that he'd written that message. "Yes, I wrote it, and it's true."

"At 5:15."

"That's what it says there, doesn't it? Five fifteen. Do I remember exactly the time, to the minute? No. You can understand that, Chief Inspector. Do you remember exactly what time today you washed your hands? The exact minute you most recently took a piss? Cut the crap. Since yesterday, I've been locked up in this filthy cell, and my son has disappeared. Those are the only details I can give you. If the screen says 5:15, then it was 5:15 when I sent the message. Technology never fails, right? I wrote it while I was driving. That's all I can say."

"Well, now I have a problem. The thing is"—Ana consciously spread out the silences between her words, so they'd hang in the air and echo in the brain of the detainee. "The thing is, I have a problem. The problem is that at that time, at 5:15, your phone was shut off and without coverage. You turned off your phone at 5:05 and didn't turn it back on until we found you, after nine that night. Did you program the message to go out at that time? Did you use some kind of remote program? How did you do it?"

Ana's job was to take the person being questioned to their limits, to the point of no return. The place where the guilty fell apart. It wasn't always easy. It didn't always happen. Often the police led the suspect before a judge without having extracted a confession. In those cases, all the weight of the accusation fell on the evidence they could assemble. And the evidence against Ricardo was too flimsy to stand.

That's why Ana had to extract a confession.

Often, to break the suspect, Ana found herself compelled to lie, to pretend she had more information than she really did. To pretend she'd found evidence she really didn't have. To pretend that an accomplice or witness had confessed to something they hadn't.

"Because the fact is, you weren't really where you say you were. You weren't wandering around the Pilar Woods, drowning in sorrow, a poor little abandoned man." Ana looked at him with a blend of sympathy and disgust. "I'm going to tell you where you were. You were following your wife. You went to the mall. You wanted to make her mad so she'd get distracted. And you took advantage of that to take Manu. Because, of course, taking him from school wouldn't work. Everyone would have seen it. And you didn't want them to see you. Right?"

Belief. You had to go into the interrogation room convinced that you were going to get a confession. A few minutes before, Ana had been more than convinced. She was almost sure that she was going to drag the truth out of this man. But it didn't happen. Manu's father went back to square one.

"You're crazy if you think I would do any harm to my son. Tell me where he is. Let me out of here so I can go look for him. Let me out of here!" He was on his feet now, as much as he could be in spite of the cuffs that attached his wrists to the table. "I want to see my wife. Bring my wife in here!"

How could you tell the innocent from the guilty? There, in an interrogation room, sometimes it was very hard to tell. And right then, she wasn't as sure as she'd been when she walked through the door.

11

INÉS

Friday was no different from Thursday. The boy again, his disappearance, The Taker. The media were obsessed with the search for Manu. The crime reporters, all of us, worked sixteen-hour days, contacting all our sources to try to get something out of them, cashing in on IOUs from every favor we were owed, and keeping a close eye on each other in case anyone came up with a scoop. It was war. A war among colleagues and friends. We politely congratulated each other over social media, all the while itching to know who the hell had leaked that fact and why our sources hadn't told it to us.

To get out in front of the others, I had only one option.

I had to call Ana again. But I knew I couldn't. Unfortunately for me, Ana was not just any old source. She had crossed over my wall between journalism and friendship. Ana was my friend, and for someone like me, that's saying a lot. My tendency is to avoid relating too much, on a personal level, with most people. This has been getting worse as I age, and I think I must have inherited it from my paternal grandmother. "You're just like your father's mother," Mama always says to me, "just like her, for God's sake! Why did you have to take after her? Mad at everybody all the time, as if the universe always owed her something." My grandmother had ended up so unhinged that, as an old woman, she thought the other residents of her apartment building were stealing her water through holes in the pipes. Or that they were siphoning her electricity. "Don't you see it? Don't you see," she'd demand of anyone who came into her house, "the way the lights are so weak? They're stealing my current—that's what it is." By the end, she was no longer on speaking terms with anyone in the building.

When we finally took her to a nursing home after she broke her ankle and couldn't live alone, she ended up in a single room because nobody could stand living with her. She accused her first roommate of stealing her stockings. The second roommate, she said, was always using her perfume. And the third was plotting to take over her bed because it was by the window. At last, even though we were only paying for a double room, my grandmother prevailed, and they assigned her a single. She was clever about things like that.

I hope I'm not headed for such extremes, but I admit that I've been getting increasingly tired of having to feign interest in certain people and situations. Maybe that's me getting older, because there are only four things that grow larger with age: our eyes, our noses, our eyeglass magnification, and our bad mental traits. And I've been starting to notice the first symptoms in myself. I worry less and less about getting along or conforming to social etiquette—except with my sources, for whom I make the effort because that's my job. And my friends, of course. I do try to take care of them, even if I can count them on the fingers of one hand.

Ana, Nori, and Joan were the closest I had to a real gang, though we didn't see Joan very much. He spent most of his time in Barcelona, though he did keep a little studio apartment here in Madrid, for when his work required him to spend some time in the capital. He didn't like hotels. He didn't trust anyone. It was important that no one knew where he was or where he slept—especially considering his ultra-secret work, which he told us almost nothing about. Suddenly I remembered I needed to call him.

"You're a big hit these days," he said as soon as he answered the phone.

"What I am is exhausted, and I've only been covering the case for forty-eight hours."

"If they don't find him soon, interest will wane. You know how these things go, Inés."

"Don't I ever? But I called you about something else."

I explained about my boss, the strange call from Manuel, which had slipped my mind completely.

"What did he want with me?"

"How should I know?"

"You don't know, but you'd like to, am I right?"

"Evidently. He's got some dirty laundry he wants you to wash, and I'd love to know about it, yeah." I felt myself smiling.

Joan promised to send me a WhatsApp message with an email address—one of his many anonymous and untraceable accounts—to which my boss could write and tell him about the problem. I told him to lay on some mystery and macabre, because Manuel thought Joan was some kind of Gollum who never left his cave, and I wanted it to stay that way. The more inaccessible he thought my sources were, the better he liked my work.

It's one of the ironies of life, that among my best friends were two cops and a hacker, although over many months we'd lost contact quite a bit. After the disappearance of Nicolás, Ana cut herself off. She lived only to find that boy and whoever had taken him. Right then I, too, was going through a bad time, so we distanced ourselves and ended up reducing our communication to emoticons. Suddenly there was a gap between us. First it was days, then weeks, then months. With each passing day, it got harder to pick up the phone, and we didn't have the courage, strength, or willpower to realign the vectors pushing us apart.

Maybe it was resentment. Maybe embarrassment, or shame, or fear. Whatever it was, something had come between us. At first, the chasm was no deeper than a curb. But as we let time slip by, telling ourselves that tomorrow or the next day we'd make the effort—that first step which, in the beginning, could have brought us back together without any fuss—that curb grew into a solid and impenetrable wall.

We spent almost a year without seeing each other. It was Joan who finally brought us together, on one of his visits to Madrid, as if we'd been waiting for someone else to take that step for us. We met up at his little place. We got Chinese takeout, so crummy and greasy that it made us laugh. That eased the tension. By the time we left, it was as if the dark chasm had never existed. But it had. And such things never completely go away.

For all these reasons, it would have been crazy to call Ana to ask her for information about the case, because really what I would have wanted to say to her was *Come on, girlfriend, let's go have a few beers, laugh, cry, and trash a few people we know. Let's enjoy each other's company and blow off steam and put ourselves back together. That's what we need. And if you can't do that for me, girlfriend, I don't know who can.*

But I didn't do that. I called other numbers and said other things. Easier numbers and easier things. I went to other contacts on the police force, even though their information was sparser and colder than what Ana would know. All of that was more antiseptic. Which meant that all of it hurt less.

Friday's live feed was no big deal. Missing for two days. All avenues of investigation open. The father making a deposition before a judge, and the country going into shock because it had to be The Taker again. The talk shows pursued the politicians and filled the roundtables with crime reporters, researchers, psychologists, psychiatrists, and anybody who could offer some filler, whether that was plastic peanuts or actual facts. We had to fill hours of programming and pages of print. Meat for the carnivores.

And not to be left out, of course, was my editor. Cursed be my soul.

"Inés, I just saw you on the news."

"Paco, I was wondering why you hadn't called. I figured you lost my number."

He didn't hear the sarcasm, or maybe he did. Maybe he was smarter than I thought, possibly the cleverest of all, and right then he didn't want a confrontation.

"Are you kidding?" he said. "Lose the number of my star? Forget to call my author who topped all the bestseller lists? Inés, you're scoring big with the kidnapper story. You're back on top of the wave, queen of the ratings, in the homes of millions several times a day."

"So?" I said while I started the car. If I hurried, I could get to the studio before the cafeteria closed. Dealing with Paco made me hungry. Starving, in fact. Dying to eat, as if a full belly would allow my brain to hit the pause button and finally take a rest. I was fed up with the guy. Damn the moment I signed a two-book deal with him. I'd regret it all my life. But I still didn't know how much.

"So? So? How can you ask me that, Inés? So you've got to seize the time, that's what. You've got to strike while the iron's hot. We could announce you're at work on another book. What do you think? I don't mean right now; we have to show a little sensitivity, of course."

Sensitivity? I had to laugh. Coming from him?

"But in a few days, we can put out the word that you're working on something new. It'll be a bombshell. Guaranteed headlines. And if you were to write about The Taker . . ." He paused to see what effect that name would have on me. "The sky's the limit."

"I've told you a million times. The topic of The Taker is taboo for me. Period."

"By the way," he said, changing the topic, "how did it go the other day at the group therapy thing?"

"That depressing place you forced me to visit?"

It was the truth, and he knew it. It seemed his only goal in life was for me to publish another bestseller.

"They didn't recognize you, did they?"

"Man, what do you think? You think they would have allowed a TV crime reporter to sit there taking in their troubles? Don't worry. I had on a disguise. And I didn't open my mouth."

"But how did it go? Did you find a good story?" Always immune to discouragement, Paco was.

"Well, really . . ."

And for a fraction of a second, that short bald guy with the round glasses, that man who seemed to have been born to spend his whole life banging his head against walls that he'd break down only through pure tenacity and being a pain in the ass—for a fraction of a second, I felt sorry for him. And nearly said yes, that I had a story, that I'd been fascinated by the horror of the young mother who'd been left to choose which of her three children to sacrifice. But fortunately it was only that, a tiny moment of weakness. If he smelled the slightest hint of blood, Paco would come in for the kill. So I backed off as best I could. I told him the attendees' lives were all insipid; their confessions wouldn't even make a short story, let alone a novel. "I don't know what you thought a place like that could inspire," I said.

"Come on, Inés. For God's sake, the whole world's waiting for your next book. I already told you I'd hire a ghostwriter, if you want. All you have to do is put your name on it."

"Yeah? And a ghost to do my TV appearances while you send me on a Caribbean vacation?" I spit back. "*That* I'd appreciate, Paco. Sincerely. I'm tired, and I've had it. I've had it with you pushing me too."

"I'll hire you that ghost and take you to the Caribbean whenever you want, babe. But you have to give me something in return. A few chapters, a sketch, a couple of pages. I'm begging you. Show me some charity. Have pity on a poor editor."

I pictured him begging into the phone, praying with his hands, raising his eyes to heaven like an old woman at Sunday mass. I almost burst out laughing.

"Look, Paco, I've had two horrible days. With this reemergence of The Taker, you can just imagine, we're full speed ahead. My boss wants me to work tomorrow morning, Saturday, to help out the weekend crew. And I've blocked out Sunday to spend time with my son, who deserves it, who's gone two days without seeing me. If you want, we can talk Monday. Right now, I've got no time for you."

"Monday, without fail, Inés. Monday. Think about the idea of The Taker. Or a novel based on him. It doesn't have to be the real case, I mean." Again I felt a little sorry for him, for his having to beg in that way. "You're good, and you write so well. You just need to get started. And to be, you know, chilled out so you can write."

"Chilled out. If I'm ever chilled out, Paco, it only lasts till you call."

So much sad news to report, so much blood, so much drama, and in the end, what was it that really drove me nuts? Human depravity? No. A short, fat editor. Why the fuck was that?

"Sorry," I said, "I have to hang up now. I'm driving into the parking lot."

"But you'll think about it, okay?"

Now his persistence made me think of Chinese water torture. So he'd leave me alone, I said that I'd think about it.

"Who were you talking to?" asked Xavi, the coordinator of the weekend news show, parking his car next to mine. "You should see the expression on your face."

"My editor."

"New book?"

"You too? Don't start, Xavi."

"No, it's just that you look like you want to strangle someone."

"Did I ever tell you about the guy I met last year while I was doing those stories on the Romanian mafia? The guy who was paid to break legs?" Judging by Xavi's expression, the answer was no. "Well, this guy told me he broke legs for money. Legs or anything else, short of murder, he said, though I think he kills, too, if somebody will pay him enough.

I kept his number in case I might need him someday." Xavi's look now said he was trying to figure out whether I was kidding. "Or if you need him sometime, I'll tell him to give you a cut rate. There are times when you need to know how to get a leg broken, right?"

"You're a psychopath. You just don't realize it," Xavi said with a laugh as he walked off. Then he turned back to say, "Just one thing, Inés. If you walk in the newsroom someday with a bayonet or a machine gun, remember to spare my life. Remember that I'm the one who brings you a bite from the bar for breakfast." He winked. "I'm going up to the office. You coming?"

"No. I'm going to eat."

Friday. Friday at last. Even though I had to work Saturday, at least I wouldn't have much left to do on Sunday. I wanted to spend the whole day with Pablo. Manu's disappearance had made me hypersensitive to my son's needs. Plus, Sam had asked for Sunday off. So it would be just Pablo and me.

I had no intention of writing about The Taker. Ever. And I wasn't planning on going back to the group therapy session no matter how much my editor pleaded. Lucía's story had made me feel, for the first time, all the pain a mother felt when her child died. It made me understand a lot of things.

I had no desire to confront that again.

12

NORI/JOAN

Javier Nori passed the exam for promotion to sub-inspector by running ten kilometers a day on the outskirts of Madrid. First, he read the entire prep course out loud—all 50 chapters, all 898 pages—word for word. It took him two whole weeks of slow, mind-deadening reading into a voice recorder, but it was worth the trouble, because then he had an MP3 file holding eighteen hundred minutes of sound. Thirty hours. That's why he took up running, because it required kilometer after kilometer of putting one foot in front of the other to listen to the entire thing, twice, which was what he had to do to master the material.

What Nori realized was that running could relax his mind. Right, left, right, left. His body went along mechanically, stride after stride, allowing his brain to reach a state of semiconsciousness in which he could concentrate on his own voice and what it was saying. Mass behavior. Social conflict and class conflict. Techniques of observation for police purposes. Police duties with respect to groups and crowds. And more—all fifty subjects. One after another, they cascaded through his neurons.

It took him some time to get used to this. Not so much to the running—over time, the aches and pains faded away—but to hearing his own voice. No one likes the way their voice sounds when they hear it for the first time. Our *real* voice, the one that people we're talking to hear. Not deep, higher pitched than what we hear ourselves. Even in the best of cases, our real voice is a disappointment compared to the one that resonates in our skull.

Overcoming his distaste for that stranger speaking to him—the stranger who really was him—Nori listened to the sub-inspectorship course again and again. Right, left, right, left. One kilometer after another. One subject after another. Penetrating his brain to the rhythm of his breathing and his strides. He took the words into his brain as he inhaled oxygen for his muscles to power another stride.

And he passed the exam.

Even now, that technique of listening to a voice while he ran allowed him to put his mind at ease so he could concentrate on the essentials and discover aspects of a case that he might have missed or connect apparently separate events that would yield the solution to a crime. These days, when Sub-Inspector Javier Nori went out to run with his earphones on, instead of a playlist of musical hits, he assembled the recordings of all his notes on the case. And he didn't need to voice-record them, because various programs could convert the notes he wrote into dictation form. Nori no longer had to hear his own strange voice that had taught him the content of the sub-inspector exam. Now he could choose the gender, the tone, and the cadence of the voice. According to his mood, Nori could choose Manuela, Agustín, Carlos, or Blanca to read to him that day.

"The two cases, Nicolás and Manu, are too similar. Maybe we need to wonder about that," Blanca began. Of all the voices available, hers was the softest and most relaxed. This was what Nori needed, someone to whisper in his ear.

Six hundred kilometers away, in his apartment in Barcelona, Joan still couldn't sleep. He'd hardly closed his eyes for the past forty-eight hours. He worked simultaneously on the digital attack against the pharmaceutical giant and the program to identify pedophiles. He'd managed to infect the computers of the thousand-some customers of the smelly panties web page. That had been easy. On Friday morning, a few dozen of them had received the shipments they'd previously ordered. Joan never would have imagined so many men buying underwear that had been worn by teenage girls. He knew the exact moment when the packages arrived because he'd also hacked into the network of the shipping company hired by smellypanties.com. He tried to imagine what type of men bought these things. *I'll wear them three days straight. I'll fuck in them, they'll get soaked with my juices, and I'll send them to you in a sealed plastic bag, so they come to you with all of my aromas. You'll enjoy them so much.* Who were the customers? Joan pictured normal men. Men who held doors open for women. Men who said hello in the subway. Men who lovingly offered bottles to their babies. But who paid forty Euros for a pair of dirty panties from a girl who could easily be his daughter or his sister?

Joan had now discovered quite a few patterns that indicated possible arousal. He'd been able to see the changes in several customers' manners of keyboarding just as they placed their order and also when they posted their reviews of the product on the site. "Pink Lady's sweet little cunt is the best I've smelled in a long time. It's driving me wild! You should try it too."

But all along, his boss never let up on him. The pharmaceutical company case was getting trickier. It was a bigger and more sophisticated attack than they'd thought, coming from several different parts of the world, and as the hours passed, it grew more intense. They'd been able to contain it so far but only through savage physical and mental effort. Some of the best hackers in the world were at work to deactivate the incursion that was trying to steal the formulas of the world's newest drugs to copy them for resale on the black market without any guarantee.

Working on both problems at once was taking its toll on Joan. But he had to stay the course.

◆ ◆ ◆

Blanca's syrupy voice was still murmuring in Nori's ear when he reached the Pilar Woods. He'd done a longer run than originally intended, and he still needed to make the return trip. He'd lost track of everything, including the fact that he was running. This happened when he concentrated hard on what he was listening to. Just when he made the turn to head back toward home, the sound of an incoming call interrupted the robot woman's voice.

It was the station.

"What's up?"

"Sub-Inspector? It's Rosalia. They asked me to call you to let you know about a meeting tomorrow at nine a.m. For all the units of the Judicial Police."

Nine in the morning on a Saturday. It had to be important. Nori came to a sudden stop.

"Something new in The Taker case?"

"I don't know. They only told me to call you and tell you to be here tomorrow morning. At nine."

"Who did? Ana or the commander?"

"Really, neither of them. I don't know where the order came from."

"What do you mean? It came from higher up? From national headquarters?" Standing still, Nori was starting to get chilly. He didn't understand this summons at all.

"Just come tomorrow, Sub-Inspector. That's all I know."

13

ANA

"Ana. Ana." It was Luis, the commander, calling her from the doorway of his office. "Ana, could you come here a moment?"

"Yes, sir," Ana answered, still unsure about who had called the extraordinary meeting.

"Come in." Luis Bermúdez closed the door. "I want to tell you something."

"What's going on, Luis?"

"Number one, someone else has been arrested. Besides the father."

"What do you mean, someone else? I'm running the case. Who the hell ordered that?"

"That's all I know. I got it from a good friend at headquarters. Let me explain something so you'll understand what's behind all this."

The commander didn't sit down behind his desk, which was there more to separate than to unite. Instead, he pulled a chair next to Ana's.

"I would rather have had more time to tell you, but with everything going on, I couldn't find a minute. Also, I didn't know whether Manu's disappearance would throw up a roadblock."

"And?"

"I'm leaving."

"You? You're leaving?" Ana had to work hard to keep her voice at a normal pitch. What Nori had told her was true.

"To be exact, they're making me leave."

"But why? Where to? When?"

"You know there are people who think these things need to be run with an iron fist."

"Sure, and with a cat-o'-nine-tails whipping us on the back while we say, 'Master, Master, do whatever you wish. Thank you for being my beloved boss.'"

"Or worse." Bermúdez moved his chair a bit closer. "The new top brass want things done differently. So they're sending me to Canillas."

"To national headquarters? To do what?"

"To think things over. Probably. Like a bad boy sent to sit in the corner." The commander grimaced. "They did promise to put me in line for a higher job."

"You're being kicked upstairs, in other words, and you know it. That's how they're getting you out of here."

"Listen, Ana, this is important, because you're going to have to handle this calmly. Okay? They're replacing me with David Ruipérez."

"Motherfucking bastards!" Ana jumped from her chair in indignation. "I don't fucking believe this."

"Ana, calm down."

"Shit, Luis. You know he's one of the last of the old guard. Unfortunately for us policewomen, part of that generation is still here—class snobs, male chauvinists, unbearable to be around. If only they'd all retire and shove their heads up their asses once and for all."

"Ana, you see what I mean? You're going to have to button that mouth. They'll be out to get you, and I won't be able to help."

Two knocks on the door interrupted the conversation. Then the door opened, as if the intruder were right at home. Because he was.

"Well, nice company for nine in the morning. Don't tell me you went out for breakfast together."

Luis shot a quick glance at Ana. *Please,* his eyes said, *control yourself. Don't throw a fit. Not now.*

"Major Ruipérez, nice to see you." The two men shook hands as only two men know how to do. As if nothing were going on.

"Are you coming to take measurements for your new office," Ana said, "with the old corpse still here?"

Truth be told, this was controlling herself, as far as Ana was concerned. A little sarcasm wasn't so aggressive. Not compared to what her body wanted her to do, which was spit in his face.

"I see your tongue is as sharp as ever, Chief Inspector Arén. We're going to enjoy working together. What an amusing post I've been given, no?" Ruipérez strutted around the desk and sat down in Major Bermúdez's chair, the chair of the commander of Madrid's Judicial Police. "Life doesn't look so bad from here," he said.

"You've got a terrific group of agents out there, Commander. They work themselves to the bone. You're very lucky to get this assignment."

"A group of terrific agents who lost a boy three days ago and still haven't found him." Ruipérez shot Ana Arén a look intended to kill.

"We've arrested the father, and today he's going in front of the judge," Bermúdez said.

"A father who hasn't confessed to anything and has nothing but circumstantial evidence against him. Turning off his phone doesn't prove anything, and you know it, Luis."

"We're working on—" Ana began.

"That's why I've taken a hand in the affair," Ruipérez interrupted. "Last night, we arrested another suspect."

"Another what?" Ana stood up so sharply she almost knocked over her chair, acting like she was hearing the news for the first time.

"Oh, sorry, Ana. I'll brief you right away." The new boss made a show of consulting his watch. "In fact, it's time right now. Everybody's waiting in the briefing room. I'll tell you both there too. I'll tell everyone at once, because repeating things tends to wear me out."

And with the same arrogance as he'd come into the room, Ruipérez left without a backward glance, convinced that Luis and Ana would follow in his wake.

In the briefing room, he didn't even give Bermúdez a chance to make the announcement. He used the tactical advantage of walking in front to stand before all his new subordinates, who still didn't know what had occurred. Chest puffed out, legs apart, chin up, shoulders back. The position of an alpha male dominating his territory. The position of ultimate power. Control. Testosterone oozed out of his ears.

"Good morning, everyone. Many of you know me already. I'm Major David Ruipérez. From now on, I am commanding officer of the Provincial Brigade of the Judicial Police. Your lord and master, just to make things clear." Incredulous murmurs and looks filled the room. "I've summoned you to this meeting to tell you that from this moment on, things are going to change. You'll see it unfold, but let me give you some advice. Pedal to the metal. All the time, all the way."

From either side of the door, leaning against the wall with their arms crossed, Ana and Luis watched him. Some members of the division turned toward them, mutely seeking an explanation.

"Right now, we need to tackle the most pressing matter—the disappearance of that boy. Some of you, those on the night shift, already know we've got a new detainee." Now the murmurs turned into a buzz. "He's in a cell. He's an employee at the mall. Officer José Barriga turned up a key piece of information. Strange, isn't it?" Ruipérez glanced arrogantly around the room, shaming every face he saw. "Yes, strange that it should come from a new agent, who's been here for, what, only three days, and shows up all the rest of you?" Barriga, seated in a chair near the middle of the room, looked like he wanted to become invisible. There was no better way to turn all his new colleagues against him.

"Chief Inspector Arén?" the new commander's eyes scanned the room for her. Ana was tempted not to answer, but finally she straightened up. "Chief Inspector, take charge of questioning the suspect. Now."

Ana gave him a challenging look, but she weighed her alternatives. She could confront him now, in front of the whole unit, or she could control herself and obey his order. Everyone could see by now that the guy was a jerk—he'd unmasked himself right away, so there was no need for her to offer further proof.

She nodded and left the briefing room, heading for the interrogation cells. Like an obedient puppy. Or at least, that's how she appeared.

14

NICOLÁS

Nicolás disappeared on the sixteenth of June. He vanished. He was somewhere, and then he wasn't. At first, he was just one more child who'd gone missing, like so many others who get lost every day. But the minutes went by, and shock turned to agony. The hours went by, and agony turned to tragedy. Nico didn't appear. His mother had been holding his hand as they walked through a mall in the outer suburbs of Madrid. Then she noticed that her son's hand was no longer in hers. She looked at her hand, puzzled, as if this were impossible. Nicolás's hand had been there. She would have sworn it was there just a thousandth of a second before. It had to still be there now.

But it wasn't.

Three days after the disappearance, one of the talking heads who by now were overpopulating TV talk shows and radio stations came up with the missing ingredient that made the case go viral: naming the kidnapper. The talking head called him "The Taker."

And there he was. The soap opera of the summer season.

Nicolás's case became front-page news, the perfect fodder to feed the headlines of the dog days. Day after day, Nicolás. For millions of readers, viewers, and listeners.

What the media hadn't expected was the extent of the panic that swept through the country. Suddenly, parents were fearful of losing their children. Children were terrified of losing their parents. In the middle of a heat wave, the streets went empty. Malls and shopping centers were hit the hardest, losing half their visitors. But also parks, beaches, and pools. Any places that children frequented were now strangely silent and empty.

The country feared a serial kidnapper.

On social media, the rumor went viral. Even though no one—not even the police—knew anything about the kidnapper's appearance, sightings of The Taker were reported all over Spain. Hashtags denoted alleged kidnapping attempts that occurred simultaneously in several parts of the country. Doctored photos were posted and reposted, passing for the real thing.

The Taker existed, he had Nicolás, and all of Spain was scared to death.

But June went by, and so did July, and August. September came, and schools reopened. Nicolás was no longer a draw, so the media couldn't come up with anything to keep the narrative current, and the story no longer sold. The four-year-old boy's disappearance was relegated to a short item, from time to time, at the bottom of a page.

Nicolás never reappeared. Life went on, in all its most humdrum and discouraging aspects. Second after second, minute after minute, day after day, time upon time. As if an occurrence like that could simply be buried away.

Two years went by.

Two years without Nicolás, without The Taker. Ana and her team had never given up, but the country soon forgot the four-year-old. Only once in a while, when the mother gave a tearful interview or the police claimed to have unearthed a new lead, did the media return to the story.

And thus, The Taker and Nicolás were gradually forgotten.

Until Manu, too, went up in smoke.

Then the headlines came back. And the fear. And the void.

15

ANA

The new suspect was a former employee of the toy store where Manu's trail went cold. The man had been fired two months ago for failing to show up for work. Also, he had a prior record of stalking. A year and a half before, he'd been arrested after a preschool teacher called the police, frightened, because for the past few days a young man had been watching the children play in the schoolyard. He'd stood there, not moving a muscle, just following the kids with his eyes in a scary way. The judge, however, didn't find the evidence sufficiently serious to warrant a jail sentence. Instead he issued a restraining order, which barred the man from coming within five hundred meters of the preschool.

"Ismael Gallardo. Twenty-nine. Record of stalking. Nice rap sheet," Ana commented with a scowl, as soon as she opened the door to the interrogation room. "Great specimen. A true son of a bitch who likes little boys. I'll make it easy for you," she said, staring him down from across the table. "Where's Manu?"

The man looked at Ana without emotion, as if he were regarding a squid on the grill.

"Cat got your tongue, or does your low IQ prevent you from putting two words together?" Ana looked at him arrogantly and spat out her words the same way. She was so angry about Ruipérez that she couldn't play the good cop who brings a cup of coffee and a sandwich to win the suspect's trust. Today she had to let out all her accumulated bile, the way a pressure cooker whistles steam through its escape valve so as not to explode.

Normally she knew how to do this, how to let the steam out slowly, right into the face of the suspect before culminating in a final, burning explosion. She'd been trained in this for years: channel your anger, direct it at the objective in a slow and precise way. If you explode right away, all you do is hurt yourself. But right now, she couldn't. She had to let it out. Fortunately, she had someone on whom to take out her anger. Someone who deserved it—a child stalker, and maybe Manu's kidnapper too.

The guy still didn't speak. He just sat there, staring at her.

"I'm sorry, my friend, but you're done. Cooked. What I've got here"—Ana lifted a gray folder—"guarantees you years behind bars. Plenty of them. I'll give you some time to think about that. If you work with us, it'll go better for you."

The chief inspector had to force herself not to slam the door on her way out. She left the detainee alone. The trick was to look unconcerned, to pretend you had the situation under control. When the nut's hard to crack, experience had taught her, the trick is to suggest you have more information than you really do.

Because you'll often get more out of a suspect with a lie than with the truth.

The secret to destabilizing a person is patience and finesse. Little by little. Opening the pores of the skin, imperceptibly, until the suspect's defenses are down and there's no going back. It's no good plunging a snail into boiling water, because it will just retreat into its shell and you'll never get it out. You must first let it swim in cold water and give it a chance to relax. Then, very slowly, raise the temperature and scald it. So it won't react until too late, just a few seconds before its skin bursts apart.

Upstairs in the duty room, she found the whole atmosphere explosive. Her team was trying to digest the news about the change of command, but they seemed to be choking on it instead. When she stepped through the door of the large gray space they shared (Ana did have an office, but she rarely used it), all eyes turned toward her. But what could she say? That they had to find a way to put up with this somehow? They already knew that.

Ana sat down in her regular spot at the table in the back of the room. She liked to be in that position, together with her agents. To get there, she had to cross the entire room, which gave her a chance to talk with the agents under her command. Also, from this vantage point, she was able to see everything, to watch how the group behaved. It was like watching the growth of a living soul, with all its struggles and contradictions.

"Hard to crack?" Luis Arcos asked.

"Have you seen him?"

"No. The new commander kept us in the briefing room a while longer." Luis sat down on the edge of her table. "And by the time that was over, you'd finished with the guy. That was quick."

"I'm leaving him to his thoughts for a while."

"And what do you think?"

"No, what do *you* think? I assigned you and the new guy to work through the list of possible suspects. How does somebody who just started working here find out about such an important lead before the immediate superior who gave the order?"

"Look, Ana, I don't know. I haven't had a chance to ask Barriga. We found out about him last night and were planning to tell you first thing this morning. I don't know how it leaked."

"You found out about him last night?"

"Yeah, about eleven thirty. Barriga was here, and I was at home, working remotely. He was the one who spotted it."

"And the two of you thought this wasn't important enough to call me about?"

"Boss, we were going to see you in a few hours. The guy was going about his life in his regular way."

"We'll discuss this later. Right now, we need to break him. Find anything you've got on him: parking tickets, minor violations. Any shit you can find. Hack into his computer and cell phone, and comb them down to the tiniest sector of their memories. Choose whoever you want to work with."

"Chief," said Charo from behind Ana. "The commander wants to see you in his office."

"What commander?" Ana said.

"Chief," Charo said, in a way that meant, *Don't get on my case, because we've already got enough to deal with here.*

If sarcasm and black humor are out of bounds, Ana thought while getting up from her chair, *what are we going to do? Shoot ourselves?* "Wish me luck," she said, heading for Ruipérez's office.

The division commander's office was at the end of the hallway on the top floor of the station. The most inaccessible office of all, the one that took the longest to get to. It had been strategically situated so that anyone heading there would have enough time on the way to worry about what was in store. Years ago, Luis had attempted to change that, to find a location closer to his subordinates, but hadn't been able to come up with any place that was free. The size of the staff had grown along with the development booms that had transformed the neighborhood into an area with more inhabitants than many of the country's provincial capitals.

Ana figured Ruipérez had taken full possession of Luis Bermúdez's office by now. Knowing Ruipérez—one of those old-timers who had risen through the ranks without taking any exams, gotten ahead by warming one chair after another—she was sure he'd already ordered new furniture to spruce up his domain. What would Luis be feeling? Who, exactly, had been the one to kick him upstairs? What had happened? A betrayal? Maybe it was better not to know yet. As with so many things in life, it's best to wait for the right emotional moment to find out who's betrayed us—at a point past anger and pain, one that allows us to respond forcefully but thoughtfully, with vengeance that's cold, not hot.

This was not that moment, so Ana would have to wait awhile before trying to find out what had really gone on. Right now, it would be a waste of energy to fight against the changes. She had no say in it and needed to focus on tamping down the swirling blend of rage and indignation inside her.

"Commander?"

"Come in, Ana, come in."

Ana didn't know how to interpret the look on his face. Or she did, but would rather leave it in some dark corner of her brain, uninterpreted for now. Not to rub salt into the wound.

"How did it go with the suspect?"

Ana was tempted to say something like, "The suspect whom I, the officer in charge of the unit and therefore the case, didn't know about until half an hour ago? Whose arrest I didn't order? Is that the one you're speaking of, Commander, sir?"

But instead, she answered, "Impassive. Cold. I left him alone to ponder, thinking we've got a lot more on him than we really do. See whether he softens. Now I'll send Nori in to heat him up, and then I'll go back."

"I hope you understand that things are going to be different from now on. I know you got along very well with Luis, but I'm different, and some things are over with. In your section, the SAF, and in the division as a whole. From now on, everything goes through me."

"That's the procedure, David."

"Commander."

"That's the procedure, Commander," Ana corrected herself.

"Of course. What do you think about the father?"

"Yesterday I thought there was a lot pointing toward him. After my last session with him, I'm not so sure." Was that a trick question?

"But you ordered his arrest."

It *was* a trick question. Ana still didn't know where the trap was hidden, the one that would snap shut on her neck, but she could smell the rusted metal, feel the teeth close to her skin.

"Yes. I ordered it. He's the kid's father. He's going through a traumatic divorce from the mother. And he was unaccounted for during the kidnapping, both before and after. Aren't those reasons to detain him?"

"The fact is, I've ordered his release."

Ruipérez seemed to be enjoying the moment. Ana could have sworn he'd just finished licking his lips. The trap was about to snap shut.

"Why? Don't tell me it's because you've got another suspect."

"Here's why." The commander tossed some papers onto the desk. "It's a witness statement."

Ruipérez crossed his arms and leaned back in his chair, enjoying this.

He'd caught her in the trap, and he was going to drag this out before devouring her. That's what she was expecting, her body taut with tension.

"Read it carefully, Ana. What does it say? What does this new witness tell us?"

"It's a bicyclist. The day of Manu's disappearance. He says he saw the detainee at the exact time the child was taken."

"What else? Details?" Ruipérez began to chew on his prey.

"The witness has just seen, on TV, the face of a man suspected of having kidnapped his own child. The witness thinks he's seen this face before. He tries to remember and does. The witness testifies that he saw Ricardo Jiménez on Wednesday between 5:10 and 5:20 in the afternoon. He's sure of this. The first time the witness saw him, at 5:10, Jiménez was leaning against a tree. Sitting down, crying. At first, the witness didn't stop, but then thought better of it and turned around.

He got off his bike and asked the man if he was okay and if he needed any help. The suspect seemed surprised by the witness's presence. The suspect seemed not to know where he was. The witness pressed him— didn't he want to call someone, perhaps? The suspect mumbled that he didn't, that he just wanted to be left alone to cry. The witness left, but he was still worried, so a half hour later, he went back, and the suspect was still there."

"So, Ana," Ruipérez interrupted. "What does this tell us?"

"How do we know it's true?" she countered.

"Obviously, Ana, we've looked into that. Maybe you didn't know, but it turns out that there are some fantastic apps that let you track your exercise. And both the app and the GPS on the witness's phone confirm the location and the cited times. And this leads us to . . ."

"The conclusion that Manu's father was several kilometers away at the moment the boy disappeared."

"Fine deduction, Chief Inspector. I couldn't have drawn a better one myself."

"I told you I had my doubts after the interrogation."

"Doubts are no good, Inspector. What we need are data, facts, evidence. We're in a police station, not an experimental treatment center. For a two-year-old, lollipops are fine, but here we're grown-ups, and we're playing grown-up games. Agreed?" Ruipérez took a deep breath before the final thrust. "So now, Chief Inspector, you need to go to Barcelona. Today."

"Barcelona?" Ana didn't understand and couldn't hide her surprise.

"Barcelona," the commander repeated. "Isn't that where you're from? Perfect. Let's see what use you can make of the Catalán you learned as a little girl."

"But, to Barcelona? Now?"

"Yes, to a meeting of the coordination group that links the Mossos to us. I committed to sending two SAF agents to a discussion of plans for joint operations in the area of crimes against children. Who better than you?"

"David, cut it out. You can't send me now," she said, raising her voice. "We've got a missing child, and time is running out. I have to question the toy store employee."

"I told you that things are going to be different around here. You're going to Barcelona without complaint, and you're taking Nori. This afternoon, you have a meeting with the Catalunya police force, and you'll be back tomorrow morning."

The commander got up from his seat, signaling the end of the conversation.

"It's just a few hours. Didn't you tell me what a fantastic team you've got? Leave the investigation to them for a little while. Besides, you've got a stupendous cell phone that all the citizens of Spain pay for with their taxes, so you can always be in touch. See you later, Ana." End of conversation, no argument permitted.

Ana got up slowly, as if the air were freezing up around her. Meanwhile her head was spinning, a thousand revolutions per minute, as she tried to calculate the value of spewing out the words piling up on her tongue versus that of winning the war, not just this battle.

Before leaving, she looked at her new commander and thought that she had to do something. She couldn't just walk away in defeat. That would set a very bad precedent. So she used the only weapon she had at that moment: the element of surprise. She put her hand very slowly into her purse—*It had to be there,* she thought while fumbling blindly, *it had to be*—and took out a small object that she pressed firmly between her fingers. Without taking her eyes off Ruipérez's face, with a fearsome concentration in her look, Chief Inspector Ana Arén opened a stick of bright-red lipstick. And very slowly, as in a ritual, she applied it to her lips. First the top one. Then the bottom. Slowly and painfully. Following the full contours. Marking territory. *You can't handle me. This isn't over yet.*

Ruipérez was disconcerted. But only for a few seconds.

"Oh, and when you get here tomorrow," he said, "send me your report on the meeting with the Mossos. In detail. Even though it's Sunday, that's your top priority right now."

Priority? Higher priority than finding a kidnapped child? Ana had known that Ruipérez was going to make her pay. He wouldn't stop until he did. And now he could, because she was under his command. But she never imagined that he'd do so at the cost of an investigation in which the lives of two children were at stake. It was clear that Ruipérez wanted her out of the way. But why?

Ana lifted her chin and left the office at a very slow walk, determinedly breaking through the ice that had frozen up around her. So she wouldn't turn around, or scream, she centered her thoughts on the advice her father always gave: "Daughter, you have to be smart. That's why we're human beings. That's what makes us human. Because our claws have moved from our hands to our brains. That's what makes us different from animals. They use brute force. We use our intelligence. Our fangs are in our brains, Ana. They're in our neurons. Use them. Don't fight with your hands. Sharpen your brain. That way, you can win whatever wars you decide to join. Or the ones somebody else puts you in the middle of."

16

INÉS

When my son, Pablo, was born, my mother was afraid I'd be a bad mom.

"Inés, Inés," she said, "what are you going to do with that child? What are you going to do, when you're such a disaster yourself?"

Quoted that way, it sounds very harsh. But given my personality as she knew it, and taking into account my unplanned pregnancy and the father living in another country, my mother worried that I'd neglect the child. Not that I'd let him starve to death, of course, but that I wouldn't feel the immense and unconditional love that it is assumed any mother should experience from the moment the sperm fertilizes the egg.

The glowing miracle of maternity, and things like that.

My mother wasn't far from wrong. During the pregnancy, I didn't feel any special emotion corresponding to the pink and blue hearts of television ads. I just felt nausea and exhaustion for nine straight months. Every day, all the time, I tasted vomit in my throat while an unbearable weight of weariness pressed on me. I had a constant sensation of being an incubator, a vessel in which another life was growing in spite of my body's rebellion against it.

Would that make me a bad mother?

When I held Pablo in my arms, after I came out of the anesthesia of an emergency C-section, I still didn't feel the cosmic connection that most mothers talk about in a kind of trance. Actually, I began to suspect that not all of them had actually felt it. Because who can confess in public that all you feel is pain and exhaustion? I loved that baby, no doubt about it. But I felt I had to care for him the way I would have cared for something very delicate left in my charge, rigorously and according to daily routines. I did everything in my power to raise him healthy and strong. To keep him warm in the winter, to make him feel loved, to keep him well fed. I would have given my life for him, too, because when all is said and done, nature programs us to reproduce the species, and one of our strongest instincts is to protect the next generation. And that's what I did.

The love that is wrenching and irreplaceable, the love that instills fear in your heart forever—that love took some months to emerge. It came, but maybe too late.

At that time, Pablo's father was living in Spain. Willie was a reporter, too, working for one of the most important papers in the United States, which had sent him to our country for a few months to try to explain to readers how we were surviving the depths of the economic crisis. The two of us met at a radio talk show one Saturday morning. I had come to talk about how journalists were making use of social media, and he, who had just finished a conversation with foreign correspondents, stayed to listen. Later he confessed that he'd made a bet with a British TV reporter that he could get this beautiful Spanish woman to go out with him for churros and chocolate. And, indeed, we went out for churros and chocolate, right from the radio station. It was a good thing, too, that we ate something, because afterward we didn't leave the bed in his apartment on Calle del Pez until Monday morning. And Willie's refrigerator contained only a bottle of vodka, some slices of ham, and a few pickles. Typical of a single foreign man.

For a while, I thought I had fallen in love with him. I'd always been attracted to men with hair the color of wheat or honey or sand, but here I was being swept away by that dark-haired giant with the body of a farmer and the mind of a philosopher. An explosive combination and very hard to resist.

I didn't tell him I was pregnant until he'd gone back to Washington. That kind of news is easier to convey when you're 6,088.67 kilometers apart. His immediate reaction was guilt and remorse. I could feel him trembling somewhere behind my computer screen. "Look," I informed him over Skype, "I'm not telling you so that you'll take responsibility or anything. Nor for you to help me or to feel guilty. It's so you'll know, that's all."

This speech confused him, but I'm convinced it laid the ground-work for our good relations later.

Willie was present at the birth, which he said he wouldn't have missed for all the world. His mother threatened to come, too, but I convinced him our story would be too much of a shock for a fervent Christian from southern Texas. What was she going to tell her friends at church? That her son had just had a baby with a Spanish atheist to whom he wasn't married? So Willie saw to it that Mummy didn't leave her house and garden in a suburban neighborhood of San Antonio.

After a season spent coming and going to visit his newborn son, Willie got the newspaper to send him on a new assignment in Spain for several more months, covering the beginnings of the movement of the *indignados*, the 15-M, a popular revolution that had already morphed into Occupy and ended up taking over the streets of major US cities, if only for a short time. He got a studio apartment in the old part of Madrid, but he came to my place every day to spend a while with his son. Pablo enchanted him.

But when the boy turned two, Willie was called back to the States for good. Spain was no longer of interest, not even to one of the papers that devoted the most space to world news. There was no way he could stay close to his son under those conditions, so he proposed taking Pablo for a while. "He's not in school yet. He's still little." Willie sprung it on me one morning over breakfast. "It would be good for him to learn other languages and see other cultures. My mother's crazy about the idea of spending time with her grandson. Just a few months—summer, if that's what you'd like—and you can come over whenever you want. In September, I'll bring him back to Spain."

At first I was offended. I got mad. What did he think? That I didn't love my son? That I was a bad mother? But then I reconsidered. Willie had as much right to be with the boy as I did.

So he took him. For a whole summer. The first few days after Pablo left, I seized every second. I had spent twenty-four months tied to a baby. I no longer knew what it was like to go to the bathroom and shut the door, or take a leisurely shower, or get into bed knowing how long I could sleep. Except for work, I'd been taking Pablo everywhere. I had opened my legs to the gynecologist—for those awful postpartum exams—with the baby wailing in his carriage. And the same for trips to the waxing center for hair removal or the endodontist for a root canal. My life the past two years had revolved around Pablo. Work, however harsh this may sound, was where I went for a break from my son.

The first few days after he left for the States, I'd get home from the studio, wrung out as always, only to find my house strangely empty and silent. It took me more than a week to get used to my time being my own again, to remember I was a person and could make many choices, even if only to drop onto the couch after dinner and fall placidly asleep in front of the TV. A most lovely siesta.

Then I started going out to the movies again. Hanging out with friends. Drinking. Dancing. Reading. Vegging out. Painting my toenails. I recovered the rhythm of a nonmother, doing all the things that seem unimportant until you miss them so much after maternity crosses your path.

I felt happy. Liberated. Free.

But before the three months were over, I started to miss Pablo terribly. One day, I broke down crying at the movie theater for no reason at all—though it was a melodramatic film, I have to say. Another night, at 3:00 a.m. in a fashionable club, I pulled out my phone and started swiping through photos: Pablo kicking a ball, Pablo laughing like crazy, Pablo covered in baby food.

By the time Willie brought him back at the end of September, I was out of my mind. It had been a terrible summer, the hardest of my life. Losing a child is the worst thing that can happen to you. When I finally hugged my son at the airport, I swore I'd never let him leave me again.

17

ANA

If anyone had been watching her, they would have thought she was nuts. With her eyes closed and fingertips caressing the walls, Ana worked her way through the Plaça de Sant Felip Neri. She walked very slowly, absorbing the horror of the wounds that festered in the stones. It was nighttime, the air had cooled down, and Barcelona was strangely empty. The plaza smelled of the humidity accumulated over centuries. In the background, Ana could faintly hear the slow burbling of the neo-Gothic fountain in the middle of the square. A random visitor would see nothing but beauty in that medieval nook of the city, accessible only through a few narrow, zigzagging alleys. But Ana's hands told her a different story.

The story of the murder of dozens of children.

Very, very gently, the way new mothers caress their newborns for the first time, Ana put the tips of her fingers into some of the hundreds of holes that perforated the façade of the church, pockmarked the stones. These were the scars of the air attack by the Italian Legion, allied with General Francisco Franco, on the morning of January 30, 1938, during the Spanish Civil War. When the attack began, the children of the nursery school in the plaza were led to safety in a basement. They survived the first rain of bombs, but a second wave killed them all. In the Plaça de Sant Felip Neri, all that remained standing was the church, scarred forevermore. Forty-two people died.

To feel those stones with the tips of her fingers, with the most sensitive part of her body, was a way for Ana to remember what really mattered in life: living.

She repeated this ritual every time she returned to Barcelona. After passing through Sant Felip Neri, Ana's route would take her behind the city's cathedral to the Carrer del Paradís. That was where her childhood was stored. And where her youth ended, too, the day she found her father's body decomposing in their living room.

Twenty-two centuries earlier, right there, had stood a small hill. Seventeen point nine meters above sea level, to be exact, the highest ground in the area. That was where the first Roman settlers had established Barcino, which would later become Barcelona. And in the place of honor, the engineers of the empire raised a temple dedicated to their first emperor, Gaius Julius Caesar Augustus, heir to Julius Caesar and shaper of the largest and most peaceful empire in the history of Rome.

Century after century, while the heirs of Romulus and Remus set about conquering the whole Mediterranean, Barcino experienced relative peace. The surroundings of the Temple of Augustus, the northeast quadrant of Barcino, became the administrative center of the city, the place where decisions about power and money were made, if it were possible to even speak of one existing separately from the other.

And there, many centuries later, in the year 1400, just a few meters away from what was left of the temple, the Generalitat de Catalunya was established, in a building purchased at a bargain-basement price from the Jews who had to flee the city overnight after the riots of the *poble menut*, provoked by an outbreak of plague. The lower classes rose up, supported by seamen and fishermen, with the green light from the king, Joan el Caçador. But, as always, those who took advantage of the victory were the richest and most powerful classes, who acquired, nearly for free, the properties of the hundreds of Jewish families that chose exile over death, or exile over conversion.

While she crossed the Plaça de Sant Jaume, Ana looked at the Generalitat's neo-Gothic façade, one of many extensions added to the building over time, as it went on swallowing up the houses and empty lots around it. On the other side of this square, challenging the Generalitat face-to-face, was the Ajuntament de Barcelona, the city hall, in whose interior could be found one of the most beautiful chambers of European Gothic architecture, the Saló de Cent, where the hundred members of the city council, a sort of popular parliament, had met since the days of Jaume I, Jaume el Conqueridor, in the thirteenth century.

It was 9:30 p.m. Ana was late, so she quickened her pace with only a few meters to go. In the Carrer Sant Domènec del Call, in a narrow, elongated room in the shadows of the old Jewish ghetto, was her favorite restaurant, La Vinateria del Call, a place that had not lost its magic despite the fact that it now appeared in the most prestigious international guidebooks.

Ana felt an electric charge when she saw him sitting there, munching on the marvelous *pa amb tomàquet* that was one of the specialties of the house. Suddenly, someone hugged her from behind.

"Baby!" It was Miguel, the owner of La Vinateria. "How long has it been? You've exiled yourself in Madrid."

"Only in body. My heart will always be in Barcelona."

"I bet you say that to all the guys."

"I still miss the barrio, really. Even if there are more tourists than residents now, it's still the old neighborhood to me."

"And your friends are here waiting. I'll sit down with all of you after I serve a few customers, okay?"

And indeed they were waiting. At her favorite table. Nori and Joan. They were laughing, a good sign. Ana needed to laugh a little, at least.

"Well, Chief Inspector, you're much better-looking in civilian clothes," Javier Nori joked.

"You, too, Sub-Inspector. I've got to say, the uniform doesn't do much for you either," she said. "But now, in that T-shirt clinging to your chest . . ."

"That's why I never became a cop, because I've got no pecs to show off," Joan said, laughing along with them. "How are you?" he asked Ana, and they kissed on both cheeks.

"I was telling him about our new friend Ruipérez," Nori said.

"What do they think they're doing, sending you to Barcelona for a coordination meeting with the Mossos when you've got a case like that in Madrid?"

"To a meeting that anyone in my unit could have covered, Joan. We're here in Barcelona to talk more of the same, yet again, and the Mossos and Madrid are never going to agree."

"How's the case coming along?"

"Not well. We haven't got anything, not even the slightest thread to follow. We've got another guy under arrest, but nothing's clear to me at all."

"Are you having nightmares again?"

Yes, even waking ones, Ana thought. Sometimes she had the sensation of being able to reach out and touch Nicolás or Manu. As if they were there, in front of her in the full light of day, pleading for help. But when she tried to touch them, they dissipated like dust between her fingers. Like her father's corpse.

"She's even lost her black humor, and that's a very bad sign," said Nori with a glass of L'Ermita in his hand. "Here, try this red. It tastes like heaven."

"To old times," toasted Ana, lifting the glass.

"To old times," echoed her friends.

"And let's put the case aside for a while, because I need a break," Ana added, and took another swallow from her glass of wine. "But speaking of losing things, how's my memory doing? It's been a few months since I asked for your report. Any sign of Alzheimer's? Are you still monitoring us?"

"Yes, I've got you all right there, all in your own folder on my computer," answered Joan. "When did I start that? Three years ago? So far, no alarms, so you're still keyboarding the same as ever. Badly, of course. And your brain's unchanged. Bad." He winked.

Everything that Ana, Nori, Inés, and a number of other friends typed into their computers and smartphones got uploaded every twenty-four hours into one of Joan's servers in Barcelona. There, neuroQWERTY analyzed their keyboarding patterns to detect changes that could indicate a possible neurodegenerative disease like Alzheimer's or Parkinson's, or a skeletal one like osteoporosis. The program monitored every active pulsation of the cerebellum, the basal ganglia, the primary motor cortex, and the supplementary motor area. Any decline would be reflected in the keyboarding pattern long before it manifested elsewhere. With advances in genetic medicine, detecting such diseases before they became symptomatic could mean having time to head them off.

But Joan and Nori had gone further than that. This was the program they had modified by introducing their algorithm to detect people who were about to launch a suicide attack.

"Just think how the pattern would change in a person who knows they're going to tie an explosive belt around their waist and blow themselves up in an airport," Joan had explained to Nori when the idea first occurred to him. "We've altered the mathematical algorithm of neuroQWERTY to notify us if any of the individuals we're monitoring are going to commit a suicide attack."

Then came the request from Ana, desperate after Manu's disappearance. That was three days ago, when she'd asked him to adapt neuroQWERTY to detect changes in the excitement of pedophiles. Maybe that way they could find the person who had taken Manu and might have taken Nicolás two years ago.

"Look, guys, we're not going to resolve the case here or solve the world's problems," Nori said. "So let's talk about something else. The night isn't so long, and we're not twenty anymore."

"Speak for yourself, old man," Ana replied.

"Yeah, don't be an asshole, Nori. I spend my days glued to three computer screens, not out there running like a demon the way you do. Which reminds me, have you got any women chasing you these days? Or any you're chasing, maybe?"

Ana could have sworn that Nori blushed, though the dim lighting of the restaurant made it hard to say. What she could see for sure was how he lowered his eyes. Something was going on.

"Aha, got you. Who would've thunk it? You've got a girlfriend?" Joan pressed.

"You know what?" Ana said. "For a while, I was thinking *this guy*," pointing a finger at Nori, "and Inés had something going. Did you ever notice, Joan, how they avoided looking at each other? What about that summer when Inés was alone, Nori, huh?"

"You're sick," he said, trying to make a joke of it. He was always shy when they talked about personal things. "I've told you, when I've got something to report, I will."

"Yeah, like a celebrity," she laughed. "You'll tell all in an exclusive on the cover of *Hola*."

"Speaking of gossip, guess who contacted me for help."

"No idea," said Nori, relieved the topic had shifted away from him.

"Inés's boss."

Nori looked puzzled.

"What boss?"

"Manuel, isn't that his name?"

"The honcho of crime and society news at Channel Eleven," Ana explained. "Inés said something about it on Thursday when she called about Manu's disappearance. She said her boss had asked how to get in touch with you." She looked at Joan. "But she didn't know why."

"Well, get this." The three of them moved closer to keep their conversation a secret. "Do you know him personally? Inés's boss?"

Ana and Javier both nodded.

"So you know that vacuous face he has, like he's never had an original thought or a walk on the wild side? Well, ta-da, he's taken one, or at least tried to, by paying for it. And now he's scared to death"—Joan paused to add to the suspense—"because he's a user of a sexual services site that got hacked a few days ago."

"No way!"

"So now I get it," Ana said. "He's scared shitless that someone will find his name and personal data in the customer list."

"Gay customers." Joan made the situation more specific. "Apparently Inés's boss goes for the guys, particularly young ones. I wonder what his wife is going to say. Or his friends in his ultrareligious church."

"So he's asked you to try to delete any reference to him from the leaked data?" Nori asked.

"Bingo."

"Are you going to?"

"I'm thinking it over. I don't know whether he deserves it or not. I'll go fishing in his hard drive first. I've already copied it, just in case, so let's see what I find hidden in there. I know he's got some encrypted files, so I'll wait till I see what's in them. I've got to cover my ass. And Inés's. You never know what kind of monster might be lurking behind a sad sack like that. Maybe there's another surprise in store."

The conversation continued into the wee hours, so Ana and Javi didn't get back to the hotel until after 3:00 a.m. One glass had led to another, calling up old times, until they realized the other customers had left and they were alone in La Vinateria. Ana's room was on the second floor, and if she opened the long, narrow windows that faced the balcony, she could reach out and touch the leaves of one of the fifty thousand banana trees that shaded the city's streets.

Two soft knocks sounded on the door. Ana froze and held her breath. Then she breathed out all the air in her lungs and tried to keep her heart from leaping through her mouth after it. She opened the door.

"Chief Inspector?"

"I thought you weren't coming."

"How could I not come, Ana? How?"

And he hugged her as he hadn't hugged anyone in a long time. He kissed her and devoured her, realizing only at the end, when he could breathe normally again, stretched out on the bed next to her, that he'd just been kneeling not only before the body of a woman, but before her soul.

18

ANA

"Do you want to come home with me?"

Joan looked in her eyes while they shook off sleep in the narrow hotel bed where they'd spent the night. Outside, the banana tree filtered the morning sunlight before it drifted through the balcony windows, sketching shadows on their naked skin. Joan had been about to ask her whether she would dare come home with him, but *dare* seemed too extreme a term.

"Home?" asked Ana, as if she weren't sure where he meant.

Obviously, "home" meant Joan's apartment, but that wasn't all. That apartment had been, and in some way still was, Ana's childhood home, the one she'd left every morning to go to convent school, the one she'd left more definitively to enroll in the Police Academy in Ávila, and the one to which she returned to find her father's decomposing corpse.

"Home?" she asked again.

"Home," Joan repeated, remembering the day he opened the door to find that small, dark-haired woman who looked at him sadly from the landing—so distant in both body and soul, standing stiff as a board on the other side of the doormat, with her feet perpendicular to the fiber weave and her arms tight against her ribs. It was almost always that way with Ana. You had to respect her distance until she decided to come to you.

"Hello," she had said. "Sorry, you don't know me. I'm Ana." When that woman began to speak, it was impossible to stop, like shaking a bottle of sparkling wine and then uncorking it. "I live here. I mean, I lived here from the time I was born. All my good and bad memories are here. One day I opened the door you're leaning against and found my father in the living room, eaten by worms. And, I'm sorry, sorry for talking to you like this. I don't even know who you are. I'm sorry to be telling you all this, because now it's your house and I don't have any right, but here I am telling you. My name's Ana—did I say that already? Let me tell you all of it, because if I don't, then I won't be able to."

And she spewed everything she was carrying inside, all that she'd been holding in since that August afternoon so long ago. She told Joan it had taken her ten years to come back and set foot on the landing outside where her father had died. For a long time, she couldn't even come near the neighborhood. Only a few years ago had she dared to walk on the Carrer del Paradís and pass by apartment number three.

When she left the Sancho de Ávila funeral home after burying her father, she hadn't returned to the apartment. She couldn't. She hired a company to empty the house and take everything away. Wherever they pleased, she told them—to a nursing home or a shelter or the dump. It was just too painful for her to look at anything of his. The only thing she kept—the only memento she wanted—was the gold medallion, that fine chain with its circular medal of the Virgin of Montserrat in relief, the one she'd always seen hanging around her father's neck. She'd found it on the bathroom shelf, where Rodolfo had put it before stepping into the shower. All the rest of his belongings, she'd given away. There was nothing left from the life that Ana and her father had lived in that apartment. Not even the home itself, not in its old form, because a real estate firm had bought the unit and remodeled it according to the tastes of the neighborhood's new residents.

And then, after a ten-year lapse, Ana showed up knocking, with no clue about who would be behind the door, just wanting to be able to take a final look that might close up her wound at last.

While explaining all this in a tumbling rush of words, Ana interrupted herself a few times to try to leave, overcome with embarrassment. "I'm being ridiculous. What must you think of me?" she said.

But Joan didn't let her leave. He held her by the wrist. "Come in, please. Won't you come in? I'm Joan. I've been here three months." Later he confessed that he'd invited her in so the neighbors wouldn't hear, because he, too, was embarrassed to have a woman whimpering at his door.

What Joan didn't know at that time was how much of an anomaly this woman was going to represent within the life plan he had constructed up to that point.

"That's right, home," said Joan, still stretched out on the hotel bed. "Do you want to come over for a while? It's not far, and your train doesn't leave till midmorning. We could have a peaceful breakfast there."

"Do you have anything to eat? I mean, anything that's worth calling food?" Ana laughed, yawning, thinking how lovely it was to shake off sleep with no hurry, purring like a cat, the sun coming through the window.

"No, but the Paki on the corner has a lot of delicious stuff."

Delicious wasn't quite the right description for everything piled up in the little store run by the Pakistani immigrant on the corner of Daguería and Hércules. Ana tried to decipher how he'd determined the order and placement of each of the products heaped together there. What was the shampoo doing next to the canned tomatoes? What were the muffins doing opposite the croissants? What allowed someone to reach up for a can of beans on the topmost shelf, jammed to the ceiling, without pulling everything down on their head?

Everything was out of place except the condoms, which were right where they should be, next to the cash register. They must have been the item in highest demand at the little store, especially by the tourists, who in recent years had been engulfing the neighborhood and displacing the old residents. When Joan and Ana approached the counter to pay for the muffins they'd chosen, they found an older couple deep in an argument, with two packages of condoms in hand.

"But don't get the sensitive ones, Carlos. Get the regular kind."

"Why not?" he protested.

"Think about it, dear. *Sensitive*, what does it mean? Feeling, sensory, sensual . . ."

"So all the better, right? They're more expensive, so what? Let's not be stingy about this," the husband argued, while his wife stabbed at the box with her finger.

"What do you think, young man?" she asked the Pakistani who ran the place.

"They're 6.35 Euros," he answered, either playing dumb or truly not understanding the scene unfolding before his eyes.

"What about you two?" The woman turned toward Ana and Joan. "Sensitive or regular?"

"Yolanda, please," the man tried to cut her off. "Leave these kids alone."

Kids was perhaps not quite the right term for these two observers well over thirty, who couldn't help but smile.

"Ignore my husband, please. The thing is, our son has a girlfriend now. A real looker, you know, and we suspect they're doing it already, if you know what I mean. And my lunkhead of a husband"—she stabbed at his chest like she'd done to the box of condoms—"gets red in the face just thinking about discussing sex with his fourteen-year-old son, so we thought we'd buy him a box of condoms and leave it on his night table, like it fell from the sky. Just in case. But you know how it is—only fourteen, how's my poor boy going to control himself? Then the party will be over before it starts, and the girlfriend just left hanging, won't she? Don't look at me that way, Carlos, because you men don't even notice, but let me tell you that a first-time teenager is the worst lover in the world. So." She turned back to Ana and Joan. "I'm sure you agree with me, sensitive is not the right thing at all. More feeling, more sensory perception? Uh-uh. The more layers, the better. Wouldn't you agree?"

Ana and Joan were still laughing about the condom debate when they got to the landing in front of Joan's door. So many years later, Ana still couldn't control her anxiety when faced with that sight. Her mind hit rewind, back to the moment when, fifteen years earlier, she'd turned the key in the knob to find the bodily fluids of her father's corpse dribbling toward the entryway. Ana grabbed Joan's hand and stepped into this home, now so different than the one she'd known. The remodeling had felled walls and expanded spaces. Natural light flowed everywhere. The entryway no longer existed, the middle hallway had become part of the kitchen, and the old living room had become much larger and opened into one large bedroom.

The smell of coffee suddenly filled the house. Joan refused to get a modern Nespresso machine, insisting instead on remaining loyal to an Italian stovetop espresso pot from his student days. Ana, who didn't drink coffee, didn't care. She was taking the last bites of a muffin that felt more like Styrofoam when someone knocked at the door. Ana and Joan looked at each other, knowing who it had to be.

"Anita must be here," Ana heard when Joan opened the door. "Isn't she? I heard you a while ago, but I didn't want to bother you. I'm going to the cemetery with flowers for Genaro. It's been four years since he died, poor thing, but I want to give the princess a kiss before I go."

"Who are you calling a princess?" Ana said as she walked over and hugged her old neighbor. "Do I look like a princess to you?"

"You look like whatever you want to be."

"How are you, Laura? How are things?"

"Good. Busy. I'm staying entertained. Listen, Joan, what did you think of the fourth season of *House of Cards*? I thought it was great. They take the cake for villains, those two."

"How can you give that series to Laura?" Ana teased Joan. "It'll give her fits."

"Her? That woman is tougher than you and me put together. Just look at her. You know she's going to bury us both."

"God doesn't want that, my children. Just so you know, in case you need to, I'm paying my one Euro a month to L'Esperança so they can bury me next to Genaro with a view of the sea. Listen, Ana," Laura said, taking her by the arm, "can you come to my place for a minute? The other day, when I was cleaning, I found an old picture of you and your father that I want you to have."

Ana and her father were posing on the street in front of the door to the building, and Ana, at eight or nine years old, was holding on to a giant dried palm frond as best she could. This was Palm Sunday, one of the few days of the year when the father and daughter went anywhere near the church. They were dressed to the nines. He had put on a white shirt and dark blue suit, almost transparent from its many washings, so fragile it was a miracle the cloth didn't come apart when he walked. She was wearing a starched white dress with a pink bow at the waist and two smaller ones in each of the pigtails that hung behind her ears, braided so tight they hurt, but she didn't care. Neither of them was smiling. More years would have to pass before Ana and Rodolfo would smile into a camera. When this was taken, it was too soon.

"How lovely you both are!"

Laura stroked Ana's back with the same caring gesture she'd repeated hundreds of times since Ana was a girl. "Laura, please, scratch my back a little," Ana would ask, resting her head against Laura's legs. And Laura would slowly rub the girl's back, in small circles, one overlapping another. It was a ritual for the two of them, a physical connection between a little motherless girl and the childless woman across the hall.

"How handsome my father was, Laura! I miss him so much!"

"He was beautiful, like you. I'm so proud of you. A chief inspector and nearly a captain. Smarter than all the other police."

"Well, not having kids or being in a couple helps," Ana answered with a degree of resignation. "I can devote all the time I want to my career."

"How is that going, Ana? Joan told me you're on the case of the missing boy."

"It's not going well. We've hardly found a clue. And my new boss sent me here to Barcelona for a pointless meeting just when I was on my way to question a suspect."

"You can't get stuck, like what happened with Nicolás."

"Sometimes I feel I can't do it anymore, Laura." Ana let out a long, deep sigh, as if trying to stop time in its tracks. Or stop the memories. Or the burden of life. "Sometimes I feel I'm breaking in two. And then I want to quit the force."

"Don't talk nonsense, girl." Laura adopted the tone of a scolding mother, as she had years before, when she was the closest thing to a mother that this girl had. "You can quit the police on your own terms, but not because somebody's trying to push you out. Look, I want to tell you something I've never told you before. Look in my eyes, look at this old woman with hardly any years left. You have a strength and courage that I've never allowed myself. I've only just started to live. Now that I'm an old widow, I'm finally doing what I want, and it's such a shame that neither my body nor my mind can manage it. You know what I mean. You knew Genaro. He didn't give me anything, not even children. He didn't take anything, either, and he never hit me, which not all the women of my era can say. But now I look back and think what a shame, what a loss of time, years, mind, and body. But you're different. You're strong and intelligent. You can allow yourself to do so much, honey. You just have to dare. Don't be your worst enemy. Don't keep yourself under wraps. You're worth more than anything. And remember, above all, that you don't have to explain anything to anyone or justify yourself! Do you see your colleagues doing that? Let the rest of them judge you however they want. Don't worry about it a bit."

Some hours later, settled into her seat on the bullet train, Ana thought about that conversation and the night she'd spent with Joan. She plugged her earphones into her phone and listened to Sílvia Pérez Cruz's heartrending version of "L'Hymne à l'amour." Ana leaned her head against the window, eyes closed, feeling the warmth of the sun. She could even feel each of the pairs of nuclei of hydrogen turning majestically to helium atoms and traveling three hundred thousand kilometers per second, at the speed of light, to end up—eight minutes and seventeen seconds later—passing through the window of a moving train on their way to her skin. The car was strangely silent, and her body rocked with the rhythmic clatter of the train as it rushed down the track at three hundred kilometers an hour. If life were perfect, that would be the moment she'd choose to frame.

But life wasn't perfect.

And a phone call was about to remind her of that.

19

INÉS

I had promised Pablo that I'd take him to the merry-go-round at the mall. He loved circling again and again on the blue horse that hardly resembled the animal. My son never got tired of the ride, but I stressed out just thinking of the impending boredom, though I handled it with the resignation that motherhood teaches us. It was better than going to the park. I hated the park above all the other things that maternity implies.

Pablo was in a bad mood. That morning, we'd had a fight because he'd started throwing his toys on the floor. All of them. Angrily. With the anger and strength children use to show that they're separate beings with their own capacity to make decisions and act on them. Finally, my son ended up breaking a small robot with movable joints that Santa Claus had brought him. Then I threatened to throw away the stuffed animal he always took to bed. "Your cow's going in the garbage," I told him. "I'm throwing it in with all the dirty things because your behavior is so bad. Look how sad Mama is because of it. Into the trash."

When we left the house, Pablo was still dissolved in tears and snot, so I tried to distract him to make him forget about his tantrum and the cow. Since it was a fabulous day outside, we walked to the mall, which was only ten minutes away. We even made a detour past the abandoned castle. Pablo loved to pretend that this half-ruined mansion surrounded by pines was the den of a dragon-tamer who chained his beasts in the basement at night so they couldn't escape. "If you stay quiet, Mama," he told me, "if you stay quiet, we can hear them roaring. Do you think we'll see fire coming out the windows?"

When we got to the mall—the same one Manu had disappeared from just four days earlier—it was quite crowded. I was surprised to see that The Taker phenomenon of two years ago—when people had shut themselves in their houses for fear that their children, too, would disappear—was not repeating itself.

I uploaded a photo to Twitter. *Everything calm,* I wrote. *Manu's disappearance does not seem to have disturbed the social life of Spain.* Was that what attracted the kidnapper? That's what I asked myself hundreds of times in the days that followed, tormented by guilt. Did that tweet draw The Taker to the mall to kidnap another child?

We went to the merry-go-round and fed coins into the bucking bronco for Pablo to play cowboy and ride. We went to the candy store and bought marshmallows and soda. Pablo was delighted. I took advantage of the occasion to go by the toy store where Manu had disappeared. I didn't yet know that a former employee with a history of stalking children had been arrested. Then we sat for a while in the middle of one of the corridors where a puppet theater had been set up.

The place was full of families spending their Sunday in the mall, and we found several other kids from Pablo's preschool. Iziar and his mother were there to buy shoes for school. "It's amazing how he wears them out in two days," she said. "Your son too?" We also saw Eli and her two girls, whom we often ran into at the park in the afternoons. They were having lunch with other friends. Later we saw Thiago, another of Pablo's classmates, who was bouncing a ball while walking hand in hand with his mother. After two o'clock, when we'd used up all the horses, all the rocket ships, and every banister or ledge fit for sliding or jumping, I asked Pablo whether he was hungry. "A Krabby Patty," he demanded, and once again I had to pretend that an ordinary fast-food hamburger had been made by SpongeBob out of crabmeat.

Have you ever tried to manage carrying a purse, two coats, and two trays of food through a crowded restaurant? What generally happens is that you drop something, and you're thankful just to get to a table without staining the coats with ketchup and soaking them in french fry grease.

When I finally managed to set the trays down on a free table and pile the coats and my purse next to them, I looked at Pablo to ask him to please sit down because the food was going to get cold, but the foolish child was still back at the cash register. My temper rising, I stood up to go get him, while trying not to make a scene. It's hard to be a mother in these technological times when anyone can take your picture or shoot a video and upload it to social media. Look how uncouth this actress is, or that announcer! There's no more privacy anywhere. That makes it very difficult to discipline a child.

I grabbed my purse and left the coats on the table, hoping they'd still be there when I got back. "Could you please keep an eye on our stuff?" I asked a family sitting at the next table. Then I pushed my way to the cash register, holding my breath and counting to ten, trying to put on my best face in front of all these people. I was thinking only about how to grab my son by the T-shirt and get him back to the table without too much fuss, whether he wanted to come or not. Sometimes motherhood was such a trial. Especially in public.

But Pablo wasn't there. There were a lot of people around, and I struggled to find him and to reassure myself, but he just wasn't there. I retraced my steps in case he'd been following me and something had distracted him. Pablo always stops and gets fixated on things while the rest of the world moves on. But I still couldn't find him. "Have you seen a dark-haired boy, four years old, about this tall, wearing a white T-shirt with blue stripes, blue jeans, and black sneakers? He was here just a couple of minutes ago."

With every *no*, I got more and more worried. I pushed my way out of the restaurant, bumping people left and right. My vision went blurry. Blood pounded in my temples, against the bones of my skull.

Pablo wasn't there.

I thought I felt a trembling in the air, a slight disruption in time and space, as if I were lost in the middle of a frozen lake and my nerve endings were starting to feel the ice cracking in the distance. The cracks were getting closer, the ice about to break beneath my feet. The whole world was going to break. And in just a few seconds, the vibrations turned into a wave of panic that rolled over me. Overwhelmed me. Annihilated me.

I had no idea I'd started to scream.

I realized I wasn't crying; there were no tears, no trembling, no understanding. Nothing. All I could do was open my mouth and scream. The rest of my body was paralyzed by panic. When I realized what had happened, I had no room for anything but horror. No heart, no stomach, no blood. Just the deepest and darkest terror.

Suffering hit me in waves, each stronger than the one before.

At some point, I had the impression I was about to faint. And I hoped I would. I clenched my teeth while hoping to lose consciousness and disappear, even for a few seconds.

Disappear from the reality that Pablo was not at my side.

20

ANA

Jumping off a train that's going more than three hundred kilometers an hour is not a good idea. That didn't stop Ana from considering it. She was tempted to break one of the emergency windows. For a few minutes, she channeled all her anger at one of the small red hammers under the *Break only in case of emergency* sign, as if she could shatter the glass simply by looking at it.

She wanted to yell, to break something, to break her skull against the walls. She was sealed inside a goddamn train and couldn't do a thing. Except wait for it to get where it was going. And she couldn't stand that. She felt like she was going to explode. A burst of energy grew inside her, a force she could hardly control. Like a star about to become a supernova, engulfing everything for light-years around.

When Nori had called, Ana almost didn't answer. She didn't want to talk; she only wanted to enjoy that moment of relaxation with her head against the warm glass of the train window on this fine Sunday afternoon. She'd call him back at the Atocha station. But on the seventh ring, she changed her mind. Maybe it was something important. Ana lived with the unceasing fear that unanswered calls could be dire. That's why she'd often answered calls from unknown numbers or returned them if she hadn't picked up. She was always disappointed. It was never worthwhile, never that important.

Except this time.

Ana figured Nori was calling to report on the questioning of the young man arrested Friday, the former employee of the toy store who had a record of stalking children. Nori had caught an earlier AVE, first thing that Sunday morning, and had been in Madrid for some time. "When I get home," he'd told her the night before while they walked back to the hotel after having dinner at La Vinateria, "I'll log in to the division's computer to see whether they've resumed questioning the ex-employee. Then I'll let you know whether it's worth your time to come by the station or whether you should go straight home to rest until Monday. And as for the report the commander assigned you, they can shove it up their ass."

But Nori's voice on the other end of the iffy cell phone connection, now, told her that something was wrong. The way he said her name, with a wavering cadence, meant bad news. Very bad news. But still she didn't imagine how devastating it would be.

"Ana?" he said again. "Are you still on the AVE? I have to tell you something."

His voice faltered a little, though not much, because he was a policeman and knew how to control himself. But Ana could hear the hesitation.

"Javi, what's going on? Tell me right away," she demanded. She was getting very nervous.

"I didn't want to tell you over the phone," he said, "but I don't want you to find out over social media or from someone else."

"What the fuck is going on, Javi?"

Ana stood to go talk between the cars where the train noise would keep anybody else from hearing her. In fact, she could barely hear herself. The noise inside and outside her head was so loud that she couldn't follow her own thoughts.

"Ana, promise not to do anything crazy," Javier said.

His silence was unbearable. Whatever her sub-inspector had to tell her, he didn't want to say it, and Ana knew she didn't want to hear it. Finally, after the agonizing silence, Nori spit it out.

"Ana, listen. Inés's son. He's disappeared. It was in the same mall where Manu was taken. Inés is in the hospital. She blacked out." Silence. "Ana? Ana! Answer me for Christ's sake!"

But he only heard background noise: Sixty-four tempered-steel wheels wearing against the rails at three hundred kilometers an hour. Eight cars shaking side to side as if about to jump off the track. The aerodynamic creaking of the hydrogen and oxygen atoms in the air offering resistance to the passing train.

And Ana's sobs.

She'd sat down on the floor of the platform, head between her legs, folded into a ball.

She couldn't answer. She had no air in her lungs, no oxygen traveling to her brain.

All her police training, the sordid cases she'd handled, the evil she'd seen, or the dozens of times she'd had to tell someone about a death—none of that had prepared her enough. Nobody, however hardened by police work, was prepared for something like this. The same way nothing prepares an oncologist for a cancer diagnosis that's his or her own.

21

ANA

Nori had wanted to tell her in person. He would have preferred to go to the train station to pick her up and be at her side when he delivered the bad news, to see how she reacted, to be able to help her handle it. Anything but calling her while she was trapped inside a train. *Our friend's son might have been kidnapped by the same man who took Nicolás two years ago and Manu four days ago.* How do you say that over the phone? How do you give that news to somebody who's locked in a cage like a rabid dog?

But hours had already passed since Pablo's disappearance, and soon all sorts of media would be buzzing with the news. Inés was a well-known TV personality. On top of that, she was covering The Taker case. Morbid interest in spades.

And, further, dozens of people had witnessed the moment when Inés had started to scream and scream and scream until she blacked out. It was a miracle the news hadn't spread already. It was a miracle no video had shown up on YouTube. Surely right now, someone was bargaining over how much money their cell phone images of Inés fainting would bring in.

As soon as the media got wind of this, all hell would break loose. So Nori had to tell her, even if she was stuck on the train. Better that way. Better a shock than a heart attack.

In the Madrid division of the Judicial Police, all leaves, sick days, and vacations were canceled. Three four-year-old boys, physically similar, were kidnapped from the same mall. This was something the country couldn't tolerate, something that struck fear into politicians because it could easily be held against them. So those running the country demanded that the ones in charge of the police give the case absolute priority. "The sky's the limit in terms of resources," the Minister told the director general of the police. "Whatever you need, you've got it. People, time, equipment. Find those kids."

The majority of the Judicial Police left whatever they were doing to focus on the disappearances of Nicolás, Manu, and Pablo. National headquarters in Canillas dispatched part of the special group on kidnapping and extortion to collaborate with the investigation.

"Where's Chief Inspector Arén?" demanded Major Ruipérez, his voice echoing through the room. "Where the fuck is the chief inspector in charge of this case? It's just been made the top priority for the entire national police force!"

One. Two. Three. Four seconds. Silence. Hands stopped typing, mouths snapped shut. Everything came to a sudden halt. You could cut the tension with a knife.

"Does anybody hear me in this place? Where-the-fuck-is-Chief-In-spec-tor-A-rén?"

The commander was turning red. Adrenaline had sped up his pulse, and the blood vessels in his face had filled, making him look like a Christmas-tree ball coated with metallic paint. His jugular vein, pulsating under the skin of his neck, threatened to burst from the pressure.

Charo started to stand up, but Nori stopped her. *Let me do it,* the look on his face said. *Let him take it out on me, since I outrank you.* Charo nodded.

"Commander," the sub-inspector said, standing up from his seat. "Chief Inspector Arén is about to arrive in Madrid on the AVE. Yesterday she was in Barcelona, at a coordination meeting with the Mossos. Remember? You sent her, sir."

Nori consciously omitted the fact that he, too, had been at the meeting the previous afternoon in Barcelona. He was standing a few meters away from Ruipérez, and he could smell the boss's rage. The sweat of an angry person is acrid and penetrating. It signals danger in case you want to flee. But the sub-inspector didn't flee. The two men stared at each other for four long seconds.

"It's three thirty on Sunday afternoon. The meeting ended last night at eight. That's"—Ruipérez stopped to count in his head—"nineteen and a half hours. Are you going to tell me she hasn't had enough time to get back to Madrid?" The commander's tone was sour and disrespectful, the tone of someone who doesn't care whether he's right or wrong because he knows he has something more important: power. "Is she crawling back on her knees along the A-2?"

At that moment, Ana came running into the room. Devastated, disoriented, distraught. It took her a few seconds to take note of the silence and the fact that everyone had turned around to look at her.

"Chief Inspector, in my office. Now. And the rest of you, I don't want any of you leaving this room until those three kids are found. Motherfucking cunts!" Ruipérez shouted at the top of his lungs, losing control. "Are you listening to me? I don't want you sleeping. I don't want you screwing. I don't want you shitting. I don't want you swallowing your spit until you first find those three boys. Got it? Look at me! I'm going to squeeze your guts in a vise until those three show up. And they better show up alive, or you're going to wish you were dead too."

In a perfect 180-degree about-face, maintaining complete verticality as if he were on parade in the North Korean army and his life depended on his posture, the commander turned and left. He didn't look at anyone, much less Ana Arén. He took it as a given that she'd follow him to his office. That's what he'd ordered. That's how it had to be.

"Quick, tell me what you know!" Ana said to the room, trying to keep the quaver out of her voice. "Facts, clues, photos. Give me a reason for hope. Something to help find those boys."

"We're gathering all the images from the security cameras inside the mall and the surrounding area. It's not easy, because today's Sunday and we can't locate all the shop owners. We've also asked for everything from the cameras in the apartment complex where Inés lives, from a half hour before they left the house to a half hour after, in case anyone followed them from home. But only the concierge has the password to the computer system that holds the video files, and we haven't been able to reach him. Apparently he's got his phone turned off. We're combing the whole area in search of any clues, and we've shut down the mall and cleared it out. We're reviewing the list of current and former employees all over again. We're also reviewing the list of sex criminals in the area." All that came from Charo in a single breath.

"Inés is still in the hospital," Nori added. "The doctors won't let us question her yet."

Ana walked toward the commander's office, supporting herself against the wall. She dragged herself there with her arm against the rough paint and her feet scuffing the floor tiles. She could hardly walk forward, unable to process the notion of Pablo's disappearance. The emotional part of her brain struggled not to blame Inés. What the hell was she doing, taking her son to the same place the two other boys had disappeared from? Was she looking for attention? Why the hell had she tweeted out the fact that she was there?

Ana needed to get a grip. Stop. Put on the breaks. Shut down her operating system and reboot. Get out of the emotional spiral so she could think clearly. She stopped walking, closed her eyes, and dug her nails into her palms. Pain always put her in her place.

Meanwhile, Ismael Gallardo was still in a cell. No one seemed to remember about him. Thirty-eight hours detained as a suspect in Manu's disappearance. Twenty-nine years old, with a record of stalking outside a preschool. Formerly employed at the toy store where the boy had disappeared. But he couldn't be the perpetrator of Pablo's disappearance, because he was already in jail. It couldn't be him. Unless he had an accomplice.

Or an imitator.

22

INÉS

I don't know whether it makes sense to talk about a state of mind, when really it was my whole body rising and falling. Head, soul, heart. When I was up, I thought everything was possible. *If you get out of bed, Pablo will come back. If you open the door with your right hand, Pablo will come back. If you put on your yellow T-shirt, Pablo will come back.* Then I went into a state of hyperactivity, where I felt I had the energy to do anything, to stand in for the entire police department that was searching for my son.

But then, without anything specific bringing about the change, I collapsed. In a fraction of a second, all that surging energy imploded, folding inward and compressing itself infinite times until it disappeared, leaving me hollow and wilted like a marionette that has lost its strings.

"Go home and wait. There's nothing you can do," Ana told me as gently as she could, when I appeared at the station after leaving the hospital that Sunday afternoon. Just four hours after Pablo had disappeared. *Go home and wait,* she told me, as if going home and waiting were the most ordinary things in the world when your child has disappeared into the hands of a maniac.

I knew that Ana had to get me out of there, that I couldn't stay in the station with the officers of the unit investigating the case, but deep in my soul, I knew I'd never be able to forgive her either. Because what I wanted then, what I needed right then, was for my friend to put her arms around me and tell me everything would be okay—they were going to find him, and Pablo was going to be all right. I wanted Ana to stroke my hair and comfort me until my son appeared. I wanted desperately for her to tell me everything was going to work out. She was a policewoman. She had to promise me. She had to swear to it. Please, please, please. But Ana didn't do any of that. She just looked me in the eye and told me they were going to run themselves ragged looking for Pablo, that she had the best officers working on the case, and they weren't going to rest until I had my son back.

"I will, won't I?" I echoed. "I will get him back?"

"Inés," Ana answered. "Go home and wait. Do you want any . . . help? Is there someone I should call? A therapist?"

What goddamn help? All I wanted was for them to find my son. And what was I supposed to do at home? Is there a worse form of waiting? All alone, shut up in the house, counting every second, one after another, so incredibly slow, while waiting for a call?

I didn't want to tell anyone. Not yet. Some corner of my conscious brain was informing me about the storm that would be unleashed when the news got out, but that was still several hours away. I had to tell my mother before the media got word, but she was in Lanzarote spending a few days with a group of friends. It would be terrible giving her the news over the phone, but it would be worse waiting until we could be together. The first flight back to the mainland wouldn't take off until tomorrow morning. The earliest it would land in Madrid was ten, still many hours away.

I went home, and then I called. Calling her was one of the hardest things I've ever done. She answered on the fourth ring, laughing, with no idea about the drama about to envelop her.

"Hi, honey," she said. "How's everything? You won't believe what a good time I'm having here. We're still going strong. Look what time it is, an hour earlier here, ha ha. An hour earlier in the Canaries—I've always wanted to be able to say that, and here I am. We're still in the pool at the hotel. Hey, you don't think I'm drunk, do you? I've only had two beers, but in this heat, you know, I think the alcohol has more of an effect. Have you ever noticed that? This is the life, Inés, this is the life. You've got to bring Pablo here sometime. You're right, the Princess Yaiza is a fantastic resort. Leave the boy at his kindergarten, and go out and have some fun. You've been looking so stressed lately. You need a break."

I let her chatter on, hoping she'd keep talking, because once I cut her off, once I told her what I'd called to say, she'd be destroyed. Why not let her have a few more seconds of joy? What harm would a few more seconds of ignorance do? That was the only gift I had left.

So I stayed quiet until she realized she was talking into a void.

"Inés, honey, are you there?" she asked. I kept quiet, still. "I think maybe the call got dropped," she said to her friends, holding the phone away from her mouth. "It's Inés, but I can't hear her. It must be a bad connection."

I hung up. I decided to give her a little more time.

Suddenly I remembered Sam. I had to tell him what had happened. I sent him a WhatsApp message but saw he'd been offline for hours. Where could he be? Probably out somewhere with his little gang of other au pairs. Or maybe he'd run out of battery. That happened to him on the weekends. He'd lose track. The late-night partying here in Spain tended to dissolve his common sense.

I decided to make sure. Just in case. If he'd come back and was in his room, I had to tell him before the media started talking about it and he found out through one of the many social media sites he was obsessive about checking. So I went downstairs to the lower floor of our duplex apartment. I knocked gently on his door. No answer. I knocked again, harder, calling his name. Again, no reply. I opened the door, in case he was asleep. It wouldn't be the first time after a weekend out on the town.

He wasn't in his room. Where the hell was Sam?

I collapsed on the living room couch. But lying down was worse, because then my mind went wild thinking about Pablo.

23

ANA

"Nothing. Not the tiniest damn thread to follow. Absolute zero. Like a vacuum," Charo said, looking at Ana with despair in her eyes. "Like the earth swallowed them up. Or they vanished into thin air. Nobody saw anything; nobody knows anything."

"But Inés told me they requested a DNA sample," Ana said, puzzled.

"Yeah, Ruipérez's order. As a precaution, I guess. In case he shows up"—Charo stopped, realizing what she was about to say and to whom. "In case he shows up . . . dead."

Ruipérez had given the order so as to keep a low media profile. If they found a corpse and needed to identify it via DNA, then notifying the parents and taking samples and comparing them to the body could alert the press, which would mean more pressure. With the DNA samples already taken and stored, the police could exercise more control over the information in the case. Or at least, that part of it.

"How's the review of the security camera footage going?"

Ana took a long swallow of coffee. Coffee disgusted her and made her want to throw up, made her feel she'd poured drain cleaner down her esophagus in free fall toward her stomach and intestines, but tonight she needed it. With a lot of sugar, for sure, so she could keep it down.

She needed a substance that would keep her body and brain reactive. Strong coffee was the only one she knew that was legal.

"We still haven't assembled all the images. It's Sunday, and a lot of businesses are closed," Charo explained, while she went on downloading images from the flash drives her colleagues had brought. "We're trying to find the owners, but now that it's ten at night, I don't think we'll have much more luck till tomorrow."

"Whatever you've got, start watching it now, right away. There must be hours and hours of footage, and it's going to take days to watch it all. Have you talked to the au pair?"

"What au pair?" Charo looked up from her computer.

"There's a British kid who lives with Inés and Pablo, an au pair who's been with them since the beginning of the school year. He takes care of the boy in the afternoon while Inés is at the studio or when she has to travel."

"Shit, we didn't know that. I'll get on it right away."

"No, Charo, you stick with the video. Have Nori help you. Tell Arcos to find the kid and bring him here. Then we'll figure out what to do with him. Right now, I've got a meeting with the headquarters kidnapping team. We're setting up a joint command."

Since the elite kidnapping and extortion team from national headquarters had joined the search, Ana wasn't directing the investigation alone. She had to coordinate all decisions, and share all information, with another chief inspector.

"Ana!" Nori stopped her in the hallway, leading her to the makeshift office set up for the new search operation. "The toy store guy was arrested Friday night, so we've only got another day to come up with solid evidence and bring him before a judge. Otherwise, we'll have to let him go."

"He was in a cell when Pablo was kidnapped. He can't be the one."

"That's assuming The Taker exists, Ana. We've got nothing pointing in that direction."

"Three kids, same age, same physical appearance, all taken from the mall, two of them four days apart." Ana crossed her arms. "Is that all just a coincidence?"

"Ana, you can't let this get to you so much. Have you thought about taking yourself off the case? Now that the kidnapping team is here, let the other chief inspector take charge. This is too emotional for you."

Ana went silent as if she'd been punched in the solar plexus.

When she could speak, she said, "No fucking way, Nori. No fucking way."

No fucking way, because deep down I know you might be right, Ana thought. *Deep down I know that my sanity is hanging by a thread, and if I want to solve this case, I'm going to have to dig my nails in until they go all the way through my palms.*

When she got to her office, she didn't recognize it. Somebody had moved her desk into a corner at the back to make more room for two big boards on a pair of sawhorses. The IT team had been quick, and six computers were already set up, though there were no chairs to sit in. Too much to ask on a Sunday night, and it was a miracle to have found the computers. How had they done that? The order must have come from very high up. The pressure from that same direction, Ana guessed, was about to become unbearable.

"Chief Inspector Arén?"

Ana turned around.

"I'm Chief Inspector Jesús Silvelo. You've heard about our unified operation, yes?" He extended his hand as part of the introduction.

"Yes, they've brought me up to date." Ana shook his hand. "Thanks for joining the investigation on a Sunday night."

"I'm a father as well as a policeman," he said, as if this explained everything.

Ana knew Chief Inspector Silvelo only by reputation. He'd had a lightning rise within the National Police Corps, going right from the Police Academy to the executive ladder. As soon as regulations permitted, he took the exam to be a chief inspector and passed with flying colors, making him one of the youngest at that rank in all of Spain. For the past few years he'd been in charge of one of the most elite divisions of the Judicial Police, always in the spotlight and working at an intense pace against the clock—the special group on kidnappings and extortion.

If you passed Jesús Silvelo on the street in civilian clothes, buying bread at the bakery or standing in line for a movie, he'd most likely be invisible to you. "People don't pay attention to boring things," he always said. "If you look like a boring person, nobody sees you, and that's a great advantage for me. To see without being seen. To be there without being remembered."

But on the job, Silvelo was different. His claws came out. He was pitiless and didn't stop for anything or anyone.

"I ordered some pizzas," he said. "For me and you," he added, using the informal pronoun. "If I may call you *tú*, with your permission, Ana?" Ana nodded with a smile, her first in many hours. "Let's dig into them before they get cold. I don't guess you have plates or silverware, but maybe something to wipe the grease off our hands?"

"Toilet paper is all I can offer," she said, responding in kind with the familiar form. "The napkins of the police force, as you know. But be gentle if you wipe your lips, the budget cuts have even affected the toilet paper. It feels more like 100-grit sandpaper than something for wiping your ass. Rubs hemorrhoids off within a few weeks."

Both of them laughed. They needed some way to release the tension. You needed to reset your brain once in a while to be able to think clearly again, to sweep away the cobwebs and see the solution. Sometimes laughter could do that, could offer a new look at a case.

"Should we sit down?" Jesús asked.

"Sure," she said, choosing the visitors' seat so he could have hers, which was softer and more comfortable. "They've brought the computers for your team, but no chairs yet. Sometimes the simplest tasks are the hardest to get done, it seems."

Ana didn't want to start marking territory in her own office. The point was to make it the whole team's office, because all of them were going to work in this space until they solved the case or the children reappeared.

Alive, she hoped.

"Well, what have we got here? Two lovebirds? Already best friends." It was Ruipérez, exhibiting his supreme talent for ruining anything he touched. The King Midas of shit and destruction. "Inviting a girl for pizza on the first date is a little stingy, don't you think, Jesús?"

"I'll tell you a secret," Silvelo responded, not even getting to his feet to answer his superior. "I ordered the pizza for you, sir. But if that's going to disappoint you on our first date, then maybe the chief inspector and I should eat it, because we've got some busy days ahead of us. And I'll ask you out another day and take you somewhere classy, more befitting, okay?"

Ruipérez's expression said he was trying to come up with a clever response. Apparently he couldn't find one.

24

PATRICIA

"Cut it out, Papa. Let go of me!"

The girl looked to be about fifteen or sixteen, but it was difficult to tell because her clothes and makeup made her look much older. Her black eyeliner and shadow were smeared. She stumbled along in bright-fuchsia shoes with ten-centimeter heels, showing off her nice-looking ankles exposed by the cuffs of her jeans, which were rolled up as if she were going for a walk on the beach. A semitransparent white spaghetti-strap top revealed small round breasts. Her long black hair had the thick, tousled look of someone who'd just gotten out of bed.

Or someone had just gotten her out of bed, perhaps.

She was on her way into the police station, towed along by a man she kept calling Papa. This was clearly a girl in too much of a hurry to grow up.

"Cut it out, Papa. Let go of me!"

But the man kept on walking without loosening the tight grip on his daughter's arm, forcing her to take uncertain steps in her high heels until they reached the station's front desk.

"We're here because my daughter has some important information about the disappearance of that boy the other day, in the mall over there."

As he talked through the intake window, the man squeezed the girl's arm even tighter, as if he was afraid she'd escape—again. White marks appeared on the girl's arm where he had a hold of her. She looked at the floor. With a perfect shake of her head, she made her mane of dark hair fall in front of her face in a gesture of indifference or embarrassment.

The rookie policeman manning the front desk that morning opened his eyes wide. Through the armored glass, his attention was nearly distracted by the transparency of the girl's white top, but what the man said left him in a cold sweat. A clue about the disappearance of one of the boys.

"Could you wait here a moment, please?" he asked them, pointing to some plastic benches where they should sit. "I'll be right back."

He turned to go in search of one of his superiors, but then thought better of it. He walked back to the microphone used for speaking to visitors. "Don't leave, please," he pleaded.

Exactly thirty-eight seconds later, a sub-inspector—the highest-ranking official present in the small station of this precinct—came hurrying through the door hidden behind the armored glass.

"Good morning. I'm Sub-Inspector Antonio Uclés. Please come with me."

They went through the door into a large, nearly empty room, where huge piles of paper covered the dozens of tables filling the space. Patricia didn't know why, but she felt anxiety in the atmosphere, like something you could breathe, as if the room had not been aired in a very long time. Not only dust particles require proper ventilation. Anxiety, too, needs to be flushed out once in a while.

"All right, young lady, what do you have to say to this policeman?" the father said in a scolding tone once all three were seated around an old round table with a plywood top. With some embarrassment, the sub-inspector tried to sweep away the breakfast crumbs his colleagues had left. "Tell him about the boy. Tell him."

The girl kept silent, staring at the floor with her hair hiding her face, as if she weren't really there, in a police station, about to confess to a crime—or so it seemed to her.

"Look, mister policeman, let me start telling you what happened, because it seems the cat's got my daughter's tongue—or her brain."

The father explained that he had, indeed, gotten his daughter out of bed and dragged her here, and that she needed to tell Sub-Inspector Uclés something she knew about the kidnapped boy. The girl withdrew, folding in on herself in the plastic chair.

"This daughter of mine is a lost cause. Look at her, sitting there like she never did anything wrong in her life."

Sub-Inspector Uclés surreptitiously signaled the policewoman on duty with him that morning. Sonia Calero came discreetly closer to the table. She'd already heard from her colleague at the front desk that the father and daughter claimed to have a credible clue about Pablo. Or maybe Manu. The man had said it was important information about the boy taken the other day from the mall. The other day could be Wednesday or yesterday. Manu or Pablo.

Sonia had been in the mall on Wednesday. She'd been among the first police officers to arrive after Manu's disappearance, and she'd taken charge of gathering the first pieces of evidence. She had also been the one assigned to tell Chief Inspector Arén what they knew when the inspector arrived.

"I'm not sure I can trust this kid, you know? I mean, how am I going to trust an empty-headed fifteen-year-old? Teenagers do crazy things."

The father was trying to engage the sympathy of the policeman. The sub-inspector nodded. His experience had taught him that the best way to empathize with someone was to subtly imitate his or her gestures, the same way the best used-car salesmen move their heads or arms in a mirror image of the potential buyers, repeating their gestures and expressions to develop rapport. But Antonio Uclés couldn't afford to turn the girl against him. So he opted for a neutral position.

"You know how kids are these days," the father went on. "So I keep a close eye on her." The man kept seeking the policeman's approval and speaking as if his daughter wasn't beside him. "I keep a close eye on her because girls even younger than her are already sending revealing pictures to boys. You can't imagine the things I've seen and the way they talk to each other. Don't think I don't sometimes have a mind to give her a beating. In my father's day, he would have already pulled off his belt for a good hard whack. But now, as soon as you raise a hand to them, the kids file a complaint."

Sonia Calero, surprised at the harsh words, looked up from her paperwork. How could he talk about his daughter like that to her face? Sonia couldn't blame her for rebelling. Luckily, the man didn't catch Sonia's reproachful expression, and he continued.

"So with a daughter like that, either I have to control her, or I'll die of shame."

The man explained that he knew everything his daughter did on her phone. It was easy. Every time she connected to the Wi-Fi network in the house, he could use his computer to get access to her phone and see everything she did, thanks to a program called TeamViewer. That morning, over breakfast, while Patricia was still asleep, he went in to snoop and saw a picture that shocked him.

"Tell him, Patricia. Tell him what you and that criminal you call a boyfriend did last night."

The girl finally lifted her head and, with a slow, tired motion, brushed the hair away from her face. She fixed her eyes on her father.

"Maybe, Papa," she started to say, in a voice that was surprisingly soft and sweet. *This father's problems,* the sub-inspector thought, *have only just begun.* "Just maybe, spying on other people's phones is a crime. The officer can tell us whether it's legal or not." She turned to stare at Sub-Inspector Uclés through the locks that still covered a good part of her face. "Isn't that right, Señor . . . what did you say your name was? Anyway, isn't spying on someone else's phone without permission a crime?"

And she was only fifteen. *Lord have mercy,* he thought.

"Look," the sub-inspector responded, "here's what we're going to do. Could you, sir, just calmly tell me what happened, while your daughter chats with my colleague? That way, we'll all be more comfortable, and I can give all my attention to what you want to say."

It would be better to separate the father and daughter. As long as they were together it was going to be impossible to get anything out of them—or, anyway, to get at the truth—because the situation between them was becoming more and more impossible. If they really knew something about one of the boys, time was of the essence. Uclés made another slight sign to his colleague.

The police cannot question a minor without the presence of a father, mother, or some other adult whom the parents have authorized. But in this case, since the sub-inspector had won the father's implicit approval, there wouldn't be any issue. Sonia took the girl to one of the offices where the complaints brought daily to the station were sworn out. Antonio and the father stayed at the plywood table in the corner of the main room.

Sonia spoke without keeping her eyes on the girl's face for very long, so she wouldn't feel pressured. "Quite the drill sergeant, your father. Mine was just like him. Even if we'd been out late at night, he woke us up at eight in the morning. Every day. Even when I was twenty-two, my father kept on marching into my bedroom to raise the blinds, open the window, and pull off the covers. It was impossible to stay asleep."

Patricia sat on the edge of the chair, with her legs apart and her body hanging forward. How to get her to lift her head and pay attention?

"But this thing today, if what your father says is true, sounds serious. I know what a drag it is at eight a.m. on a Monday. But, Patricia, I need you to help me, please. If you know something, I need you to tell me so I can help those kids."

"I didn't do anything, okay?" At last, she was talking. "Not me and not my friend. Before I tell you anything, you need to guarantee immunity for both of us."

What movies had this girl been watching? Immunity? For both?

"Patricia, I'm sure you're right that you didn't do anything, but you have to help those boys. Maybe what you tell me could save a life."

"No, what I tell you isn't going to change anything, because they're already dead."

25

SAM/PATRICIA

Luis Arcos found Sam at eight o'clock on Monday morning, about the same time that the girl with the fuchsia heels was being dragged into the station by her father a few kilometers away. Detective Arcos found Pablo's au pair walking down the street with his hands in his pockets and a vacant look on his face, very near where Inés lived with her son. Arcos couldn't say whether the paleness of the youth's face had to do with the habitual color of his Britannic skin, or imbibing too much alcohol, or exhaustion from a long weekend.

Or with fear and remorse.

That's what they'd have to find out once he brought the kid into the station.

Arcos hadn't spoken any English since Margarita Sorolla, his high school teacher, gave him a passing grade in senior-year English out of pure pity, because otherwise he'd be ineligible to take the college entrance exam. In the end, though, Sorolla's D-minus did him no good. He crashed and burned on the entrance exam, so no university would accept him.

Since his English was less than rudimentary, Arcos approached Sam with badge in hand and a single repeated word: "Police, police." For further explanations, he was tempted to pull out his smartphone and connect to Google Translate, but that seemed tacky for a detective of the national police force. Instead, he tried in primitive Spanglish to explain that Sam needed to answer some questions about Pablo's disappearance down at the station, but to all appearances, the approximation of *desapareixon* did not mean anything to Sam. Nor did *interrogueixon* or *comissariii*.

Sam did, on the other hand, understand Pablo's name, and it seemed to terrify him.

"Let me speak with Inés, please," he said in English. "I need my phone. Let me talk to her. Where's Pablo? What's going on?"

And that was all. Repeated more than once. "I need my phone. Let me talk to her. Where's Pablo? What's going on?" Out of all that, Arcos understood only *Pablo, Inés, please*, and *phone*. In sign language, Arcos indicated that Sam should follow him to the car, and the youth did so, obedient as a lamb.

◆ ◆ ◆

"They're already dead."

The phrase echoed through the brain of Officer Sonia Calero, seated in front of a girl of fifteen whose father said she had information about the missing boys.

"Who's dead, Patricia? Who?"

"The boys, those boys who disappeared, the ones everybody is talking about."

The girl closed her eyes and covered her face with her hands, her elbows resting on her legs, her body curled up like a snail without its shell for protection. Sonia wasn't sure whether to touch her lightly, to establish some kind of contact, or not. She decided to wait.

"Help me, Patricia, please. Help the families of those boys. Imagine their poor mothers. Their poor fathers too."

"What's going to happen to me?"

Patricia raised her head, pushed the hair out of her face, and looked the policewoman in the eye. Finally, Sonia could establish some kind of connection with her.

"What have you done, Patricia, that anything could happen to you? Have you done something wrong?"

Sonia leaned down so her head was even with the girl's, because she didn't want to seem too authoritarian, addressing her from above.

"I don't know," Patricia said.

In a different station, much bigger and better equipped, phone calls were made in search of a certified English interpreter so Sam could be questioned according to the law. Although an interpreter was easily found, showing up was another matter. It was nine on a Monday morning, the first day of the month, in Madrid. And it was raining. In other words, hell on wheels.

While Luis headed toward provincial headquarters with Sam in the back seat—his hands were free, as Arcos had decided not to cuff him, since he wasn't under arrest—Nori stepped into one of the interrogation rooms to try to get something out of Ismael Gallardo. Only hours remained before they'd have to let him go for lack of credible evidence. Which meant that, if he was guilty, he'd be able to destroy any incriminating evidence. Or do something to Manu, if Manu was still alive.

The suspect had demanded a lawyer, and a public defender was assigned to him. "Pedro de Francisco," Nori read in the visitors' ledger, just as the door to room number three opened.

"Pedro de Francisco?" the sub-inspector asked.

"Yes. I've just been talking with my client. And you can let him go."

"That's for us to decide, isn't it?"

"He just offered a solid alibi for the afternoon Manu disappeared. And as for Pablo, you know full well you were already holding my client then. I suppose you're clever enough to draw the right conclusion on that one."

Badly done, Nori thought. *Badly done, Señor Attorney. Too young, too impulsive, too hungry. You're better off not burning your bridges with the police. Now you'll learn the hard way.*

"What's the alibi?" Nori asked.

"That afternoon, at about five o'clock, he went to a site for sexual exchanges on Calle del Desengaño, in central Madrid, more than a half-hour drive from the suburb where the boy disappeared. This site is an underground operation, an apartment where all kinds of sexual practices go on. Uncommon ones, shall we say, at least as far as public knowledge goes. Only couples can go there, so my client hired a hooker off the street to accompany him. You can ask her, too, though I guess you won't value her testimony much. They got caught for trying to deceive the club, were told to leave, and there was a fight. The local police intervened after a call from the neighbors. You can ask for the report, which ought to contain everything you need to know. They weren't released until ten that night, by which time the boy had been, let's see . . ." He paused dramatically. "Missing for almost five hours. There are many things you could say about my client, but a talent for being in two places at the same time still eludes him. So you need to let him go. Immediately."

Ismael Gallardo was innocent.

They were back to square one.

"Fuck a duck," Nori said to himself.

◆ ◆ ◆

"Patricia, I can't help you if you don't tell me what happened. Patricia."

Officer Calero was still trying to get the dark-haired teenager to tell what she knew. Repeating the name of the person you were speaking with was a common tactic for seeking contact and rapport. *I'm here with you, I know who you are, and you matter to me. Patricia. Patricia. Patricia.* But Patricia offered only two words in response.

"I'm scared."

Scared. Of what? Of what she had seen or what she had done? Or maybe scared of the repercussions that would follow if she told? Did she know The Taker? Did she have some suspicion about who he was?

Then the door opened. At the worst time. Just when Sonia was convinced she was about to get Patricia to talk. It was the father. Shit. Shit. Shit. Shit.

"Don't say a word, Patricia. Keep quiet. I mean, what's going on here? My daughter's a minor, and you can't question her without my consent and a lawyer present."

What could have happened out there? Sonia gave Sub-Inspector Antonio Uclés a sharp look when he entered the room. The sub-inspector mimed holding a phone to his ear. "Lawyer," he mouthed. The father must have gotten a call.

He grabbed his daughter by the elbow and yanked her out of the chair.

"Look, sir, you authorized us to speak with your daughter," the sub-inspector said.

"I haven't authorized anything. You took my daughter into another office. She's a minor, and you're not going to pin anything on her that she didn't do."

The father began to drag the girl toward the exit, followed by Antonio and Sonia, who legally couldn't do anything to prevent it. But the sub-inspector did try a parting shot.

"If you leave, I can arrest you for obstructing justice."

The man hesitated, but either he was a good negotiator, or he'd seen too many police shows.

"I'm not creating any obstacles. We came here voluntarily. All we're asking for is our rights as citizens. And protection for my daughter, who's a minor."

Sonia tried to establish visual contact with the girl, but she'd gone back to hiding behind her hair.

"Patricia, listen to me," Sonia tried. "I can help you."

Father and daughter were now halfway out the door. He was pulling her the opposite way from ten minutes before, once again making the girl trip over her fuchsia heels. At the last moment, Patricia turned around and looked at Sonia, about to say something, but her father interrupted.

"When you guarantee us all the legal requirements due a minor, we'll be delighted to tell you what we know. We'll be at home, so you know where to find us." The heavy glass door closed behind them.

Sonia was already dialing the number of the SAF. She had to speak with Chief Inspector Ana Arén right away.

26

RAMÓN

Fog again.

In the half-light of early morning, a blanket of fog carpeted the little suburban city. Or big suburban town. What did you call a place that had grown, in forty years, from barely three thousand inhabitants to upward of seventy thousand? Two hundred years ago, these lands— once the hunting grounds of King Philip II—had been sold off by the crown to the nobility at a bargain price. Six generations later, at the turn of the twenty-first century, the great-grandchildren of these courtier-speculators had reaped obscene quantities of money from selling the land during the building boom that nearly tore Spain apart. Asphalt and brick now covered nearly all of Majadahonda. What remained of the former hunting grounds was just a small part of the Pilar Woods. Which was a lot better than many other neighboring towns could say.

That morning, the fog was heavy and blurred everything. Ramón turned off the bike path that bisected the town center, veering suddenly into the Woods, trying to get to work before it started to rain.

Access to the Woods was closed at night, but by this time, the gates would be open. He entered the pine forest through the gate next to the Cerro del Espino, one of the last subdivisions developed during the boom, one that had come dangerously close to the Woods. He took the path that led toward the train station and wound its way downhill for a few easy kilometers. It would do him good to saturate himself with cool, fresh morning air, because he'd spend the next eight hours underground. At least he was on the day shift this week, so there would still be some light when he emerged.

His job wasn't difficult, quite the contrary. The hard part was to avoid succumbing to boredom. He had to concentrate on the array of automated machinery, instrument panels, computers, buttons, and switches that left him daydreaming most of the time. What a way to waste his life, he sometimes thought. When everything was working well, all Ramón had to do was make sure the technology didn't go haywire. Unfortunately, there was always some resident who had to screw things up. Damned grown-up spoiled brats. During the eight years he'd been working at the pneumatic garbage depository, Ramón had seen it all—but never anything like what was about to appear that day.

The alarms went off just when the system was beginning to inhale the garbage from the Cerro del Espino, adjoining the Woods. The sounds and lights of the alarm filled every cubic centimeter of the small underground room. *Fucking pipe number three clogged again,* he thought.

"Alberto! Alberto!" he yelled without getting up. "Check on number three, please."

"Three? Did you say three?" yelled his coworker at the other end of the room, trying to make himself heard over the din.

"Yeah!" Ramón yelled back, while double-checking what his computers were telling him. "That bitch of a pipe, number three."

"Can't hear you! Did you say three?"

It had to be the same resident as always. Instead of taking his yard debris to the dump like any upstanding citizen, this guy insisted on tossing tree branches and brush into the suction system for household waste. Without bagging them or anything. Naturally, the branches built up in the underground pipes that connected the neighborhood with the central system and ended up creating a bottleneck that blocked the rest of the neighbors' bags of garbage, which had been deposited correctly in their designated pneumatic receptacles.

"Three it is." Alberto had finally gotten his ass out of the seat and was standing next to Ramón. "Number three again?"

"I swear, I'll shove that guy into the pipes myself. I'll stuff him in so tight he'll learn what it's all about," Ramón muttered while manually turning off the alarms.

At last, the noise stopped.

"Phew," he said. "That's over. Those alarms are enough to bust your eardrums."

"Should we use the backup motor?" Alberto asked in his usual high-pitched whine. Sometimes, on the phone, he was mistaken for a woman.

"Yeah, rev up number four. Get it going, because I don't want to be leaving late today. I bought movie tickets."

Ninety percent of the time when something got stuck in the pipes, the power of the extra fourth motor managed to get the garbage flowing toward one of the system's five central repositories. In this case, Ramón and Alberto wanted to push the blockage to the tanks situated just one level down from where they were, connected by hundreds of pipes to each of the real estate developments in the southeastern zone. All the residents had to do was open the doors installed on the pipe intakes and put their garbage bags inside—much like using a front-loading washing machine. Some of these inlets were located in the parking garages of the newer apartment buildings, some outside on the sidewalks of the subdivisions. Simple and clean. But only if they followed the rules. Some people thought you could stuff in anything, up to and including your Christmas tree. And that produced the obvious result: a blockage in some point of the network of pipes would shut the system down.

"What's going on with pipe number three?"

The shift supervisor, who had his own office, had come to Ramón's control room. It's never good news when the boss comes to you.

"Stuck. It's got to be that jerk with the pruning shears again," Ramón explained, not turning around. "It's blocked in the same place as always. We're going to fire up number four, to see if we can get enough suction to pull it out."

"Until they get serious about levying fines, we're never going to get anywhere. They should mount security cameras at every intake to see what each person is tossing in. Then you'd see how fast all this gets taken care of," the supervisor said, "because around here, everybody tosses in whatever they want. And someday we're going to have an accident."

Nori was still watching video. Everybody in the unit was wearing out their eyes searching for Inés's son in the footage from every camera within a radius of several kilometers around the mall. There were hundreds of hours of video, and it would take days to watch it all. Even with the help of the members of the special kidnapping unit, they couldn't cut that down to less than seventy-two hours. The child seemed to have gone up in smoke.

Like Nicolás two years ago.

Like Manu the week before.

Meanwhile, fear of The Taker traveled like a bubble of fright through streets and squares. Just a little pinprick, and panic would break out. It would be hard to control, like the human mobs that, once set in motion, could end up trampling and crushing themselves.

That Monday, many children were kept home from school. The elite private schools near the mall where the three boys had disappeared hired private security firms. Television cameras recorded images of guards at their doors. Shopping centers and recreational facilities were strangely empty, even though they, too, had visibly reinforced their security.

For the twenty-four hours following the news of Pablo's disappearance, life retreated indoors. How long could the country handle this level of fear? Would it get worse? Everything depended on an investigation that seemed entirely cold.

"Coffee?" Arcos asked Nori. He got up and counted out coins for the machine.

"If I drink any more caffeine," Nori said, wearily brushing the hair from his forehead, "it's going to start sloshing out of my ears. Not even a half marathon would burn it up."

"You ought to take a nap. How much have you slept in the past couple days?"

"How'm I going to sleep? Two kids just disappeared without a trace. One's the son of a friend of mine. Not to mention the one from two years ago. What are we dealing with? A serial sexual predator? A kidnapper shortening the interval between crimes? A pedophile whose appetite is demanding more and more food?"

Arcos had no time to answer, because Nori suddenly seemed to go berserk. "I've got him! I've got him! I've got him!" Nori screamed. "Here. Here he is. I've got the kid. Here. It's Pablo. Take a look! He's right here!"

The image was blurry, but it was Pablo, without a doubt. White T-shirt, blue stripes, blue jeans, and black sneakers. His face was hard to make out, but the clothes matched what he'd been wearing when he disappeared, and both his size and complexion also matched Inés's son. The time fit too. And the place. The image was from the security camera of a drugstore just five hundred meters from the mall. Pablo appeared in the lower left corner of the screen. He was walking, apparently calm, looking at something or someone to his left. A something or someone outside the frame.

◆ ◆ ◆

"So is that motor doing the job or not?" the supervisor of the morning shift at Majadahonda's garbage collection center asked.

Ramón could feel the boss's sour breath in his ear. He had to concentrate to keep from retching. How could such an awful smell come from inside a living person?

"I've got it at 60 percent, but so far, pipe three isn't coming unclogged. That bastard must have thrown in half a cypress tree. There must be a pretty thick branch caught crosswise." Ramón was starting to get nervous, both from the blockage and from the smell emanating from his boss's mouth.

"Rev it up to 90," the supervisor said.

"Up to 90," Ramón complied. "Here's hoping it doesn't explode."

"Here's hoping, yeah."

27

PATRICIA

"Turn on the siren, Charo. Turn on the siren, and let's make some tracks."

Monday morning, first of the month, and raining. Madrid was like a rat's nest. Not even a police car with a blaring siren could make any headway in the bumper-to-bumper traffic. However much the other drivers tried to maneuver out of the way, it just couldn't be done.

"If we were cops in an American movie, we'd already be up on the sidewalk," Charo joked, "though I don't see any fruit stands to knock over. It's always best to have apples and melons flying through the air. And a terrified fruit vendor, of course."

"But life isn't that spectacular, Charo, and you know it. Life is dismal and difficult, not a Hollywood circus. Life is the real Hollywood that lurks behind the camera."

Ana was banging her fist against the window of the car as she spoke. Bang, bang, bang, bang. Rhythmically. It was another way to work off the stress and tension. Finally they had a lead, a thread to follow. And it was slipping through their hands.

Fifteen minutes before, when Sonia Calero had called from the Madrid West station, Ana couldn't believe what she heard. But she understood right away. She didn't even let Sonia finish telling the story of the teenager's interrupted report. Clearly that girl dragged into the station by her father was an important clue to the kidnappings.

"They're dead" was as far as the girl had gotten, before her father had thought better of allowing a voluntary statement and had taken her away. He wanted legal guarantees. Apparently his lawyer had woken up to the client's frightened message on his voice mail and found he was already too late, because the man and his daughter were at the police station. "Don't say another word," the lawyer had ordered over the phone. "Get Patricia out of there. Any statement has to come with legal guarantees."

So Sub-Inspector Nori was on that now, finding a legal defender for minors so it would be possible to get a statement from the girl. Although the majority of the lawyers in the children-and-youth group were good, all of them specially trained to work with children, Ana had given Nori three names she thought could best handle the case and the girl. If The Taker were someone inside the girl's social group, would she dare betray him?

Meanwhile, Ana and Charo were on their way to the minor's home to try to convince the father to go with them to provincial headquarters for a statement. But they were stuck in the traffic jam.

Ana's phone rang.

"Jesús, hi, good morning, yes. You've heard, haven't you?" It was the chief inspector in charge of the kidnapping and extortion group from national headquarters assigned to work with them. "Yes, I'm on my way to the girl's house to try and convince the father. I've got my sub chasing down the best children's lawyer, to talk with the parents on the phone and convince them to come down to the station." Ana looked up from the phone. "That way, Charo," she said, pointing toward a small street on the right. "Let's cut through the university district. Try to get to La Coruña highway, where maybe we can move a little faster. Sorry, Jesús, we're in a nightmare of a traffic jam." Ana was quiet for a few seconds. "Sure we do, can't you hear it? Siren and lights too. Listen, could you tell

Ruipérez? The last thing I want to do is to speak to him." Ana stopped talking for a moment. "Yeah, sure, I'll let you know as soon as I'm with the parents. Maybe I'll send a WhatsApp message, if I've got them in front of me and can't talk."

It took them forty-five minutes to get to the girl's house—a townhouse, though not so grand as the word implied, more like a sliver shoehorned into a row of several dozen identical houses on the right side of the street. Each house was strangling the others, growing upward in search of a little breathing room.

"Number twenty-three, this must be it."

Each one had a ridiculously tiny yard in front, where no resident had set out even the most woebegone chair. What for? It would have been like sitting in the street, or in the middle of the sidewalk, in view of the entire world.

"Hello, I'm Chief Inspector Ana Arén. We spoke on the phone a while ago. This is my colleague Charo. May we come in?"

Inside, the house looked even smaller because the stairway ate up a good part of the space. The residents had to spend all day going up and down. More times than they wanted, for sure—down to the living room where they'd left the phone when going up to bed. Up to the bedroom to get the keys when they went out. Down to the garage in search of the extra toilet paper when they got to the attic bathroom and found an empty roll. Up again, down again, all day long.

Just as Ana and Charo took seats on the couch, Ana got a message and gave her phone a discreet glance.

Eva's not on duty today, but she's agreed to come as soon as you confirm you're bringing the girl. You can call her, and she'll explain the procedure to the parents.

That was good news. Eva was one of the best children's lawyers in the Spanish judicial system.

"Would you like something to drink? Coffee?"

That had to be the girl's mother. She seemed older, as did her husband. Patricia must have been a surprise after they'd concluded they weren't having children. She wore her hair short, a pale chestnut color, painstakingly curled to give artificial volume on the sides and top, as if she were using a hair-restoring fiber treatment to make herself look taller. She was dressed too formally for a Monday morning. Ana figured she had put herself together to face the police.

Twenty minutes earlier, while trying to dodge the traffic, Ana had requested background information on the family and learned that the mother hadn't been employed for several decades. She'd stopped working when she got married. The husband was retired. Two old people with a teenage daughter. A potentially explosive combination.

"No, thanks," Ana said. "You're very kind. We'd like to speak with the two of you before talking with your daughter."

The couple sat down. The man seemed to have lost the aplomb with which he'd charged into the police station only an hour before.

"As I told you over the phone, I'm in charge of the investigation of the disappearances of Nicolás, Manu, and Pablo, labeled by the press as the 'Taker' cases. I understand your daughter has some important information for us."

The woman looked at her husband as if asking permission. They knew it. Whatever their daughter was mixed up in, they knew what it was.

"What I'd like you to do is speak with Eva Galán. She's a fantastic lawyer and a specialist in children's cases. She'll be with you and your daughter when your daughter makes a declaration. If you'll agree, I'll call Eva so she can explain the whole procedure. All we want to do is talk to your daughter, nothing more. She's not accused of anything or being arrested. All we need is her help."

Fifteen minutes later, four of them were in the police car on their way to the station. The mother had stayed home. The mother would

Carme Chaparro

have liked to accompany Patricia, Ana thought, but the father wanted to be the sole person in charge.

The conversation in the car consisted of small talk. Ana didn't want to force anything. She wanted the girl to get used to her.

"Okay, here we are. Patricia"—Ana turned to face the girl—"this is the station where I work, where we're coordinating the whole operation for finding the boys. What you tell us will help a great deal. Now we'll leave the car in the parking lot, and I'll introduce you to Eva. She'll help you with the declaration. Okay?"

Ana's cell phone rang again. The chief inspector blanched at what she heard on the other end.

28

JESÚS/RAMÓN

Nori's fingers flew over the keyboard. The rest of the detectives in the unit stood behind him, watching the computer screen. Attracted by his shouts, some members of the kidnapping group working out of Chief Inspector Arén's office had gathered there too.

"Look, do you see him? At 2:13 yesterday afternoon, just ten minutes after he disappeared, according to the witnesses."

The boy looked calm. Pablo was walking with a determined gait, as if he knew where he was being taken. The quality of the image was poor, and enlarging it only produced a blur, but it looked like he had a half smile on his face.

That wasn't normal. If the child had been taken by force, he wouldn't have looked even halfway content. So he had to know his kidnapper. Had to know them well and want to go with them. Just then, Chief Inspector Jesús Silvelo entered the room. Nori brought him up to date.

"What other cameras are in the area?" he asked.

"We're waiting for the stores to open. Yesterday was Sunday, and a lot of them were closed. Now we've sent a team out there to go store by store and request the images."

"I'm going to send out two more cars to help. And none of you better even think of leaking this to the press. I don't want to see this picture in any paper or on any TV show. Understood?" *What was going on?* Silvelo asked himself. If Pablo went peacefully alongside the kidnapper, it had to be someone he knew. The Taker had to be someone from the neighborhood, maybe a teacher, someone from a store, or a neighbor—someone the boy knew. Besides, kidnapping a child on a Sunday afternoon and walking as calmly as that? Something was wrong, but they didn't know what.

"Commander." Jesús Silvelo knocked on Ruipérez's door. "Commander, we've got some news."

Ruipérez was reading a paper on his desk. Or pretending to. He was perfectly aware that the chief inspector was standing in his doorway, waiting. But that was exactly what made him happy, to be in control. To make his subordinate beg.

"Hello, Inspector," Ruipérez said without raising his head, once he'd decided to extend the waiting time longer than might be prudent, coming close to the edge of danger. "How was the pizza? Good?"

"I have some news," Silvelo answered, ignoring the provocation.

Silvelo approached the desk. He waited for the commander to ask him something, anything at all, just to demonstrate a smidgen of interest. But Ruipérez only raised an eyebrow and adopted a bored look that said, *Okay, get it over with. You're not important, and my time is too valuable to waste.*

"We have an image of Inés's son taken ten minutes after the kidnapping," Silvelo said, still standing on the other side of the enormous wooden desk in the commander's office.

They called this desk "the wall," because it seemed made to separate two worlds. The boss from the subordinates, the one who commands from those who obey. Nobody could remember how long it had been there or which of the past division commanders had acquired it. But there it still was. Intimidating.

"Is anyone alongside? Can you make out the kidnapper?"

The commander stirred in his chair, which was as oversized and ostentatious as the desk, matching the ego of the man sitting in it.

"No. The boy's walking in the lower left corner of the screen. The shot's from the drugstore camera. He looks calm."

"Where's that drugstore?" Ruipérez asked.

"Near the mall, on the south side, across the street. The times match perfectly. It's just a few minutes after he disappeared."

"And how come it's taken us twenty-four hours to realize that Pablo was recorded by the security camera of that store?"

Ruipérez cracked his knuckles. One by one.

"The usual reasons, Commander." The chief inspector had to struggle not to shift his weight from foot to foot, which would betray a sense of insecurity—the last thing he wanted to suggest. He projected all his body weight into his feet equally, making a conscious effort to anchor them to the floor and stay still. "The usual, you know. Many hours of footage, and it hasn't been easy to find all the store owners. Yesterday was Sunday, and a lot of places were closed. We've also got the video from the traffic cameras for several kilometers around. That adds up to thousands of recorded hours to review."

"And the boy doesn't appear in any other camera?" This time Ruipérez did meet Silvelo's eyes, almost without blinking, trying to intimidate him.

"We're checking right now. Concentrating on the cameras closest to the drugstore."

From here on, this was going to be a matter of dueling stares. Quite a while ago, Jesús had mastered a trick of his own, which was to stare between the other person's eyebrows. Your opposite would believe you were continuing to look them firmly in the eye, but you were really concentrating on the triangle formed by the eyebrows and the upper part of the nose. This freed your brain from the pressure of continuously meeting the eyes and allowed you to focus on the conversation instead.

"We've got everybody working on this," Silvelo continued, "staring at the screens to the point of exhaustion. In a few hours, we'll have more images of Pablo. We're trying to reconstruct the path he might have followed."

"Hurry it up. We can't waste a second." For the first time, the commander's voice sounded strangely upset. Maybe the societal pressure around the case was getting to him, or the pressure from the top levels of the police and the government, or—who knew?—maybe somewhere deep down, David Ruipérez was a human being too. "In cases like this, a few hours can make the difference between finding the child alive or dead."

"I don't need you to remind me of that, Commander. We've got men and women on our staff who've gone five days without sleeping since Manu disappeared. They're wearing themselves thin. And now, if you'll permit, I'll go back to looking for those boys, because right here, with all due respect, I'm not helping the investigation at all."

Chief Inspector Silvelo had to restrain himself in order to keep his tone agreeable and not slam the door, which was what he really wanted to do.

◆ ◆ ◆

The fourth motor roared at maximum velocity. It couldn't generate any more suction than this.

"Ramón, it's not working."

The supervisor of the pneumatic collection center now had his cell phone in hand to call the central office. *Better that than overtaxing the whole mechanism,* he was thinking. *Let the higher-ups decide, so I can wash my hands of the thing.*

"Wait another minute," Ramón urged. "Let's see what the neighbors dumped in there. The blockage must be starting to move a little."

And suddenly, *boom*! The force of the suction had done its work, pulling away whatever had been clogging pipe number three. It produced a deafening sound. They'd never heard anything like it here.

"What the hell did they throw in there? Ramón, Alberto, go down to the tank and see what fell in. And I swear, I'm calling the police to find the jerk who caused this," the supervisor roared, without imagining how true his words were going to be.

The garbage depository was an enormous underground room where the refuse from the homes of ten thousand residents flowed into two huge tanks, one for plastics and the other for organics. Glass, paper, and the rest of the materials were collected in the traditional manner, from containers placed on the streets.

Ramón and Alberto turned on the lights. The problem pipe was the one carrying plastics—this wouldn't be the first time some idiot had thrown bulky yard waste into the wrong receptacle—so whatever had caused the blockage should have landed in tank number two.

"Have you got a mask, Ramón? And gloves? Be careful with what might come out of there."

It wouldn't be the first time that rats had appeared, though they tended to prefer the tank for organics, which provided more food.

"How many days since we emptied this? Three? This thing"—Ramón pointed to tank number two—"has to be swimming with bacteria having more fun than rock fans in a mosh pit. With the cutbacks, we're emptying it less and less often. We ought to call Public Health about that."

But he knew that wasn't going to happen. Too much pushback from the bosses. No, his job right now was to open the safety hatch and look at whatever was inside.

"Wait, grab this. At least wear my bandanna before you climb up there. The smell alone will be enough to knock you off the ladder."

But what almost made Ramón fall from the ladder wasn't the putrid smell that emerged from the hatch of tank number two as soon as he opened it. What made him jerk backward, three meters up, was what he saw.

Inside was a child.

And Ramón didn't know whether the kid was dead or alive.

29

ANA

"Wait for me, Jesús! Wait for me!" Ana Arén shouted into the phone. "I'm turning into the lot now. I'll be there with you in three minutes."

"What's going on?" asked an almost childlike voice from the back seat of the police car.

Ana had completely forgotten she had company. Shit. The teenager and her father were back there. But after what she'd just heard, questioning Patricia was no longer the top priority. One of the missing boys had been found in a garbage repository very close to Patricia's house and the mall where all three boys had disappeared.

"Patricia, they just told me something very serious and very important."

The chief inspector turned toward the back seat, trying to decide how to tell the girl and her father that she had to leave them there. Given how hard it had been to get them to this point, she didn't want all that work to go down the drain. Besides, Patricia might know something that could help them catch The Taker.

But now Ana had to go. She had to get moving as fast as she could to focus on the boy who'd appeared in the hydraulic garbage collection system at Majadahonda. Was he really one of the three kidnapped by The Taker?

"Patricia, can I ask you for a favor?"

People tended to accept orders better if they came disguised as requests. Not just because granting a favor made them feel good, but also because the other party would owe them something in return.

"I need you to go with Charo. She'll take you to Eva, the lawyer who already talked with your parents on the phone. I'll be back right away. I promise."

"You're the boss, right? You're in charge of all this?" the father said.

"Well, I'm directing the investigation, yes."

"Then we'll only talk with you."

Great. More problems, just what she needed.

"Perfect, fine. The lawyer can start by telling you how all this works. Okay? I'll be right back. I promise. It's very urgent. Please, take my word for it, Patricia. Trust me, this is a matter of life and death."

Half an hour later—the traffic jam had loosened up a bit—Ana was once again in Majadahonda, seventeen kilometers from central Madrid. The southern repository of the garbage collection center was halfway between the mall where the three boys had disappeared and the row house where Patricia and her parents lived. Did the girl have something to do with the disappearances? Who knew? All the way there, Chief Inspector Silvelo was filling her in. When they arrived, Ana bolted from the car.

"Where's the body? Has it been identified?" she asked the two policemen guarding the entrance to the repository.

"What body, Chief Inspector?" the shorter one, a redhead with a beard, replied.

Ana looked at his insignia. A crown and an ear of wheat. An intern, still in training. Didn't they teach them at the academy what a corpse was?

"The body of the child who was found here," she answered, hurrying into the repository without looking back.

She didn't have time for nonsense. What did he mean, "What body"? She followed a trail of smells, taking the metal stairs to the right of the entrance two at a time. There wasn't even a reception desk. What for? Who would come visiting a giant warehouse full of garbage?

Two floors down, she came to an open door. That was where the smell was emanating from. Inside, a scientific team was busy looking for clues.

"Chief Inspector," one of them said, "nothing so far. Although the repository has a capacity of several tons, it's going to take us a while to classify it all. We're waiting for them to send us a fiber-optic unit so we can put a camera down the pipes and see what's inside the one where the kid was stuck."

"Where's the body?" Ana asked.

The forensic examiner couldn't have come and taken the corpse already. Physically impossible. The examiner would have taken at least a half hour to get there. Behind her, Ana heard rapid footsteps on the staircase she'd just come down.

"What body?" the technical specialist asked.

"There's no body," the voice of Chief Inspector Jesús Silvelo said.

The two voices mixed, chorusing in stereo, one in each ear, so that Ana heard something like "What body isn't there?" Her brain separated the messages. There was no body? Then what the hell was all this? If it was all a joke or a false alarm, what was the scientific team doing here?

"Ana, look at me." Silvelo stood in front of her now. "He's alive. The boy's alive. Critical condition, but alive. They just took him to Puerta de Hierro."

Miraculously, whoever he was, that boy had come out alive after being trapped for hours or days in a narrow pipe. He'd even survived the powerful force of the suction of all four motors of the garbage system running at full capacity.

It was a miracle.

But, for whom? For what parents? For what grandparents? For whom?

"Who was the boy?"

So far, no one could say. The three missing kids looked a lot alike, and the two workers who found the body couldn't give a very precise description. Besides, the face was swollen, bloody, and badly bruised.

Ana didn't want to call any of the parents to give them false hope. She would rather go to the hospital herself and try to identify him. She had known Pablo all his life, even before he was born. And she'd pored over so many photos and videos of Manu and Nicolás that she felt she knew them too.

The hospital Jesús Silvelo had named was less than two kilometers away. She could clear this much up, at least, very soon. Whoever the child was.

If he turned out to be one of The Taker's three victims at all.

30

ANA

"Chief Inspector Ana Arén." Ana waved her badge at the ER desk of the hospital. "I've come to see the boy they brought in an ambulance from the garbage collection dump."

Ana placed her badge against the glass that separated her from the three women processing patients for the emergency room. They were seated strangely, way below the level of those who came up to the window, which meant they were constantly craning their necks to look their clients in the face.

"Let me check," the woman closest to Ana answered. "No, I don't have anything like that. If they brought him in an ambulance, he didn't come through here. They would have taken him right inside, or maybe to an operating room. Do you know the boy's name?"

I'd like to know it, Ana thought. *That's what I'm here for, to find out his name.*

"No, we haven't identified him yet. That's why I'm here, to find out who he is."

The receptionist kept typing, looking down, making it impossible to know whether she had heard Ana or not.

"I don't have any record," she said at last, after a minute that seemed to stretch into an eternity. "But that's not unusual. If he came by ambulance and hadn't yet been identified, then the doctors couldn't fill out the intake forms. Wait out here, please, and I'll get somebody to come for you."

Ana took advantage of the break to call Joan. Not even a full day had gone by since they'd said goodbye in his apartment in Barcelona on that bright and happy Sunday morning in which everything seemed possible. Twenty hours ago she'd nearly felt guilty for feeling lucky. Since then she'd slept a couple of hours at most, and the world was no longer the same one in which she'd allowed herself to lean her head on the warm window of the train and listen to music. The world had gone back to being a shithole where everyone sank deeper and deeper each day.

"Ana!"

"Hi."

Suddenly she felt terribly tired, as if all the strength had drained out of her, as if her body and mind had said, *Enough, this is as far as we can go.* Maybe that was because, with Joan, she didn't need to pretend. He was one of the few people with whom Ana let herself appear vulnerable. She took a quick look around the brightly lit waiting room. Full. Barely an empty seat. Could this many people have medical emergencies on a Monday morning? She walked to a less crowded part, in the corner formed by one of the walls and the enormous plate glass window facing the parking lot, and sat down on the floor. She could hear the rain hitting the glass.

"I'm in the hospital," she said.

"Are you okay? What's going on? How's Inés? What have you learned?"

Joan let loose a barrage of all the questions that had been on his mind, but Ana couldn't tell him much. She was, above all, a good police-woman, and good police officers didn't share what they weren't allowed to share. Not even with family. Although, lately, some members of the force were telling too many secrets to other colleagues in WhatsApp groups, and the information—and photos—jumped too freely from one chat to another. Someday there was going to be a big surprise. One of those crime scene photos, or one of a wounded officer or an officer doing something he or she shouldn't, would leak into the press, and an internal investigation would ensnare everyone involved.

"I'm not here for myself, Joan. I'm in the hospital as part of the investigation." She was dying to tell him, to spill everything, to get the opinion of someone who could see from the outside. But she couldn't, so she used all her willpower to change the topic. "It's raining here. An awful day. Is it raining in Barcelona?"

"No, it's sunny, just like yesterday."

Now Ana was on the verge of tears. And over what? Not the child, not The Taker, not the case, but for something so foolish—because she was yearning for the sun shining through the window of the train. For a moment of peace. For a life free of shit.

Joan was accustomed, by now, to her excluding him from anything that smacked of police business. Or almost.

"I guess," she said, "that no alert has popped up in your program for monitoring pedophiles?"

"No, though I've got two habitual ones I'm keeping my eye on, because I think they could be starting to consider producing their own material, with kids. I need to send this over to Nori for him to send it on to the TIU." Joan sighed. "Ana, you have to think about yourself."

"No. No. I have to think about those kids."

Always the same argument. How many police officers had this argument with their spouses, girlfriends, boyfriends? *Almost all of them,* Ana thought. At least, almost all of them who were worth their salt. Some cases took you over, leaving no room for anything else. Just the case. The victims. The guilty parties. But, above all, the solution. Fitting the pieces together. Solving the puzzle. Though this could be hard to admit, it was also your own ego fighting to win the game.

"Are you the police detective?" asked a young woman in a white coat who had come up to Ana without her noticing.

That was a sure sign the case was taking its toll. For a moment, Ana had stopped paying attention to her surroundings and hadn't seen the woman approach. She could have been anyone.

"Joan, I've got to go. They're looking for me. I'll call you later."

The young woman led Ana through a double door that opened when she pressed the red button with her elbow. "It's a habit," she explained when the chief inspector gave her a quizzical look. "This is the door we use for the most urgent cases—car crashes and such—and since we can't use our hands for fear of contamination, we use our elbows to push the button. The boy is in critical condition in intensive care. Sorry, I haven't introduced myself. Dr. Mariña Tribiño. Yes, too many ñ's, people always tell me that." Suddenly her expression changed. "Sorry. I'm sorry. I always make the same joke, but this isn't the time. You're here about the boy in the garbage system. He came in less than an hour ago. We're taking care of him."

They were walking toward an office in the emergency treatment area, a white and glassy place with a giant exterior window that would normally let in an abundance of light, though today only the gray and the rain showed through. A desk and a cot were the main furnishings. On the walls hung childish drawings made by boys and girls as thank-yous for the treatment and comforting they'd received.

"The child has suffered a lot." The doctor closed the door, pointing Ana to a chair. "I don't even want to imagine it. He's unconscious. His body was under pressure for many hours. He has two broken ribs, and we're afraid his brain has suffered from lack of oxygen. Besides which, the force of the suction they applied to get him out could have damaged an internal organ."

"Does he have any injuries that weren't produced by the pneumatic garbage system?"

"I can't say. It would be difficult to figure out, because while he was being pulled through the pipes he could have been hurt by a number of things. A medical examiner would need to do a lengthy exam. So far, we've just tried to stabilize him."

"Will he recover?"

"It's hard to say. We have to see how things evolve over the next forty-eight hours."

"I need to identify him. May I see him? I have to know who he is so I can tell his parents. You can understand that, Doctor."

Dr. Tribiño hesitated. In any other case, she would have said no. For anyone other than immediate family to enter the pediatric ICU was forbidden. And only one person at a time, and only a few hours a day. But this was an exceptional crime, and the parents of the child hovering between life and death had to know he'd been found so they could be by his side in case these were the last hours of their child's life.

"Could you identify him through a window in the ICU?" she asked.

"I think so. Let me give it a try."

The pediatric ICU was one floor above the emergency room. As a shortcut, to avoid going back through the public area of the hospital, the doctor led Ana through a stairway restricted to health personnel. As they neared the ICU, Ana's heart began to race.

"Room three. The third window on the left, facing the nurses' desk. Do you want me to come with you?"

"I'd rather go alone. Thank you."

First she saw his feet. They were covered in bruises and cuts. The hands rested along the body, also painfully banged up, although someone had washed off the blood and cleaned the wounds. If it weren't for all the lacerations crisscrossing his skin, he would have looked like a child peacefully sleeping after an exhausting day of school and games.

Ana forced herself to look farther up the body, though uncon-sciously she was delaying the moment of finding out who he was. She was afraid. Acid rose from her stomach and burned in her throat. She made her eyes keep moving until they finally reached his face.

Her lungs suddenly expelled all the air they'd been hoarding.

It was Pablo.

31

INÉS

Maybe you can change the proportions, but a hospital still smells the same.

Blood—oxygenated by contact with the air—is the first thing the body's warning system perceives. A smell of old iron, a smell you can almost taste. Thick and repugnant.

The smell of danger.

In a biological animal reaction that has allowed the human race to survive, the oldest parts of our brain, the limbic system and the hypothalamus, associate the smell of blood with an emergency. Either we're wounded, or we've wounded the prey we came to hunt. The message says to hide or attack. To treat the wound, or kill.

That's why a hospital puts us on alert, because it smells like blood. Or so we think. In truth, the hospital smell is a mix of blood, alcohol, disinfectant, and chlorine, alongside the ketones given off by certain sick bodies—very volatile and thus very expansive—and gases like oxygen and nitrogen, and of course the medications used to treat the patients.

However you alter the proportions in that mix, strangely enough, all hospitals smell the same.

Of blood, fear, anxiety, and despair.

Very rarely does a hospital smell of miracles. Not because there aren't miracles going on. There are. But we don't smell them, because pain is always more intense than joy. Lamentation more intense than laughter, sorrow more intense than hope. Miracles go right by, unperceived by those who aren't included in the good news.

That day, running through the spacious lobby of the new Puerta de Hierro hospital, recently relocated to Majadahonda from central Madrid, I did smell hope. In fact, it penetrated every pore of my skin. Pablo was alive. Alive! I didn't even hang up the phone, just ran out the door of my apartment. I ran down the stairs—no way was I waiting for the elevator—out of the building, and onto the street to grab a taxi. I ran through the corridors of the hospital. Pablo was alive, and that was all that mattered.

That day, to me, blood smelled like hope.

My child had survived.

My genes would go on replicating, one more generation.

32

INÉS/ANA

There wasn't much more Ana could do at the hospital.

She was the one who'd called to tell me my son was in the ICU. And on a strange, nearly absurd kind of guard duty, she waited for me outside his room to make sure Pablo was never without a loved one looking over him, as if my little guy were conscious of what was going on around him.

But after that, there wasn't much else she could do.

Pablo was alive, but he wasn't out of danger. I had to redeem myself. Ana had to find the son of a bitch who had done this to my son.

And she had to solve the puzzle. Where were the other two boys? Where were Manu and Nicolás?

"I have two more children to return to their parents," she said by way of excusing herself, before she, too, took off at top speed.

Ana had left the car just outside the emergency entrance, behind the hospital. That meant she didn't have to go out the front door, which was now occupied by dozens of reporters. Someone had given them the news that one of the boys stolen by The Taker had been admitted to the hospital. Did they already know that the survivor was my son, the son of the star TV reporter and bestselling author? An almost perfect journalistic storm.

While I—wrapped from head to toe in sterile cap, gown, and booties—was running my fingertips over my son's wounds, as if a mother's love could work a miracle, Ana suddenly remembered about Patricia and her father. She hoped Eva, the lawyer, had been able to keep them at the police station. What was the girl going to say about Pablo? Had she seen who stuffed him into the hydraulic pipes used for collecting garbage?

◆ ◆ ◆

In her office, the chief inspector found only Jesús Silvelo.

"Where's your team?" Ana asked, surprised by the silence and emptiness.

It had been only seventeen hours since part of the kidnapping group had moved in there, but it felt like weeks. Ana had to struggle to remember what her office had been like just twenty-four hours ago. The day before.

"They're in Majadahonda, looking for possible witnesses to whatever happened to Pablo. Also we're trying to find more security camera footage from the stores that were closed yesterday. How's the boy?"

"Bad. Very serious. The doctors don't know if he'll make it or not."

She sank into her chair. Sometimes she felt that all the weight of the world had fallen on her, without realizing that she was the one who'd taken it up. She wanted to do everything. Wanted to take charge of everything. Wanted to solve everything. And that wouldn't change until she chose to lighten the load.

But not today. The decisions Ana would make on this day could save someone's life. Everything would depend on what she did in the coming hours.

"And the store employee? Is he still being questioned? We're almost out of time."

"And we've got nothing. We confirmed his alibi and had to let him go. He made a statement to the municipal police about some trouble that broke out in a spouse-swapping club." Silvelo made a gesture with his hands, somewhere between despair and disgust.

"Another blind alley," Ana said, standing up with regret. "We've got Patricia here. Let's see if we get lucky and she can tell us something about who threw Pablo into the garbage chute."

And just like that, without knowing it, Chief Inspector Ana Arén was on her way to saving a life.

I just wanted to sit there, in that chair, looking into my son's face, holding his hand, and stroking his arm. I knew the map of his skin by heart, the curves, the folds, the freckles and moles. I would have recognized it anywhere. Even blind, deaf, or mute, I would have known just by touching him that this was my son.

I just wanted to be there like that. Just the way I was. Caressing Pablo for the rest of my life.

But people won't leave you alone.

They come with the best of intentions. But what can anyone say to a mother in a situation like this? Just empty words. *Pablo will pull through this. He's a strong little boy. You have to have faith.*

And so forth, in infinite variations.

All these phrases just bounce off and land like specks of oil floating on the water, as if they had nothing to do with you at all. Is there any point? I don't know. Sometimes, out of pure survival instinct, you grab on to one of them, trying to trust in the idea that so many people can't all be wrong. If so many people keep saying the same thing, that must mean it's true, so everything really *is* going to be okay. Everything is going to be okay.

"I don't want to pressure you, but you need to think about this."

Manuel, my boss, had been one of the last to show up. Of course. He had a news program to run, and I say that without irony. Almost nothing can make a journalist leave a post when there's a crisis to cover. Even if, in this case, the crisis was mine.

The police—on Ana's request, I assume—had sent several officers to guard the floor that held the pediatric ICU, to keep the curiosity seekers away. Also, they told me later, there were plainclothes police stationed at various points in the hospital, in case The Taker decided to come by. Criminal profiling experts said he was a man between twenty-five and forty-five, without a college education, a white man with an athletic build, or at least, one given to exercise. It was also likely, the experts added, that he was unemployed or had a job with flexible hours. Millions of men fit that profile.

But the police deployed in plainclothes around the hospital were looking for something more. They were trained to identify suspicious people. They worked primarily in airports and at border crossings. They knew how to recognize the movements and gestures that signaled a bundle of nerves or someone with something to hide.

No one could enter the area where Pablo was without identifying themselves first. They didn't even let my mother through until I vouched for her. The friends and colleagues who came to see me had to wait through the same process: an officer had to show me their ID cards so I could verify that I knew them and wanted to let them in.

I would have liked to say that I didn't know anyone and they should all leave me alone. But at the same time, I needed some friendly arms to sustain me.

Seeing my mother was the hardest of all, though the most comforting. Nobody else can wrap you in her arms without your having to give any explanations. At last—I really had no other choice—I had called her to tell her that Pablo had disappeared, but I waited until 4:00 a.m. Monday, just as she was packing for the airport. There was no point in telling her Sunday evening and leaving her to a sleepless night waiting for the plane that would take her to Madrid from her vacation in Lanzarote. She had landed in Madrid and was collecting her luggage from the baggage claim when Pablo was found.

With her, no words were needed. She asked me only two things: how was Pablo, and how was I. Nothing else mattered to her. Then she sat on the other side of Pablo's bed and started rhythmically stroking his hand with all the love in the world.

"I don't want to pressure you, Inés, but you need to think about it," my boss repeated. "You need to end the speculation. When all's said and done, this is your job, and you know how much power you have right now. Everybody will listen to you."

"Listen to what? What do I have to tell them? That my son is hanging on by a thread?" I raised my voice. "That I don't know whether to feel relieved that he appeared or devastated because I don't know whether he's going to survive? What? Tell me, Manuel, *what?* What do the people need to hear from me?"

"This has cost us a day of our lives, shut up in this police station—a whole day lost. Does that seem okay to you? We've got rights, don't we?"

It was going to be a difficult conversation, for sure.

"Patricia," Ana said, sitting down at her side, very close, and looking her in the eye. She addressed the girl directly. *You're the only one who matters to me. All I care about is what you have to say. I'm here for you.*

"Patricia, I'm very sorry you've had to wait so long. I don't know whether my colleagues told you, but we've found one of the boys."

The girl's eyes widened behind the barrier of her cascading hair.

"So, so, now there's nothing for me to say, right? If you've already found them, then you don't need me anymore."

Them? Was there another boy in the garbage chute? Or two more? Were all of The Taker's victims in those damned hydraulic garbage collection pipes?

"Patricia, are you talking about two boys? We've only found one. Just one. I need you more than ever. What you saw is fundamental to solving this case."

"Who did they find? Which one?"

"What do you know, Patricia? What did you see?" Ana didn't want to give out any details that could affect the girl's statement.

"Chief Inspector." The lawyer interrupted to give Ana a hand. Eva looked nothing like a stereotypical attorney. She wore blue jeans, a T-shirt, and sneakers. She didn't wear makeup, and she sported a ponytail with one—any one—of the colored stretch bands she always wore on her wrist. She was forty-four years old but could easily pass for twenty-five, not that much older than the young people she had to protect from the system. "I've already told Patricia and her father that they don't have anything to worry about, that they're here because they want to collaborate with the police, and that they aren't charged with or accused of anything. We're very grateful that they're helping us to save these boys."

Save? The last thing Patricia had said was that the boys were dead—although the latest events had shown that at least one of them was alive. In critical condition, but alive.

"I'd never been there. It's shut down at night, you know?"

"What's shut down at night?"

"The Woods. They close the gates at night, but there's a way to get in."

"There's a way to get in," Ana repeated, to help her keep going.

"Yeah, a friend showed it to me."

"Tell them. Tell them about that friend," the father jumped in from the other side of the small office. "A good-for-nothing delinquent, one of the worst in her school. It's like my daughter has some kind of magnet for the ones with a screw loose."

"Please," the lawyer said. "Let your daughter tell us. Patricia, listen to me, you haven't done anything wrong. We're listening to you."

"The T-shirt," the girl went on at last. "That's how I recognized him. I'd seen it on TV."

◆ ◆ ◆

"Thank you for respecting our privacy."

It was strange to be there on the other side, being the news instead of reporting it. It was strange to stand up in front of my colleagues and act in the expected way. Seen from my perspective, it was scary. And at the same time, ridiculous. Two dozen reporters were kneeling on the ground, a melee of hands, cameras, microphones, and voice recorders all pointed at my face. And twenty more behind me. Together, we were like a multi-cellular organism in precarious equilibrium. And I was the magnet, the center of gravity around which they moved.

Finally, I had decided to step out of the hospital and speak to the journalists, videographers, and still photographers I worked with every day or was always crossing paths with at one scene or another, the people with whom I'd shared so many stakeouts like this. They'd spent the whole day waiting for me, and somehow I felt I owed them something. At least a few words.

I waited until they were all in position, the cameras rolling with good angles, all the microphones on. So nobody would miss anything. They watched me in silence, letting me set the pace.

"Thank you for your caring. Thank you for all the messages of support that keep coming in. There are a lot of things I can't tell you because, as you know, the investigation is under an order of secrecy. Pablo is in critical condition in the ICU. The doctors say that the next few hours are key to seeing how his condition evolves."

"How did he end up in a garbage dump?"

"What hypotheses are the police working on?"

"Was it The Taker?"

"Have they found the other boys?"

The questions rained down like rocks in a ritual stoning. Once the first one was hurled, the avalanche was unstoppable. There had been a few seconds of silence, the reporters courteous and embarrassed, because how were they supposed to treat a colleague—a friend, in some cases—who had become a victim? But then they all began talking at once. I couldn't make out most of it. I listened as if they were on the other side of the glass wall of a fish tank. *Glug, glug, glug.* Who were these people? What were they saying? What did they want?

What was I doing there?

"The truth is, I can't tell you anything more. I don't know much myself, and everything is under an order of secrecy. Thank you, truly, for all your support and for respecting our privacy. I'm going back to be with my son. That's all that matters to me now. Pablo needs me. Please."

I made a nearly superhuman effort to turn around and walk toward the hospital door without my legs buckling under me.

33

ANA

Manu's T-shirt turned out to be the key. The T-shirt he was wearing when he disappeared, the one the mass media and the social networks had shown and posted over and over again. An enormous Superman logo printed on the front with the word *SuperManu* stamped underneath. A shirt his father had specially ordered. And a shirt that, by now, half of Spain had seen.

When Patricia and her boyfriend climbed over the fence that enclosed the Pilar Woods that Sunday night, all they were looking for was a place to drink, smoke marijuana, and have a little sex without anyone bothering them. Nothing out of the ordinary for two teenagers like them.

They had barely walked five hundred meters, using their cell phones to light up a narrow dirt path through the Woods, when they glimpsed the abandoned Palace of Cotoblanco, a three-story mansion that was never put to use and, after decades of neglect, retained only some walls and part of the roof. The rest had fallen in on the lower floors and formed big piles of rubble, at least as far as could be seen from the fence that surrounded and protected the house. In what had once been envisioned as an ornamental garden, a swimming pool had been constructed, but it was filled only with rainwater.

"This is a little freaky."

"Don't be a chicken. Let's check it out. Nobody ever goes in there. We'll probably be the first to set foot there in twenty years."

After scaling this fence, too, Patricia and Hugo walked hand in hand, while she used her free hand to shine the phone light on the unstable ground, and he held a plastic bag with a bottle of gin and some glasses, just bought in the twenty-four-hour store on the Avenida de España. They entered the house by going up four enormous steps to a ruined front porch and then through a large opening designed as a main entrance with an imposing door, which had either vanished or was never installed. Inside, the hallway and salon of the mansion were impassable. The teenagers had to walk very carefully to avoid falling among the rubble and the bushes that had poked their way through. Trying not to stumble, Patricia and Hugo got as far as what must have been the kitchen, surprisingly well preserved. Through a doorway, they found a windowless room intended as a storeroom or pantry.

There they sat, drank, smoked some pot, and got down to business.

And that would have been the end of their excursion that night, if they hadn't heard a strange noise, something that seemed to be crawling slowly somewhere beneath their feet.

"Rats! Ugh! Rats!" Patricia screamed.

But it wasn't rats moving underneath them in the basement of the house. It was something that, startled by Patricia's scream, darted out of what seemed to be a heap of dried-up bushes. Something with two legs and two arms that took off running like the devil was after it.

As if time had frozen around them, Patricia and Hugo were paralyzed, almost not daring to breathe. For a few seconds, nothing moved except their pounding hearts. A few minutes later, still in complete silence, the boy's hand slowly felt its way through the rubble to find hers and squeeze it tightly, as if this link could form a lightning rod to channel all the fear away from their bodies.

Patricia was the first to speak. "Where did that man come from?"

And she was the first to get up. "There has to be a trap door around here."

She turned the phone's flashlight app back on and traced a line along the ground floor. The man had come out of some kind of hole in a corner of the kitchen.

"Look. There it is."

There was an open trap door, indeed. Through the hole, they could see a narrow cement stairway, built against a wall, going down into a compartment that must have been intended as a storeroom or cold cellar for food.

"Patricia, shit, for Christ's sake, come back here. Don't go down there. Let's get out of here."

But it was too late. Patricia had already set foot on the first step, and then the second, and then the third. Later she couldn't say why she'd done it. She was scared to death. She kept her right hand against the wall for support. The stairs had no handrail and were open on the left side. She didn't want to fall. On the first step, she stopped and crouched to see what was underneath, sweeping her phone light along the basement floor.

"What do you see? What's down there?" Hugo had come as far as the edge of the trap door.

"Nothing, just some scaffolding along the wall. But the stairs and the floor are clean, like someone just swept them."

Patricia went down one step farther, still crouching, until she could light up an area right next to the stairs.

"Holy fuck! Holy fuck!"

"What's going on? What do you see?"

"Holy shit! Two boys!"

"Will you get out of there? Will you get the fuck back up here? Okay?" Hugo yelled, crouching at the top of the stairs himself.

"I'm coming, shit, I'm coming. Just taking a picture first."

"You're crazy, girl." He grabbed her hand to pull her up the two top steps. "Let's get out of here. Damn."

When they were through the trees and thought they were safe, Patricia sat down on the edge of the sidewalk. They were on a block full of restaurants. She was still breathing hard.

"Look."

And there in the picture, lying in a corner and partly covered by a blanket, were two kids. The bodies of two kids. And one of them they recognized, because his story had been repeated over and over on television for the past several days, and his mother had never stopped showing the pictures she'd taken the day he disappeared, just a few minutes before he vanished. "My son, Manu, please give him back to me, please. You're a good person, and Manu is so small and so afraid, and he needs his mother, please." That dead boy in the basement was wearing his T-shirt. *SuperManu.*

34

ANA

For the third time that day, Ana turned on the lights and the siren and covered the seventeen kilometers that separated Majadahonda from central Madrid, this time at suicide speed. This time, she was at the wheel and driving like a madwoman.

"Ana, you're going to kill us. Or worse, you're going to kill somebody else. Those kids are dead, and ten minutes' difference isn't going to save them."

Silvelo was next to her, in the passenger seat. Behind them, two more patrol cars followed. They were talking with Patricia and her father on speakerphone. He was the one guiding them.

"Park the car once you get past the Atlético practice fields—you see them? Okay, go a little further down the street, till you get to a traffic circle. There, on your right, is a dirt road that goes to the fence around the Pilar Woods. See that? Okay. Follow it to the left, and soon you'll see a gate."

Ana and Jesús were already running through the Woods, looking for the entrance that Patricia and her father had described. Some distance behind, five more police officers were following them.

"Okay, we're here," she said, out of breath. "Now what?"

The father directed them to the house. Once they got over the fence, Ana asked for Patricia to get on the phone.

"Okay, Patricia, tell me exactly where I have to look, where the entrance to the basement is."

And there they were, two boys, one lying next to the other. But the blanket that had been in the photo on Patricia's cell phone was gone. One of the boys was Manu, no doubt about it. He seemed to be smiling. The other one looked mummified. The skin of his face was shrunken, and there were no eyes in the sockets. But Ana had no doubt. She looked at Chief Inspector Silvelo.

"I'm too late. I'm too late, and I couldn't save them," she said.

She put on a latex glove so she wouldn't disturb the evidence. She touched Manu's face. It was surprisingly warm.

Warm and alive.

35

ANA

Soon, rumors began circulating among the reporters camped out at the entrance to the Puerta de Hierro hospital. It was almost time for the nightly news, but they couldn't drop the bomb without a confirmation. A second body? Had a second Taker victim been brought in?

"Lola, do you remember me? It's Ana Arén, the chief inspector in charge of the case of your son's disappearance."

Ana could hear how Lola froze on the other end of the line. She could almost see the woman leaning against the wall and sliding to the floor, where she rolled up into a ball. Getting ready for what she was about to hear.

"I have good news, Lola, good news. We just found Manu. He's alive. Can you come right away to the Puerta de Hierro hospital? Come in through the emergency entrance because the main door is jammed with reporters. A police officer will be waiting to escort you. I'll be there soon. I'm very happy, Lola, very happy for Manu and for all of you."

But first, Ana had to fulfill a much more painful obligation. And she had to do it in person. There are things that can't be said over the telephone, that shouldn't even be said face-to-face, because they shouldn't happen at all. But they do. And someone has to inform the family.

She parked in front of the house. From the street, she could see them in the kitchen, maybe making dinner. Their silhouettes showed through the white linen curtains. What Ana was bringing them was still a hypothesis, not a certainty. But she knew that forensic tests would confirm the boy's identity. She had no doubt about that.

"Ana!" The woman was surprised when she answered the door.

"Chief Inspector," her husband greeted Ana from behind his wife, as he came from the kitchen into the hall. "It's been so long. We expected you might call, but not to see you in person. We saw the news about the son of that reporter. Does that have anything to do with Nicolás?"

"May I come in?"

"Yes, of course, we were just making dinner. Would you like to eat with us?"

"Thank you, but I've got a long night ahead of me. I just came to tell you something."

Propped behind the door, the bike was still there. The old blue BH bicycle that had belonged to Nico's father; the boy had inherited it on his third birthday. The training wheels were still attached. "We wanted to take them off, but he was afraid," the parents had told her during the earliest days of the investigation. She could see the spots of rust that had accumulated with humidity and the passage of decades.

"We just can't move it," the woman explained when she saw what Ana was looking at. "We just can't take it down to the basement. This is where Nico left it that morning." After all this time, Nicolás's mother still didn't dare say the word *disappearance*. For her, it was always just *that day*. "And we want him to find his bike there when he comes back."

In this house, time had stopped, waiting for Nicolás. His toothbrush was still lying next to the bathroom faucet, just as he'd left it the night before he disappeared. Spiderman was still locked in battle with a dinosaur on the night table by his bed. His pajamas were still folded under the pillow.

Ana had been there scores of times since Nicolás had disappeared. She knew all the nooks and crannies of the house. She'd tried to get inside the parents' heads—in the majority of cases of disappearances of minors, someone in the family or very close to the child is involved—to find Nico alive, but she'd ended up lost in a labyrinth that threatened her own sanity. The memories of those first difficult weeks erupted like a lava flow in her head, and she had to grab on to the back of one of the living room chairs.

Now came the worst part.

"As you've heard, we found one of the missing boys. The son of Inés Grau, the reporter from Channel Eleven News. I can't give you many details, but we're still investigating the connection between that case and your son's."

The couple, who had sat down facing Ana, looked at her with the deepest sadness. Another dead end, they were thinking. One more.

"But there's something you don't know because it isn't public yet, and so I'm going to ask you for complete discretion. We've found the place where the kidnapper may have been hiding the children all this time, an abandoned house in the Pilar Woods, in Majadahonda. Two teenagers found it by accident last night."

Ana knew she was delaying the moment of telling this couple that she thought the corpse she had found matched the description of their son.

"I'm very sorry to tell you this. In that hiding place, we found a body." Ana never used the word *corpse* when talking with the families of the dead. "And we're analyzing its DNA to see if it matches that of your son."

The moment when the world comes crashing in on you with all its weight—that's what Nicolás's parents felt. Crushed by an avalanche, struggling through the snow without knowing whether they were going upward—toward a way out, toward oxygen, toward life—or digging their own graves deeper still.

36

INÉS

Nothing can prepare you for something like this. It doesn't fit in any of your frames of reference. Not even remotely. Our human brain has evolved so much, has gotten so far beyond the animal one, that it doesn't remember how to survive such a blow. When it receives an impact of such magnitude, it folds in on itself almost to the point of disappearing, leaving just the bare minimum of automatic neuronal connections to allow for survival. The heart beats. The lungs breathe. The blood circulates. But not much else. The eyes don't open. The legs don't hold up the body. The stomach doesn't tolerate food.

The brain shuts down because it's incapable of withstanding such anguish. Curled up in a corner of the skull, it stops thinking and cedes all its tasks to the unconscious realms of the body, the mechanical parts, so they can begin to stitch up the wounds without so much pain. It's as if our platelets and fibrin have the capacity to form a protective barrier, a scab that can separate us a little from the emotional abyss into which we've plunged. Months or years later, when the brain begins to wake up, gray matter rebuilds itself around this clotted pain that will never go away, that intersects with every thought and every dream. For the rest of your life.

Until you die. And even after.

I woke up in a hospital bed. That's the first memory I have—the first, at least, that's remained engraved on the other side of the scarred-over abyss in my memory. In the time After. In my body After. In my brain After.

After Pablo.

The hospital staff told me that, before coming fully into consciousness, I had opened my eyes two or three times. For some reason, my brain didn't record that. My brain must have been completely in the dark, deactivated. The tranquilizers they injected into my vein must have helped as well.

I woke up in a hospital bed. In the same hospital where Pablo had just died.

I remember a sense of peace. Maybe that was the moment in my life when I was most at peace. There was just the void and me, suspended out of time, floating without friction.

Then came the first pain. It was physical. The first thing I remember is the light scratching at my eyes. It hurt to open them. A lot. It was a slow process, consciously slow. Little by little, my pupils contracted, reducing the glare from the fluorescent bulbs in the room and letting me, at last, open my eyes a bit to see.

Then came the second pain. It was physical too. I saw the IV line in the cephalic vein of my right arm. I was so conscious of the needle that my body reduced itself to the round, elastic wall of a vein pulsing around the strange object inside it. A plastic taste from the 22-gauge needle and its long, sharp bevel flooded my mouth, filled my palate, flowed through my bloodstream, everywhere. We were just a vein and a needle in a hand-to-hand fight.

But the third pain was the one that destroyed me. It knifed directly into my spinal cord, spreading to every atom of my body.

The third pain was Pablo.

My brain established the necessary connections for me to remember what had occurred. I wanted to scream, but my voice box didn't respond. My tongue, my mouth, my lips, my teeth—none of them wanted to assume the right position to pronounce his name. My two lips together, a little bit pursed, and the incisors a bit separated, for the *P*. My tongue flat on the base of the mouth, my lips open and projecting, for the *a*. My lips together again for the *b*, making my vocal cords vibrate a little more. My tongue forming an upside-down toboggan, letting air escape through the sides of my mouth and making my cheeks vibrate, to sound the *l*. And at the end of his name, the phonetic apparatus at last relaxes. You only have to let the air travel from the lungs to the mouth, let it slide downhill along the tongue and escape between the incisors and the lips to make the final letter. The *o*.

But neither my lips nor my mouth nor my vocal cords nor my tongue would respond to my orders.

So I let out a silent scream that, instead of forming sound waves and spreading through the room, remained inside my skull and exploded in my brain like a million shards of glass.

Pablo.

37

ANA

Pablo survived in the hospital for only a few hours. He didn't even make it into the next day. His injuries were too serious, and his brain had been deprived of oxygen for too long. Almost better that way, the doctors said, than a whole life in a vegetative state.

We tend to think that the worst thing about a corpse is its smell. But for Ana, the worst thing about a corpse was its color, that sensation of its becoming a pale and baggy-eyed thing, already starting to disappear.

When you go into an autopsy room, the smell of a cadaver is something you expect. You prepare yourself to be overwhelmed by it. But that's not what pursues you every time you close your eyes for the next few days. For Ana, it was like a mixture of baby's vomit and the rotten food you find when you come home from a summer vacation and discover that the refrigerator has broken while you were gone.

That's what a corpse smells like.

But eventually you forget the smell. It ends up decamping from your head, leaving behind just a few traces that can suddenly take you to a good or bad moment from the past. However, what you can never get rid of—what will always stay with you—is what you see on the two metal tables in the morgue. On one rests the corpse. On the other, the medical examiner places everything that accompanied the body when it went from being human to being a corpse. The comfortable shoes put on in expectation of a day with a lot of walking. The old underwear grabbed from the bottom of a drawer because all the presentable pairs were waiting to be washed. The sweater bought on sale—at a price too good to resist—that from now on will always be stained with blood. The bracelet chosen that morning for good luck. The wrinkled Post-it Note in the pocket, a reminder: *half a kilo of tomatoes, chocolate, butter, milk.*

The trivial choices of an ordinary morning become our shrouds. Would we have dressed differently for the day of our death, if we had known? Surely we would have, yes.

Looking at the objects on the table, Ana imagined the lives the victims had lived and the moment life slipped through their fingers. This brought her the same distress she felt when she saw a bloodstained shoe in the middle of the road next to the remains of a horrific traffic accident. The shoe led to a foot, the foot to a person, the person to a family broken forever.

That was why the table of personal objects always made a deeper impression on Ana than the table holding the body—taller, fatter, younger, hairier, lighter, darker, whatever it might be. The objects were what always returned in her nightmares. Sometimes in the morning, when she chose a pair of pants, she couldn't avoid asking whether those were the pants she was going to die in and how they would look on a metal table in the autopsy room. And some mornings, before leaving home, Ana would be hit by an inconsolable grief, an urgent need to leave everything clean and neat. *If I die today,* she would think, *I want whoever comes here to see that I'm an orderly person, that I left this place in good shape.*

Chief Inspector Ana Arén forced herself to go into the room where they would soon slit Pablo open—Pablo, a boy she loved even before he was born. As she entered, the medical examiner and his aide were finishing up their inspection of the body of the little boy found in the abandoned house in the Pilar Woods, the boy who almost certainly was Nicolás. They had already sent a DNA sample to the laboratory for identification.

"The body is quite well preserved. The cold in the basement, the constant temperature, and the dryness of the air all helped to mummify it," the examiner said without lifting his eyes from his work.

"Anything in the clothes?"

"Some hair samples. From at least two different people. Maybe three. They were caught in the threads of the woolen sweater. Not that it was easy to find them. We've had the sweater under the microscope, looking for the smallest sign. Paula"—Paula was one of his assistants—"spent the whole afternoon working on him. Wool is an extraordinary material for getting things stuck to it, which sometimes makes life easier for us."

Ana had known Yon, the examiner, for years, and she'd never been able to understand how a man whose Facebook wall was full of pictures of kittens could be so cold about dissecting cadavers. So many years in the profession, probably. She'd ask him someday.

"If the hair samples are from several people, can we establish whether they were all left at the same time?"

"Are you thinking several people may have taken part in the crime?"

"At this point, I'm not rejecting anything," Ana answered.

"It's hard to say, but we could try. Also, if we could find the people the hairs belong to, we could tell, by comparing them with a current sample, when they lost them on the corpse."

"What?" Ana didn't follow this.

"Think of hair like a tree, but instead of growing in rings around a center, it grows lengthwise. In a tree, every ring is a year, and the rings tell us a lot about how the tree fared during that period of time. Hair works the same way. Each layer tells us a lot, and each one is unique. If we knew who the hair came from and could compare it with a current sample, we could tell you when it fell out or was pulled out."

That would be incredible. But it would require a match between the DNA from the hair and that of someone in the police database. Unlikely they'd have such luck.

"Any signs of sexual assault?"

"Hard to say given the state of the body. We've sent some remains to the lab, in case they show traces of semen. But if there was any aggression, it wasn't physically traumatic."

"Cause of death?"

"Apparently none."

That was Yon's favorite joke when a body didn't show external signs of violence. But today it hit Ana like a punch in the gut, and Yon saw that on her face.

"Sorry, Chief Inspector, just a habit. Nothing in this first exam suggests what this child could have died from. Maybe the toxicology report will shed some light. He must have been four or five at the time of death. It's true that he was very thin. Was Nicolás a skinny child? Below average weight for his age?"

"Not that I remember. I'll have to check the records. I'll ask his parents too. Anything else that stands out to you?"

"He seems to have been well cared for."

"What do you mean?" Ana asked, surprised.

"Well cared for is well cared for, Ana. His hair was combed. I don't know whether you noticed when you found the body. His hands were clean, and his clothes were not dusty. We didn't find anything under his nails, or in his hair, or on his pants. Only the woolen sweater retained anything external to the body."

"As if they were trying to wipe away any clues?"

"Could be. But it could also be that someone was watching over him. The position of the body when you found it suggests something like that. That child was important to someone. Has been important to someone for the past two years."

38

ANA/JESÚS

While Ana was in the autopsy room, Chief Inspector Jesús Silvelo was directing the processing of the evidence found in the area where the two children were discovered. Detectives were still there, combing through every centimeter of the house and its surroundings. The girl had said that she and the boyfriend saw a man go running out of the basement. A man—or so they thought—whose face they couldn't see, but who must have been nimble enough to climb two fences, the one surrounding the house and the one surrounding the Woods. He must have left behind some particle of his clothing or, if they were very lucky, some DNA. In order to limit the search area and not have to examine all the surrounding barbed wire, they were using dogs to follow the suspect's trail.

Already, they had set up one of the basements of the division complex as an area for receiving evidence. Silvelo had asked for rubble from the house to be brought in to be carefully analyzed. The tiniest piece could provide an important clue to locating The Taker. But that meant several tons of material needed to be examined under a magnifying glass. That would require more staff. He called Ruipérez.

"I can't authorize that," the commander said.

"What do you mean you can't authorize it? It's going to take at least two weeks to process all this if we don't get any help."

"Look, Jesús, you've found all three of the kids, right? All three are accounted for. Two of them dead, that's true. Because you didn't get there in time. But as a result, the case is no longer so urgent."

"Isn't it?" Silvelo growled back. "No? And if the kidnapper strikes again, if now that he's lost those three he comes back to snatch another, then it'll be on your conscience. Not only your conscience, but I personally will see to it that the whole world knows."

"Are you threatening me, Silvelo? Are . . . you . . . threatening . . . me?"

Jesús Silvelo, one of the most serene and tranquil members of the police unit specializing in kidnappings, hung up before he started to curse.

In the autopsy room, Yon pushed the button that activated the video and audio recording system. For some years now, all autopsies had been recorded in case a judge demanded the footage as a form of expert testimony.

"Pablo Grau Schmidt. Born April 20, 2012. Weight, eighteen kilos. Height, one meter seventeen centimeters. Multiple external injuries in the form of cuts and bruises."

Ana thought she'd be able to handle this, but her anguish was deeper than in all her years of experience, so she gave the child one last look and left the room. It seemed foolish, but she wanted to remember him that way, whole, not after he'd been slit down the middle. Once out of the room, she leaned against the wall, closed her eyes, and focused on her breathing. She couldn't allow either pain or anger to blind her.

While a second truck unloaded rubble from the house where the two boys had been found, detectives were at work placing the fragments in long lines on the floor, which had been covered in plastic. They had tried to reproduce the design of the house with duct tape, placing the remnants from each room in the corresponding part. They looked like a team of archaeologists with a long summer ahead of them.

Chief Inspector Jesús Silvelo let his staff do their work and went to try to light a fire under the laboratory team. The evidence they could provide had absolute priority, trumping all their other cases, but sometimes it was important to remind the technicians about this and give them a little push.

Why was it always cold in the labs? Did these scientific types have a different body temperature than the rest of humanity?

"Hi," Silvelo said. "We've got a team processing the remnants of the house. If they find anything important, we'll bring it right over."

It seemed that the inspector had spoken into a vacuum, as if the laboratory air lacked the capacity to transmit sound. Only one of the technicians even looked up—the one Silvelo expected to respond, the director of the lab, Pedro Sanz, an institution within the force.

"Have you found anything more in the garbage dump?" he asked.

That was another thing. They not only had to process tons of rubble from the house, but also the tons of garbage in which Pablo had been found. Nothing was easy about this case.

"Your guys still haven't brought us anything from there. Are they losing their grip?"

It was hard to imagine Sanz himself at a crime scene, ever. Blood made him nauseous. He would prefer never to leave the realm of his lab, where everything was under control. Although they worked with the grimy residues brought in from every crime scene, they saw it all from behind screens, protective glass, gowns, and gloves. Everything antiseptic as could be.

"The medical examiner has requested priority for some samples he found on the body from the house," Sanz went on. "Basically hair on a woolen sweater."

Silvelo didn't know anything about that. He hadn't gotten the preliminary autopsy report yet, because the examiner wouldn't compile it until he finished with both of the boys.

"Four hairs, to be exact, more than I have on my head," Sanz joked. "But we're lucky. Two of them come complete with the root, which means they've got DNA. We're processing them right now. When we finish, we'll enter the result in the database and see whether we're lucky again—enough to find a match."

That would be a miracle. In any case, they'd know soon enough. Silvelo wondered whether there was just one killer or two. And would any of them be in the records at all?

39

INÉS/ANA

When the girl with the purse rang the bell, I was lying on the floor. I couldn't remember how I got there, to that particular spot in the right-hand corner of the kitchen, farthest from the window, in the coldest and darkest part of the room. Nor could I remember why the house was empty. I figured I must have thrown everybody out, because otherwise, why would everybody desert a mother whose four-year-old son had just died?

Since I'd left the hospital, I hadn't been alone for a second. It was hard to convince the people buzzing around me that they could at least let me close the bathroom door. I guess they were afraid I'd do something crazy. It had been a strange conglomeration of people that swarmed into my house. Coworkers from the TV station, friends, neighbors. I was almost convinced I'd never exchanged a word with some of them and that they'd shown up out of pure morbid curiosity, because nothing is more reassuring than the suffering of others. When someone suffers more than we do, it makes us feel shamefully lucky and alive.

She must have rung the bell several times.

"I heard you from out in the hallway. Calling your son's name and crying," she told me later. "That's why I kept ringing. Sorry for my persistence." Once I heard the bell, she must have waited a long time for me to gather enough strength to get up and open the door.

When I did, she gave me a long, gentle look, full of a calm that's hard to describe. For the first time, I felt someone truly understood me. More even than my mother, who right then was distracted by all the paperwork for the funeral. At first, we didn't speak at all. Without taking her eyes off me, she just took my hands in hers with a mixture of tenderness and sorrow. I don't remember how long we stayed like that, me inside the apartment and her outside, the doorway between us, looking silently into each other's eyes. Maybe it was only a few seconds, but time had slowed down around us.

"The first thing you have to do is let go of all your guilt." By now we were sitting together on the couch. She was turned to face me, leaning forward and getting as close as she could. "Until you can free yourself of the guilt, you won't be able to move forward," Lucía said.

Yes, Lucía. Her name popped suddenly into my head. Lucía, the mother who got caught with her three little boys in a flash flood in the middle of the night. The mother who tried to save them, struggling against the current in the darkness. The mother who had to decide which child she'd sacrifice to save the rest. The mother who opened her arms and let go of the littlest one, her baby, so she could pull the others from the torrent of water swollen by the downpour, threatening to carry all of them to their deaths. *Goodbye, baby, goodbye.*

"I Googled your address," she explained. "You can find anything online, you know? Everything's on Google, except what really matters. A group of your fans tagged themselves in a photo in front of your building. I hope you don't mind my coming. When my son died, it was all hugs and words of consolation, but I felt nobody really understood, that nobody could possibly imagine what I was going through."

"Will it ever end? The emptiness and the cold, will they ever go away?"

◆ ◆ ◆

"This is just about the worst part, isn't it?" Ana stepped into her office while taking sips of the vile hot chocolate from the machine at the end of the hall. "The waiting. Waiting for the lab techs to get in here and turn on their machines, waiting for those devices to start spitting out results."

"And waiting for forensics to find something on the ground among all that rubble from the house," Silvelo said. "Waiting for all that security footage to shed some ray of light. Yesterday we didn't have a thing. And today we've got, literally, tons of potential evidence to sift through. Did you just come from the autopsy room?"

"Yeah. I stopped by to see you before I go talk to Charo. I've got three missed calls from her. Do you know what they're about?"

"No. I just came down from the lab."

"And?"

"Nothing. Did you know Yon sent out a few human hairs they found on the boy's sweater? Judging by the length, one of them seems to be from a woman."

"Yes, he told me that. The body was well cared for, as if someone had been watching over it all these months. It's almost a miracle that we found a biological trace. We still haven't confirmed that the body is Nicolás, although the clothes match what he was wearing the day he disappeared. Anything in the rubble?"

"Ugh. We're talking about tons of stuff. It's going to take time. And that bastard Ruipérez won't assign us any more staff. He says the case is no longer a priority."

"Can I go punch him in the face?"

"Ana, sit down."

Jesús had to take hold of her arm to stop her from charging up to the commander's office. He felt the same way, ready to go after the man with a hammer, but that wasn't going to solve anything. If it got them pulled off the investigation, everything would be much worse. What they had to do now was catch The Taker before he could strike again.

"I need to go out for a minute," Ana said. What she needed to do was call Joan. Maybe he'd found something through his pedophile-monitoring computer program.

"Ana, thank God," Joan said when he picked up. "I don't know how to get hold of you anymore. I was about to jump on an AVE and set up shop in Madrid."

"That wouldn't help anything, and I'm almost never home."

"I realize you're only thinking about the case and nothing else, and you won't have a personal life until you solve it."

"Well, that doesn't sound very attractive."

"If I didn't know you so well, it would be easy to hate you. Sometimes I want to, to tell you the truth."

"To hate me?"

"Life would be simpler that way." Joan sounded resigned. "I don't guess you're calling me to see how I am. You want to know whether any alarms have gone off."

The silence at the other end of the line told him he wasn't wrong. Ana was incapable of having a personal life when faced with a case like this.

"You know how I am," she said, her timid attempt at an apology.

"It drives me crazy. Especially not knowing how you're feeling. But let's get to the point, since you don't have time for anything else. No, nothing from the computer program. If I'd found anything, you'd have two hundred messages from me. But nothing shows that the people under surveillance have done anything out of the ordinary."

"Out of their disgusting ordinary, you mean."

"Right, nothing outside of what generally gets them off, which is watching kiddie porn. Or making it."

Apparently, then, The Taker wasn't among them, nor had he ever done anything to make a blip on the radar. So who could he be?

◆ ◆ ◆

"Will it ever end? The emptiness and the cold, will they ever go away?"

Right then, that was all I cared about. Whether the pain would ever subside. Whether I'd ever be able to live without Pablo.

The woman I'd thought of as "the girl with the purse" took me by the hands and spoke very slowly. She had needed to learn to live without her little boy and to bear the weight of the guilt for having let him die. For her, it had been the only way to save the other two kids.

"The emptiness and the cold never go away completely. Even when you think you're over the worst. Even when you finally manage to laugh for once, that black hole is still there trying to drag you back in. But a time will come when you can stand to live without constantly thinking you want to die."

When I'd first laid eyes on Lucía, the Wednesday before—less than a week, though it felt like an eternity—my life had been almost perfect. A good job, a successful debut novel, but above all, a child who had taught me to be a different person, to depend completely and without limits on the love of someone who now had been irremediably taken away.

I hadn't started needing Pablo in that desperate way in which you only love a child, until his father took him to the United States for those three months, when he was two years old. And I'd never loved and needed him so much as in that moment when I'd lost him forever.

"Why did you come here?" I asked Lucía. "I deceived you and everyone else the day I came to the group therapy—especially you, because you were the one who told your story."

"There was a moment when you left the room, and then you came back. Right then, I don't know why, I recognized you. You looked different, but I recognized you. And something made me think that the story I was telling, about the death of my son, filled you with a pain few people feel, as if you'd had a violent experience in your life. I wanted to ask you, but you left before the meeting was over."

I froze. Does a mother who has gone through the traumatic loss of a child have some special sensitivity that lets her see what others can't?

Pain. Guilt. Fear. This woman saw inside me better than any of the people with whom I shared my life.

Though, right then, that didn't matter anymore.

The moment would remain recorded in every pore of Ana's skin and every neuron of her brain, as if she were a clock that had stopped at the moment of the tragedy. It was 1:38 a.m. when her telephone rang. She had decided to go home and sleep a little because the searching and sifting for evidence still had a long way to go. She needed a clear head to keep pursuing the child-killer and make sure the bastard didn't get to strike again.

In the hospital, Manu was still unconscious. He was the only child to survive The Taker. His testimony, if he could manage to come out of the coma, would be key. Who had taken him? How? What had happened during the five days he'd been missing?

Ana hated the waiting.

So when the sound of her cell phone woke her, she knew something big must have happened. Maybe Manu had regained consciousness and remembered something. Or maybe some piece of evidence had surfaced, one that could lead somewhere.

The telephone kept ringing on the mattress next to her. Ana was no longer leaving it on the night table so she wouldn't risk knocking it on the floor. Years ago, in another case of life and death, Ana had gotten a crucial call at 2:30 a.m. The killer had found her private number and called to toy with her. But when Ana reached for the phone on the night table, half-asleep, she knocked it to the floor, and it broke, sending the call to voice mail. By the time she heard the message, it was too late. A golden opportunity had been lost.

Before picking up, Ana tried to see who was calling, but her vision was too blurry from sleep. So she was surprised to hear the voice of Jesús Silvelo, sounding nervous. Very nervous.

"Ana, you've got to get down here right away."

"Jesús, what's up?"

"Ana, listen. Drive as safely as possible, but get down here fast."

"Has another kid disappeared?"

"No, no, take it easy. The machine analyzed the DNA of the hairs found on Nicolás's sweater. They're from three different people, and there's a match. Get down here before I have to call Ruipérez and tell him." What the inspector didn't want to say over the phone was whom the hair belonged to. Because if he did, there was no telling what Ana might do.

40

ANA

Nobody knocked on the door like that if it wasn't something important. Much less in the middle of the night. There was no time to put on a pair of pants or even to grab the T-shirt lying at the foot of the bed. It was either open up right away, in nothing but underwear, or let them kick down the door.

In the twelve seconds between being woken up by the pounding and opening the door, the rush of adrenaline did its work, like being on amphetamines. Among the many swirling thoughts, one was paramount: *Who the fuck is coming for me?*

It took, as always, four turns of the key to undo the latch. There in the doorway were seven SWAT team members ready for action, for whatever crazy thing the suspect might do.

Then, there was Charo, behind the arrest team, apparently trying not to faint. But she wasn't the one who spoke. It was the officer who accompanied her.

"I'm sorry. I have a warrant for your arrest."

"What?"—looking at Charo, trying to force an answer out of her—"What are you talking about?"

But Charo kept her mouth shut. She pointed to the handcuffs hanging from her belt.

"For my arrest? What the hell is going on here?" Now he started to raise his voice. "Charo, look me in the eyes. Are you really arresting *me*?"

Charo knew she had to speak, but she couldn't. The words wouldn't come out. How could she say what this man was accused of? It was so serious she didn't want to pronounce the words, because pronouncing them would make it true. And it couldn't be true.

"Are you going to handcuff me?"

"Do I need to?" she managed to say, dropping her eyes. The SWAT team was still fixated on every move he made.

"You know you don't," he said, yielding. "Let's go."

He left his home, under arrest, at 2:20 a.m. The evidence pointed to only one suspect. Him.

"Can you tell me what this is about?" he asked in the car on the way to the station.

Nobody answered that.

◆ ◆ ◆

Chief Inspector Jesús Silvelo was right about not telling Ana who the DNA match was over the phone. It would have taken a straitjacket to contain her rage. She got to the office in record time, barely twenty minutes from when his call woke her up. She must have driven at suicidal speeds.

When she came in the door of the shared office, she was breathing hard. She had to inhale and exhale deeply, several times, to speak.

"What the hell is going on? What? What do the DNA samples say?"

"Sit down, please."

"I'm not sitting down. Tell me what the fuck is going on!"

"Okay, Ana. Calm down."

The inspector was slowly moving to get between her and the door. The last thing he wanted was for her to go charging out before he could calm her down a little.

"It's Nicolás. The DNA confirms that. Should we call his parents now, or wait till the morning?"

She looked baffled, disoriented, as if she didn't understand anything. But she reacted soon enough. The identification of the body couldn't be the only thing. Silvelo wouldn't have dragged her down to the station in the middle of the night for that.

"That's what you made me come down here for? I'm not an idiot. Tell me what's going on, now!"

"The lab was able to extract the DNA from several of the hair samples that adhered to the wool of the sweater."

"As if I didn't know that. Get to the point."

That was a good sign. The policewoman inside Ana was beginning to come out. Silvelo led her a little further down the analytical and rational path before he dropped the bomb.

"The DNA from the hair belongs to three people. Two men and a woman."

"Identities!" Ana demanded.

"We've been able to process one of those from the men. And there's a match." The inspector kept delaying the moment of truth.

"Tell me."

"The match came from CODIS. One of the men is registered there. But not for any crime. His genetic profile is in the database as a preventative measure."

Ana began to understand what those words implied. And she didn't like it. Someone whose genetic profile was in the Combined DNA Index System, but not because of committing any crime, could mean only one of two things: Either that person was a police officer whose DNA samples had been taken to rule out contamination at a crime scene. Or else it was a victim's family member.

"Who? Which one of us?"

"Ana, please, what I'm about to say will hurt you very much." She looked at him, her eyes vacant, not understanding, or maybe because she was actually starting to understand. "I need you to calm down, at least a little, before you pick up the phone or leave this office. All right? I need you to listen to this with your detective mind, not with your heart."

Silvelo came closer to Ana, nearly intruding on her personal space.

"Right now, a group of police is arresting Sub-Inspector Javier Nori García at his home."

It was the last thing Ana expected. The brutal punch to her solar plexus doubled her over, as if she had taken an actual blow. For a few seconds, she couldn't breathe or think. It was impossible. Simply impossible. Her mind refused to accept it.

"The evidence is there. The sub-inspector's DNA was on Nicolás's sweater. And he hadn't been to the crime scene, so it can't be a case of contamination."

"But he must have been there, Jesús. He must have been. Nori is innocent. I'd put my life on the line for that man. Nori didn't do it."

"I know he's not only your sub but also your friend. I know you've been working together a long time. But it's not just the hair. There's more."

It wasn't just the DNA of the hair found on the sweater that incriminated Javier Nori. It was also the alibis. Or the lack of them. When each of the disappearances occurred, the sub-inspector had been off duty. Jesús Silvelo had checked that in the system. When Nicolás disappeared, in the middle of summer, Nori was on vacation. He'd spent the time alone in Madrid, as Ana remembered perfectly well, because they'd met over a beer a few times and also because she'd asked him to come back to work early when the boy stayed missing and they didn't have any clues. In the second case, the sub-inspector likewise had no alibi. At the time of Manu's disappearance, Nori hadn't yet started his shift. On top of that—Ana remembered as Silvelo was reporting it—he'd shown up late for work. And when Pablo disappeared, Javier Nori was back in Madrid after spending the night in Barcelona. He had changed his train ticket to get back early in the morning, while Ana had stayed till noon in the city of her birth.

Three kidnappings, three windows of opportunity. Too many coincidences? Jesús Silvelo didn't believe in them.

"He'll have to show us where he was on those three days. Let's see how it goes. And, even with solid alibis, he could still be an accomplice. DNA doesn't lie."

"It has to be contamination. The evidence has to be tainted. It can't be anything else." Ana struggled desperately to find some logic to all this.

"Anything's possible. It wouldn't be the first time we found tainted evidence. Science is science, but human beings process the evidence. In this case, though, your sub has never handled the body or the clothes the boy was wearing. So it's almost impossible for there to be contamination at the scene of the crime."

"Almost, but not completely. And I'm going to prove that."

Ana rushed out of the office, leaving Jesús Silvelo the job of calling Major Ruipérez, waking him up, and telling him whom they'd just arrested. He would have rather jumped out a window, but he didn't have a choice. He couldn't wait until the morning.

Javier Nori had been working in this building for ten years, but when he came in under arrest, everything looked different, as if he were there for the first time. He had time to notice things he'd never seen. The light, the odors, even the air felt different, as if he weren't the same person he'd been before.

Charo hadn't spoken to him during the ride to division headquarters. Nor had Nori spoken to her. They knew silence would be better. It meant they wouldn't voice what they didn't want to say out loud or make promises they couldn't fulfill.

◆ ◆ ◆

Chief Inspector Ana Arén paced like a caged wolf. She took long strides around the main room of her unit. She sat down. She stood up. She sat down. She stood up. She was so nervous she didn't even know what to do with her hands. She wrung them until the pain made her stop.

She went to the adjoining building, where the forensic units were based, to see whether she could find anyone in the DNA lab. The lights were on—the machines continued processing information twenty-four hours a day—but there seemed to be no one inside. The door was locked. Looking through the small peephole, she couldn't see any technicians. That was strange. Just as she was returning to her building, she got a phone call. She knew who it would be.

"And you call yourself a cop? You're a policewoman, you had him right in front of your nose the whole time, and you couldn't even see it?"

Ruipérez's hostility was on overdrive, awake or asleep. Ana's was at peak level, too, but somewhere at the bottom of her despair, a warning light flashed, that same light that has saved human beings from extinction, though lately it seems to have malfunctioned, like a brake light out of order. It told her she needed to be on good terms with the commander if she wanted to stay on the case. She couldn't leave Nori without any help. Not like this. Not now. *Hold on. Nori needs you.*

"Commander, we don't know whether there could have been contamination. That's the most probable hypothesis at this point."

"Maybe *your* most probable hypothesis, Chief Inspector."

"But—"

"But nothing. Listen to me, because I'm not going to say this again. Think like a goddamn police officer. Forget it's Nori. Imagine we arrested a stranger. What would you think? What does your analytical mind tell you? What do your years of experience say?"

Ana couldn't answer. Because the answer was obvious. If the suspect were a stranger, she'd think he was guilty. Nearly 100 percent sure.

41

INÉS/ANA

There's nothing worse than looking at your son through glass.

There's nothing worse than seeing him there, in a coffin, behind a window in a funeral parlor, not being able to reach out and touch him. When you open the door and your eyes grow accustomed to the dark—"Your relative will be ready in room six in a few minutes," they told you at the desk—the first thing you see is your silhouette outlined by the light leaking through the door frame. But it's still dark, and you don't dare turn on the switch, as if the darkness made everything less real, so you can't see what's behind the enormous window at the back of the room where you see your own reflection. You can guess, though. In fact, you know. Behind that window is a curtain. And behind the curtain is your son's coffin.

After a few seconds, someone draws the curtain aside.

And then you see him.

On the other side of the glass. Alone. Alone now and forever.

And you, too, alone, on this side.

On the wrong side of the glass.

My mother and I grasped each other's hand and began taking small, hesitant steps that tore us up inside. So far, no one else had come. The funeral home had just opened for the day. Willie, Pablo's father, was changing planes in airport after airport, trying to get to Madrid from some remote town in the United States where his paper had sent him to cover a sordid scandal involving an important congressman—something about teenage prostitution; I didn't really get it when he told me, nor did I care. Four years ago, calling the same number, I had experienced the same fear. That time I had called him to tell him I was pregnant. Now I called him to tell him his son was dead.

When we reached the panel that separated us from my child, my mother and I were still holding hands. I can't say who was squeezing tighter. Or who needed the other's hand more. Five or ten minutes later, I raised my eyes and looked at her. Or maybe it was an hour later, I don't know, because for me minutes and hours no longer counted. I do know I raised my eyes, looked at my mother, and she understood without my having to say a word. She said, *Yes, go ahead. Do it if it helps ease your pain.*

So I did.

I got up and opened the inconspicuous door in the corner of the room. It led to an ordinary, anonymous passageway, with a floor of poorly buffed cement and white-tiled walls—they're easier to clean, was what came to my mind, but how could I think that in the midst of such pain? It was cold in there. Or maybe it wasn't cold, but I was cold inside. The kind of cold that seeps into your soul and never lets go. I looked to the right. It had to be that one. I opened the door, and there I was, on the other side of the glass.

On my son's side.

The side where I should have been, long before him.

I reached out my hand. I saw how my fingers shook, which was strange because I couldn't feel the trembling, as if that were someone else's hand, practically in the dark, reaching out. Or as if something had separated my hand from my body. I touched Pablo. I was surprised at how cold he was. His skin had not only lost its warmth but also its elasticity. My son was icy and stiff, as if he'd been sculptured in marble and death had converted him—for all eternity—into one of the statues above the tombs of kings and nobles to remind the living of the dead who were rotting below. I slid my fingertips along the curve of his nose. I touched his lips. I stroked his cheeks. I kissed him. *Goodbye, my son. Goodbye. I'm sorry I couldn't protect you. I'm sorry I wasn't the best mother in the world for you. The mother you deserved, the mother I didn't know how to be.*

I lifted my eyes. On the other side of the glass, Mama was looking at me with tears in her eyes. Her tears had formed a streak of mist that grew like her grief.

Ana spent the night trying to gather evidence that would prove Nori's innocence, but Ruipérez had thrown a blanket of complete secrecy over the case. No one could know that the sub-inspector was under arrest. The officers who had participated in his arrest or processing got direct calls from the commander ordering them to keep their mouths shut. Ruipérez also barred anyone from going down to the cells to speak with or question Javier Nori until further notice.

That prohibition expressly included Ana Arén. She wasn't allowed to be in contact with the suspect or speak with anyone about the case. The commander was trying to limit the damage before the bomb exploded in his hands. To have a presumed pedophile, kidnapper, and child-killer on the police force was in itself a scandal sufficient to end his career. But if, on top of that, the accused officer belonged to the unit charged with combating those exact crimes, the dismissals would rise through the chain of command like a strip of firecrackers going off. And in such scandals, you never knew where the final explosion would sound, how far the trail of gunpowder would reach. It could even immolate the Minister of the Interior, who this time, perhaps, wouldn't be saved by divine intervention or all the medals he'd donated to the country's holy Virgins during his incomparable service of national protection.

The prime objective was to control the crisis until there was sufficient evidence to take the bull by the horns and come out with the news.

At the hour she considered prudent, which was eight in the morning, Ana began making phone calls in search of an alibi for her friend. She didn't want to scare his mother, an elderly woman with heart trouble who lived in a small town in the mountains of Huelva. Of the sub-inspector's friends, she knew only a few members of his soccer team. In general, police officers ended up relating mostly to other police. It was a very endogamous profession. Coming up with the phone numbers of the soccer players had taken quite a while.

"Alejandro? Sorry to bother you at this hour. It's Ana. Ana Arén, Javier's colleague. Yes, you've got it. No, nothing serious, don't worry. It's just that I've got the Internal Affairs Department all over me—you can't imagine how annoying they are—and I completely forgot about a report I should have turned in last night. Yes, police stuff, you know how it is. We end up wasting more time on paperwork than we spend catching the bad guys. Yes, you're right. So anyway, excuse the hour and the hurry, but they're making me fill out a report about my unit, and the members can't know anything about it. Yes, a mess, exactly. So what I need you to tell me, if you can remember, is about June 16 two years ago. Yes, two summers back. That's right, the summer your daughter was born. Well, so what I need to know is whether that day, which was a Sunday, do you remember whether you had a game or practice or whether you were hanging out with Javier for any reason? You don't remember? That makes sense, given how much time has passed. But do you keep your calendar on your phone? Could you take a look? Also, could you tell me what league you play in?"

Ana tried the same thing with the days that Manu and Pablo disappeared. But Alejandro hadn't been with Nori or called him, nor did he have any idea what Javier might have been doing then. Ana was sure that as soon as she hung up, Alejandro was going to call Nori to tell him about the strange exchange he'd just had with Nori's boss. But Javier Nori was deprived of his phone, incommunicado in a cell in his own police station.

Maybe Joan . . .

"What do you know, Chief Inspector Arén calling to wish me good morning," he joked, surprised, and failing to hear the gravity in her greeting.

"Joan, something very serious has happened."

She stopped, unable to say what she needed to say, the words stuck on her tongue.

"Ana, you're scaring me now."

"Nori's been arrested," she blurted.

"Arrested? What for? Slapping your new commander in the face?" Joan went on joking, trying to lighten up something whose full seriousness he didn't yet grasp.

And, in spite of the gag order imposed by her superior, Ana told Joan everything. She didn't care about the consequences. She needed to feel better, even just a little. Talking helped. Trusting in other people helped. Not always. Not with everyone. But it did with Joan. She was just starting to learn that. It felt good. She hoped it wasn't too late for her own sanity.

"Do you want to help?"

"Of course! How can you doubt it?"

"Then I'm going to ask you to do something."

"Anything."

"Are we still connected to the Parkinson's experiment?"

Joan knew what Ana wanted, without her having to say it.

"You know they aren't likely to accept those results as evidence. The program hasn't been certified. Only we know about it, and we thought it up as a preventive measure, never as evidence for or against a suspect that could be presented to the police or in court."

"I know, but at least this way you could give me something to use."

"And if it doesn't turn out well? Have you stopped to think what would happen if the dates actually match the symptoms?"

"How can you think that about your friend?" Ana raised her voice. It was the first time she'd raised her voice to Joan.

"I don't. It's just that someone has to be the voice of reason here. I can't imagine Nori doing anything even remotely like that, but you have to realize that the result isn't always what you might expect. We all have some kind of monster inside us, who only needs a push, sometimes a very small one, to come out and devour the world." *Isn't that what it means to be a detective?* he was on the verge of saying. *To find the monsters, whoever they may be?*

But he didn't. And Ana remembered she had an even more difficult task. She had to tell two parents that their son was dead.

After the whirlwind of the past week, it felt like someone had hit the slo-mo button. Really, people and things had returned to their customary rhythm, but the contrast made everything seem slower in Ana Arén's unit. Very few people knew that the presumed guilty party was locked in a cell a few floors below them, much less that he was one of their own. But the three boys had reappeared—although two of them were dead—which reduced the pressure somewhat.

"Have you heard anything about Nori?" José Barriga asked Charo in a whisper.

Charo looked up from the computer screen. Barriga could see that her eyes were swollen and her face flushed, which her makeup couldn't conceal, meaning that she'd spent the night crying. She felt alone and disoriented. She'd been in the unit only four months but had become good friends with the sub-inspector. And this was her first real case since graduating from the academy. In her previous post, all she'd done was stand watch over embassies and their staff.

"I'm new here, too," he said, trying to comfort her. "Just a week, and I don't know which end is up, with everything that's happened. But you can't let things get to you so much."

Was there really a way to manage that, Charo wondered. How did a police officer do that? How did anyone?

Barriga pulled one of the old, wheeled office chairs up next to her. He sat beside Charo and reached out his hand.

"Take this," he said.

"What is it?" she asked.

"Besides a flash drive?" he tried to joke. "Something to occupy your mind. Images from the security cameras near the garbage chutes that Pablo could have been stuffed into."

"How many cameras? Scare me."

"A hundred and five. We've downloaded twenty-four hours of recording from each, between the time Pablo disappeared and the time his body was found."

More than twenty-five hundred hours of video. Not to mention tons of rubble from the house. It was overwhelming. But best to keep on digging.

The thought of her father's body decomposing and of the long agony he must have suffered lying alone on the floor for more than a day, trying to get to the phone, changed Ana Arén irrevocably when she was only twenty-two. It made her a difficult, elusive, and evasive person. Someone who held herself apart.

Except with victims.

When she talked with victims, Ana changed. In her years in the SAF, she had needed to convey the bad news of dozens of unexpected deaths to relatives who couldn't imagine what they were about to hear. Ana always watched them carefully beforehand, trying to draw out the moments of normalcy she was going to destroy forever. *One more minute,* she'd say to herself, *I'll give them one more minute.* They never knew of the gift the policewoman was trying to offer them.

The family eating dinner in front of the TV. The parents sleeping late on a Saturday morning. The son studying in the university library. *No, no way he can be dead,* everybody told her, or *I spoke with her just this morning,* as if such a conversation were the magic potion of immortality. As if a few seconds couldn't break off a life forever. *He's there. He must be there. How can he not be? No, she isn't dead—it's impossible!* And Ana saw in them her own image from years before, that police cadet walking on tiptoes, clutching the wall, step by step, knowing her father was dead at the end of the hall, but trying to delay the moment when she would see his corpse and the fact of his death would be unavoidable. "Let's go inside," she would say to the parents. "Let's sit on this bench in the sun," she would say to the student. "Kids, can I put on some cartoons for you while I talk with your mother?" she would say in a family's living room.

And she'd take them by the arm, or offer them her hand, or embrace them. Each person needed a different type of contact in the face of pain, and Ana knew how to detect, each time, what it was. Some people wanted to be hugged to keep them from fainting. For others, any type of physical contact produced a lightning bolt of pain. "I just spoke with the medical examiner. Your son died in an ambulance on the way to the hospital. He was in a car accident. I'm very, very sorry. Is there someone I can call for you? Can I help in any way?"

With Nicolás's parents, it was both easier and harder. Easier, because she was putting an end to their doubt, worry, and the agony of not knowing. Harder, because as long as their son was "missing," they could hold on to the hope of seeing him again.

Abruptly, Ana was going to do away with that hope.

42

ANA/INÉS

"I have to go to the funeral home. Any news?"

Ana had called Silvelo from the car. Her hands were still shaking. She had to concentrate just to keep a good hold on the steering wheel.

"How did it go with Nicolás's parents?"

"One of the worst things I've ever had to do. Let's just try to catch this bastard as soon as we can."

He should have reminded her that, most likely, this bastard was already in a cell three stories below her office, but Silvelo thought she needed to purge her own pain in her own way. It had to be terrible to see your fellow detective, and your friend on top of that, arrested for a crime that had been driving you nuts for two years. The perpetrator was there all along, and you didn't see him.

Ana was torn between denial and guilt.

"Want me to come with you?"

"No, it's something I need to do by myself."

"I don't need to take you for an idiot and remind you not to say anything to Inés about the sub-inspector's arrest, do I? That's her name, right, Inés?"

"And I don't need to take you for an idiot who would think I'd do that."

The funeral home on the M-30 piled depression on top of death. It was an indigestible gray concrete hulk built right next to the busiest and most often gridlocked highway in Madrid. The building had been commissioned in the heady days after the death of Franco, by the city's mayor, the man who pulled Madrid out of the mental and urbanistic torpor of forty years of dictatorship. His intentions were surely good, but the tastes of the eighties were equally terrible in both architecture and fashion, dominated by big hair and impossible shoulder pads.

So the mortuary would have been a depressing place even if its function were not to hold the recently dead and the people crying over them.

Inside, there was a long central court with an atrium roof. It wasn't hard to tell which of the doors led to the room holding Pablo's coffin. Children's funerals are always the biggest. In a strange paradox of life, the longer you live and the more people you know, the fewer come to your funeral. Maybe because the less space you take up in the world, the less time you have to disappoint or hurt others.

Ana couldn't avoid scrutinizing the crowd in search of anyone suspicious. She did so out of inertia and out of habit, the same way she never sat with her back to a restaurant door. Besides, maybe the child's murderer could really be there. Her mind struggled to take Nori out of the equation.

In a corner of the main courtyard, lost and lonely, Sam was crying in silence. He was sitting on a small concrete ledge and leaning his head against the wall. He looked like a Caravaggio painting of the mourning mother of Christ. Tears flowed down his cheeks in a hypnotic rhythm, piteous to look at.

The au pair had been released as soon as his questioning was over. He said he'd spent the weekend partying around Madrid with a group of other Brits. They all confirmed his alibi—which wasn't even necessary, because he fell apart completely when he heard that Pablo had been kidnapped. That kind of pain could not be faked.

◆ ◆ ◆

I saw Ana when she came into the room where I was watching over my son. I was still pressed against the glass, watching him, feeling him. It was the last time we'd be together, close to each other, and I didn't want to leave. I had to store up each of the final seconds alongside my little one. But, however much I clenched my fists, time flew out of my hands. There was less and less of it left before he would be taken away from me.

Ana came toward me slowly, watching all the time. "I'm sorry, I'm sorry, I'm sorry." That was all she was able to say. "I couldn't save him. Forgive me, please." I could see her shaking.

We hugged for a long time. Sometimes it's easier to give an embrace than to look someone in the eyes and feel you have to fill the silence with words. We hugged until we were interrupted. More people, more condolences, more embraces, more *you-have-to-be-strong*.

There were too many people around us. And perhaps too much pain about not having been able to save my son. Ana lowered her eyes and left without saying goodbye, while I continued to receive embraces. I watched her leave, her back to me, as if dragging weights tied to her ankles.

Once she got to the courtyard, I couldn't see her anymore, but just then she caught sight of Willie, Pablo's father, in the crowd. He had arrived after more than twenty hours of travel.

"Ana, tell me you'll catch the guy."

Those were his first words, while the two of them fell into a sustained and painful embrace. In spite of living more than six thousand kilometers way, Willie had spent long periods with his son and had been in continuous contact. A week never went by without them talking over Skype.

"How are you doing?"

"I still can't believe it." His eyes, red from so much crying, could barely focus.

"Go to Inés," she begged him. "She may not show it, but she needs you. You're one of the people who know her best in the world. And I have to go. I have to catch that son of a bitch. Call me for whatever you need, okay? And above all, call me before you leave. I want to see you before you head back."

Outside the building, there was quite a crowd of press—more than twenty television cameras, dozens of photographers, at least fifty reporters. Ana lowered her head and circled around the edge of the melee.

Her phone rang just as she pushed the unlock button on her key fob.

"Ana, are you watching TV?" Silvelo asked.

"No, I'm just coming out of the funeral home; you caught me about to get in the car."

"Get in and turn on the radio. Any news station. Fucking sons of bitches."

Four words were all it took. Minister of the Interior. *No way,* she thought, *not even that band of bastards was capable of holding a press conference to give Nori's name to the public.*

"Right now, it's still too early for us to tell you any more," the Minister was saying, "but we can assure you the evidence is more than sufficient. Specifically, a piece of forensic evidence found on the body of one of the boys."

"Can you completely eliminate the possibility of a tainted crime scene?"

"Completely. Sub-Inspector Javier Nori had no contact at all with the crime scene, the body, or the laboratory where the evidence was examined. That remote possibility has been totally ruled out."

They were plunging Nori into a puddle of shit from which he could never completely emerge, even if proven innocent. Ana could imagine how and why the idea for the press conference had emerged. With all the top brass and politicians assembled, they'd decided to strike first, getting ahead of any potential leak. In a crisis, it's always better to take the initiative, and additionally, with this dramatic announcement, they were sweeping the deaths of the two boys under the rug. "Yes, they're dead, but we've solved the case. We've caught the bad guy, and the rest of the country's mothers and fathers can rest easy." That was what this press conference from the Minister of the Interior was supposed to communicate. Someone in that kind of position only offered explanations in special moments. And this was one of them. He could be a star. He could shine. Another medal. Another notch on his gun.

When the press conference ended, Ana realized she was sitting in the car, in the dark, in the parking garage of the mortuary, and hadn't even turned on the engine. She checked for cell phone coverage just as a call came in.

"Joan," she said.

"I just heard about the press conference where that lowlife crucified Javi."

"We'll prove he's innocent. I swear it, if it's the last thing I do."

"Have you talked to him?"

"No, they won't let me. They're holding him incommunicado. But I'm still in charge of the investigation, as far as I know. I'm going to call Silvelo to see whether we can push the commander into letting us question him."

Ana drove toward the exit. People were still arriving. Among all those coming to offer condolences, how many came out of curiosity? How many came with real pain? And how many were faking it? How many came out of morbid fascination?

"At least they'll relax now that the pressure's off," Joan said.

"Maybe, but those people don't think like the rest of us. All they care about is their chess game, and the game is about politics, nothing to do with us. Have you been able to run Nori's neuroQWERTY data through the pedophile program?"

"That's what I wanted to talk about. There's a problem. I have to go to Paris right away. Some kind of bug was inserted into the central computers of a Europe-wide institution, likely an inside job. They discovered it by accident, but they have to stop it before it executes because they don't know what kind of damage it will cause once it runs. I'm leaving for Paris now."

"Fuck. You can't say no? This is more important."

"I thought about it. But no, I can't. If I could, I would have done it, believe me."

An uncomfortable silence of truth opened between them. "But look, I've figured out what we can do. I'll give you remote access to my home computer where I've got the program running. I'll try to connect, too, but I'll be on the plane for about two hours, then stuck in a high-security bunker, probably with no signal. They haven't given out any details, which means it's a big deal, so most likely they'll confiscate our phones and computers. You're going to have to help me. I'll send you the instructions on how to do it. I'll write them in the taxi on the way to the airport."

When she got to her office, Ana opened the email from Joan. She did it from her personal cell phone so no trace would be left on her work computer. She read the instructions, but she'd have to reread them to fully understand. From what she could gather, she'd need a computer to calibrate the data. Since she couldn't leave any hint on the police computers, she'd have to do it on her laptop, which was at home. Once again, she'd have to drive across town.

"Boss, boss." Charo came running out of the main room. "Ana, Manu woke up. He's talking. You have to get to the hospital right away."

Ana leapt from her chair, but when she got to her office door, she stopped suddenly and went back. She turned on her desktop computer and logged in to the police database. She had something very important to print.

She left the building clutching a folder to her chest. If she'd been able to remember a prayer, if she'd believed in God, she would have prayed that what was in there would do the job.

43

ANA

"Manu, honey, I'm so happy to see you awake. You're a very strong boy. Stronger than Superman, don't you think?"

Ana's sneakers squeaked against the polished tiles of the hospital floor. An annoying noise, as if they were calling for help or amplifying the pain that bubbled through the chief inspector's veins. It must have been the sound of the shoes, in a part of the hospital where even the silence was antiseptic, that alerted Manu's parents. Lola stuck her head out of the door to her son's sickroom, perhaps surprised that anyone would be hurrying down the hall. The police had closed off this part of the ICU to protect the boy and his parents. No one except authorized medical personnel was allowed in.

"You saved Manu. Thank you. We can never thank you enough."

Only one, Ana thought. She'd been able to save only one. Two children had died because she had not been able to solve the puzzle in time. But that wasn't something you could say to the parents of the only survivor.

"They told me Manu has woken up."

"It's a miracle. You've given our son back to us."

Lola kept holding the chief inspector's hands in hers as if they were delicate objects to be worshipped. The hands that had given her Manu back.

"Do you think I could talk with him for a minute? I'd like to ask him a few things. It's important to the investigation. May I come in?"

Ricardo was there, of course. Manu's father. The man she'd arrested as the prime suspect in the boy's kidnapping. The one she'd believed to be guilty, whom she'd interrogated almost with hatred, harassing him terribly to try to get at the truth. During the questioning, she had said horrible things to him.

"Ricardo." She approached and offered her hand.

"I see, Chief Inspector, that now you can remember my name without any trouble," he said, still hurt.

"It's my job."

"And on top of that, you had the murderer in front of your nose and couldn't see him. Some cop you are! We saw what the Minister said about your detective."

"I can't discuss details of the investigation with you. Please understand."

"Ricardo, please," his ex-wife scolded him.

The walls of the hospital room were painted with princesses and dragons. Cute drawings that, nonetheless, might not be very pleasing to a boy who'd worn a Superman shirt—his favorite—on the day of his disappearance. That shirt likely saved his life.

"You know what, Manu, I think Superman is missing from this wall. Maybe we can ask the doctors to paint him on?"

Ana stood on one side of the bed. The parents had stepped back against the wall and were watching from there. Ana had asked them not to stand too close so as not to influence the boy's answers.

Since her assignment to the unit of the SAF that attended to minors, Ana had needed to learn how to talk with children. She'd spent a lot of time trying to learn the secrets of the delicate technique of questioning minors. Kids Manu's age thought adults, especially their parents and caretakers, had superpowers. They could do anything. They knew everything. They'd never lie. Therefore, it was important to keep their influence at a distance.

"My name is Ana. Could I stay here with you awhile?"

Ana responded to Manu's half smile by moving closer, to the edge of the bed.

"I'm not wearing my uniform, but do you know what my job is?"

The boy shook his head.

"I'm a policewoman."

"Police, like the jerks that give out fines?"

The answer surprised everyone in the room. Ana laughed, but Lola elbowed her ex-husband. "You see? He watches you and copies everything you do," she whispered. "You can't talk like that in front of the boy."

"No, I don't give out fines, Manu. The part of the police force where I work doesn't do that. I chase bad guys."

"But my papa's not bad, and they give him fines."

"Well, maybe he drives a little fast sometimes."

"If he doesn't," Manu argued back, seriously, "we'll be late for school."

"Well, don't worry about that. Since I work for the police, I can take care of the problem of the fines, you know?"

The boy smiled, looking at his father. *See, Papa, how I'm taking care of things?* In a traumatic situation like the one he'd been through, children develop a vital need to be loved and appreciated by adults. Ana couldn't let this influence his answers.

"Manu, what I need is for you to help me. Can you do that?"

"Yes." He looked toward his parents for approval. Lola nodded, encouraging him.

"Do you know why you're here?"

"Because I hurt myself."

"You hurt yourself?"

Ana didn't know what the parents had told Manu in the two hours since he'd come out of the coma. Small children tend to fill the holes in their memories with the subsequent information they collect from their surroundings, which they store up like experiences they have lived. Had Lola and Ricardo unintentionally shaped what their son was going to say?

"I was scared. Really scared."

"What scared you?"

"The boy who wasn't moving . . . I had to stay next to him . . . I had to play with him . . . But I couldn't do it. He wouldn't move."

Manu looked like he was about to dissolve into sobs.

"He broke when I touched him," he went on, an expression of terror crossing his face.

"I think that's enough of an interrogation for today," someone said over Ana's shoulder.

A doctor had just come into the room. Ana supposed it was the doctor in charge of Manu's case. Maybe the nurses had told him she was there.

"Doctor, please."

But she couldn't convince him. She walked into the hallway, asking him to follow for a minute. He did, but remained unbending. "Probably tomorrow," he said. "The boy has gone through a very difficult experience, and we have to let it come back to him little by little and in the least traumatic way possible."

The doctor promised to let her know as soon as possible, after the psychologist had visited Manu.

"I'd like the psychologist to be with you the next time you talk with the child. All right?"

"Just one more thing, Doctor, a very important question. Please," Ana pleaded.

She went back into the room. Manu's parents had returned to the head of his bed.

"Just one more thing," Ana said while facing them. Her expression was pleading again. "Manu, I'm leaving, but I promise to come back tomorrow with a Superman for the wall, okay?" The boy looked at her with a strange mix of joy and suspicion. Why was the doctor throwing this policewoman out of the room? "But first I need to ask you one last thing. I'm going to show you a picture. I want you to tell me whether you know the person in the picture. That's all. Just if you know the person or not. Okay?"

The polyurethane soles of Chief Inspector Arén's shoes wheezed again against the polished floor tiles of the hospital. But now they weren't calling for help. It was a cry of hope.

44

ANA

No way. Ruipérez wasn't answering the phone. He was probably still hiding under his desk, in fear of her wrath about the Minister's press conference accusing Javier Nori. Ana tried Silvelo's number while merging into the traffic of the M-30.

"What did the boy tell you?" he asked.

"That it wasn't Nori," she answered confidently.

"What do you mean, that it wasn't Nori? Did he name anyone?"

"No. I showed him a photo of Javi, and he said he'd never seen that man."

"Shit, Ana, he's a four-year-old. That won't do. It doesn't count as evidence. I don't mean in front of a judge. I mean even for you. The kid is very young and just went through something that would leave its mark even on the sanest adult." *How could this woman be so stubborn?* Ana figured Silvelo must be asking himself.

"He was very emphatic," Ana said. "It's not the person who kidnapped him."

"What's emphatic is the DNA evidence. You've got to find something better."

Find something better. But it wasn't only about proving Nori innocent. It was more complicated than that, because she'd have to find a way to explain how a hair with his DNA got onto the woolen sweater on the corpse. A sweater that came from who knew where. They were trying to trace it, but it was impossible. There were tens of thousands of practically identical ones, from a cheap, quickly manufactured brand that had gone on sale in May two years back. Nicolás had disappeared in June, when the weather had already turned hot. He'd been wearing a T-shirt and shorts. Someone must have put the heavier garment on him, which jibed with the idea put forward by the medical examiner: someone had been taking care of Nicolás, or his corpse, that whole time. For two years.

Furthermore, even if they found the real killer, Ana would still have to dispel any possible doubt as to whether her friend might be an accomplice or involved in a cover-up of the three kidnappings and two deaths. Could she do that?

While driving toward home, she tried Joan, but his phone was off or out of coverage. Was he already on the plane? That left the two-hour flight to Paris, during which there was no way to contact him. This reminded her about the remote access to his computer, which held the neuroQWERTY program with Nori's file. Ana would have to follow the instructions Joan had emailed her and run Nori's keyboarding pattern through the program for the emotional states of pedophiles. If there were no changes, her friend would be innocent.

When she got home, she collapsed on the couch. Adrenaline had kept her going for almost twenty straight hours, without eating or even thinking about food, but right then, she felt incapable of making the slightest effort, even to turn on her side. She let her mind drift. When she was on the point of fading into black, her whole body shook with a spasm as if hit by an electric shock. One fleeting thought had been enough to wake her. She had to find more favorable evidence in support of her friend. She had to get up and keep working. *No sleep for you, Ana Arén.*

When she turned on her computer, the light of the screen seemed brighter than usual and surprised her. She had to rub her eyes to focus. Her eyesight was clearly declining, and she'd soon need glasses to see close-up. She reread the instructions from Joan.

It was going to be more complicated than she thought.

In half an hour, she managed to download, install, and start up the programs needed for remote access to Joan's computer. Ana had never used a remote desktop, and it didn't come easily. But miraculously, it worked, and she was able to open a window on her MacBook Air that showed she was now inside Joan's computer. Luckily it had the same operating system as hers, so she had no trouble navigating folders and finding the one with Nori's data inside.

Her eyes closed. She had to make a superhuman effort to keep on working. She dug her nails into her palms to keep herself alert.

She opened the program that read the emotions of pedophiles and typed in the dates that the boys had disappeared. As Joan had recommended, she included a date range from seven days before to seven days after each kidnapping. She also tried using the dates the children had been found. The killer must have gotten very nervous when he learned about this.

Now all she had to do was drag Nori's data to the program and wait. But she made a mistake and, along with those of the sub-inspector, sent all the files in the folder, which held the keyboarding patterns of all the friends whom Joan was following to detect possible neurodegenerative disease, including her own. Shit! This was going to take longer than she thought. In the upper left corner of the program window, she could see the progress bar. It estimated six hours and thirty minutes for the whole operation.

Her eyes closed, and she let herself wander off to sleep.

The first thing she felt was an intense pain in her neck. Then she noticed the light; was it morning already? She sprang up from the couch. She'd slept there all night while the laptop, open on the floor, went on processing.

She hit a few keys, but the screen didn't respond. The battery had died over the course of the night. She plugged the charger into the computer, then the wall socket, and managed to start it up. Still another half hour left to finish the analysis, so she went to take a shower. God, how good a torrent of hot water felt on her back! Ana conceded herself the luxury of bathing without hurry.

When she got back to the living room, a box of cookies in hand to quiet her growling stomach, she sat down on the floor with her legs crossed and put the laptop on her knees. What data had the program obtained? Ana was convinced this would exonerate her friend.

Completely convinced.

She called Joan. She wanted to talk with him. She missed him. And, of course, he could help her analyze the charts in case she had trouble. She hadn't heard from him since the day before, when he was about to get on a plane for Paris. But again she only got his voice mail. His phone must still be turned off.

She looked at her watch. She was late. She'd keep the laptop in her purse, until she could succeed in catching up with Joan.

And suddenly, in a painful flash, it occurred to her.

45

INÉS/ANA

I felt the way you do when you're in the middle of nowhere and suddenly the sky opens in a downpour. You look around and don't see anywhere to take shelter. All you can do is stand there, absorb the water soaking deep into your bones, and let the pain go on killing you. But without dying—you just feel like you're about to.

Bear the brunt of the storm without being able to do a thing.

Because there is no shelter after the death of a child. Not even, you suspect, in your own death. Your bones will keep crying in your grave.

However many hands hold you up, however many words of consolation are whispered in your ear, you're still alone in the worst tempest of your life. Soaked through with no way out.

"Remember that you're alive, that you have a right to live and shouldn't feel bad about it," Lucía had told me, but I was not so convinced about deserving to live.

That morning, I had to say my final farewell to my son. Within a few hours, the hearse would take him—my poor son, alone in that car—to the cemetery where the funeral would be held. And then we would cremate him.

I still hadn't thought about what to do with the ashes.

The idea burned through Ana's cerebral cortex with the intensity of an electric shock. So fiercely that it hurt, because of what it was and what it implied.

It couldn't be.

Still, at this point, she couldn't reject any possibility. Not even the awful thought that had just crossed her mind.

She grabbed a set of keys that had been lying for years in a small cabinet in the living room, keys she'd never, ever used. If she'd believed in God—how many times in her life would it have been useful to believe in God!—she'd have prayed for a sign that what she was thinking was completely nuts.

She was paranoid. She was sure that hallucinations were beginning to get the upper hand over logic. But, what if she was right?

"Pedro?" On her way, she called the director of the lab. "Are you in the lab?" Ana was running down the street toward the parking lot where she kept her car.

"It's eight in the morning. Where are you going, panting like that?"

Ana needed to ask him a personal favor that would require him to skirt several strict norms.

"Right now, I'm stepping through the door of your favorite bakery, to get you a tray of your favorite mini-croissants. Should I grab you a couple with filling too? Chocolate, butterscotch, or cream?"

"Ah women, food in return for favors. I'd prefer sex, to tell you the truth, but I guess I'll have to make do."

"Don't make me beg, Pedro. You know how much I hate that. You're the only one who can help me, and I trust in your discretion."

"Here. Here he is. Look, here he is," Charo said, urging Luis to come over to her desk.

She'd found something in the security camera footage. After Pablo appeared out of the garbage collection pipe, they'd concentrated on finding the entry point where he could have been thrown in. There were more than five hundred such receptacles in the whole area, but the company in charge of the service had limited the possibilities to about a hundred, because the pipe in which Pablo had gotten caught served only one particular sector. But there was a problem: in that part of the city, the majority of the receptacles were inside the buildings, especially in the garages. In those developments, none of the security cameras focused on the garbage chutes. What for, after all? Who would want to rob them?

So the police had to work in reverse. Jesús Silvelo sent several patrol cars to the receptacles where anyone could have put Pablo, and they retraced their steps from there, to see where Pablo and his murderer might have passed by a camera.

"Are you sure?"

"Look, I've got the whole sequence put together. We're lucky, because I could have started anywhere. But then I thought, *Just what if?*"

"Shit, shit, shit. This changes everything. How could we have been so wrong? Do you realize what this implies? You have to call Ana right away. Do you know where she is?"

Ana hadn't gotten to the station until midmorning. Finding what she was looking for had taken longer than she thought. Her stomach twisted with disgust, but she overcame her nausea, like so many other times, although no other investigation had been so personal as this. So intimate. So painful. She had gathered several possible DNA samples from the small studio on Calle del Nuncio and put them in the evidence bags

267

she always carried in her purse. When she got to the station, instead of going up to her office, she went to a building next door. She was hysterical. She thought she'd throw up at any moment, but she had to control herself. She needed to know the truth. As painful as it might be.

"Should we go for coffee?" She held out the delicately wrapped package from the pastry shop, trying to keep her hands from shaking.

"I could smell them all the way down the hall. Let's go."

Neither of them talked while the machine mixed powder with water to produce a diluted substance far from a half-decent cup of coffee. Ana's lemon tea was also a joke, as if it contained more plaster than tea leaves. *Hadn't someone told me,* Ana thought, *something about mixing some ingredient with plaster to make stupas? Reliquaries for Buddhist monks and nuns? Now I'm jumbling concepts, like my brain can't keep each idea in its place!*

She and Pedro made small talk while they walked out to one of the courtyards dotting the police complex. The belt highway ran right next to this one. The noise of the cars on the M-30 would keep anyone from overhearing.

Ana set the tray of croissants on a concrete ledge. She slowly removed the lid.

"You bought the expensive ones. That's a bad sign."

"They're what you would have bought," she said. "I know they're your favorites."

"Okay, let's cut the crap," Pedro said. "You don't have to seduce me in order to give it to me up the ass. I'm an easy guy." His confidence, or trust, could be repulsive at times. "Ana, what do you need?"

"This."

The chief inspector took three evidence bags from her purse. Perfectly sealed, but unlabeled.

"What's that?"

"Evidence," she answered, as if it were the most natural thing in the world.

"I bet it is. What of?"

"I can't tell you, Pedro. But please, and believe me, it's like my life depends on it, can you extract the DNA and see whether it matches anything in the database of criminals or links to evidence from some unsolved crime?"

"Like The Taker case?" the lab director suggested. Ana's silence told him what he needed to know. He relented. "How do you want me to label it?"

"Don't make me beg. You know you can't label it. You have to take the utmost precautions not to leave any trail. You know how to do it. Please."

Ana's personal phone went off in her purse. She let it ring until it stopped. A little later, the phone sounded again. Ana opened her bag and looked at the screen. It was Joan. She almost dropped the phone.

"Pedro, I've got to take this. It's important," she said while stepping away. "Please call me when you've got something. Whatever time that is. Please."

Her hands shook. She was drenched in sweat. She had to swipe her finger on the screen several times before it would pick up the call. She couldn't do it. Fucking smartphones. The call went to her voice mail. She called him back, but the line was busy. Joan must be leaving her a message. The two and a half minutes that went by before the "new message" signal lit up seemed eternal.

"What a mess," Joan had said on the voice mail. "Very serious. I can't tell you much more. It doesn't have anything to do with what I thought. They've locked us in a bunker with servers and cut off our access to the outside for security reasons. This is the first time they've let us make a call, but they're listening in. Have you been able to access my computer? Anything there? Be safe, Ana. Take good care of yourself."

As soon as she finished listening, she called him again. But again his phone was shut off or out of range. The voice mail came on.

"Joan, where are you? I've been calling you for hours." Ana was whispering into the phone so no one could hear, but even so it was probably clear how angry and nervous she was. She realized she was on the edge of tears. "Call me whenever you get the chance. Even if it's the middle of the night, I don't care. It's urgent."

She hung up. But she called again.

"Please," she said the second time. "Please."

It wasn't until several minutes later, just when her brain was again able to focus on the reality of things, that she realized she had three missed calls from Charo. She went up to their unit to find her.

"Where were you? I've been calling for half an hour. Look at this. You won't believe it," Charo said, pointing at the computer. "We've been wrong from the get-go. All this time."

When Charo hit play and Ana saw what had been recorded by the security camera, her hands flew to her head. She had to watch the images three more times to believe what she was seeing.

Click. Click. Click. One part of the puzzle began to fit together.

She looked at her watch. If she hurried, she could still get to the funeral. Although she wasn't sure she could handle telling Inés what had happened to her son.

46

INÉS

"Come back in a few hours, after lunch," the man at the mortuary said to us, in the same tone that might be used to ask restaurant customers to wait at the bar until their table was ready.

Even now, when I try to remember something about the funeral, all I see is Pablo's coffin disappearing into a hole in the floor, toward the cremation oven, in a sequence where I can't hear any sound at all, as if it had been recorded without audio in my brain. Or as if it had happened in complete silence.

And then, always, I hear a voice. *Come back in a few hours, after lunch.* That's all I can hear of what happened that morning. The only sound my memory plays back. A voice telling me when my son's ashes will be ready for us to pick them up.

Just that one voice.

Until Ana came.

Because what happened after that, yes, keeps echoing in my mind. Even now, after so long, I remember the moment and hear those steps behind me again. The steps of some feet that aren't lifting very high off the ground, that even drag sometimes as they approach, as if they had to support the weight of a very heavy conscience. Sometimes they make the gravel crunch. And sometimes they make it pant.

That was Ana. Just as we were leaving the building where they'd incinerated Pablo. And with her came sounds—thunderous and deafening—that I'll always remember.

"Inés."

She hugged me tightly, but I had the sensation that she was the one trembling, not me. I could hear her joints creak under the layers of living tissue around them, with a squeaky sound that drilled into my nerves.

"Inés, I'm so sorry. I'm so sorry."

"Thank you."

She didn't know what to say to me. What could she say, when she should have saved my son? That was her job. Her fucking rotten job that she hadn't been able to do.

"I'm here to tell you something."

I'd spent two days gone, crazy, out of it, as if someone had taken my body to the death zone, over eight thousand meters up, where our cells start to die for lack of oxygen. But instead of running back down, I kept climbing toward the summit of Everest. Mountain climbers say you have to get out of there within forty-eight hours, because otherwise the process is irreversible, and your body won't recover. You'll die. But I'd gone over the limit, and I was still alive. Curse my luck. For some perverse reason, my body refused to succumb.

And for the same reason, I had found enough energy to listen and remember a name. Nori. It was Nori, someone told me. Or someone told someone else, and I heard it. But I couldn't even react. I felt so much emptiness and pain that the arrest of my friend didn't find a place to lodge. It was a name that came and went.

"I came to tell you what happened to Pablo."

We had sat down on a bench in the sun. I was listening to her with my eyes closed. I could hear my mother and Willie and Sam moving away, maybe because Ana had given them some sign to leave us in peace. I knew what she was going to tell me, but I still kept quiet to let her say it. For her to make the effort. *Nori killed Pablo.* Let her tell me that. Let her have the balls to say it out loud.

But no. That's not what she came to tell me.

That wasn't it. And, in spite of everything, she had the courage to come and tell me in person, even knowing that after that confession, nothing would ever be the same. We'd never be able to be friends because every time I saw her—every goddamn fucking time I saw her—I'd remember that moment. Her face, her hands, her voice—every subatomic particle of her body—would be irremediably associated forever with that terrible news. Until that moment, I had thought that nothing could hurt me more than the death of my son. Never. Nothing. Nothing in my life. Nothing even in death.

But I was wrong.

"Why did you go to the mall with Pablo that day?"

"I don't know." That was true. "I don't remember."

"You told me you argued with him before you went out, right?"

Why did she have to remind me of that? Why did she have to remind me that one of the last things I did with Pablo was scold him and make him cry? I struggled to hold back the tears. Yes, we argued. Pablo was in a bad mood. That morning, we'd had a fight at home because he'd been throwing his toys on the floor, and then he broke one, and to punish him I pretended I would throw his stuffed animal, the cow he took to bed with him every night, in the trash. "Your cow's going in the garbage," I said. "I'm throwing it in with all the dirty things because your behavior has been so bad."

"Inés, listen to me. It wasn't your fault. Please, don't blame yourself. It wasn't your fault."

I knew that already. Even in the middle of all the pain, I knew my son's death wasn't my fault. I knew that some depraved person had taken him from me. But I was wrong.

Ana shifted closer, almost touching me. She reached out to take my face in her hands. I felt a shock running through my marrow.

"Nobody kidnapped your son. We think it was an accident. He went home by himself. Several security cameras recorded him."

Pablo could be seen walking calmly but with determination, Ana told me, although I wasn't listening to her, all I was hearing was noise. It took him twelve and a half minutes to get from the mall to our building. The lobby door was open, and he went in. For thirty seconds, no camera caught his steps. Then he reappeared, down a flight of steps, in front of the entrance to the underground garage that served all the units.

"We think he went over to the garbage chute and opened the door to try to get his stuffed animal back. He thought you had really thrown it away. He must have climbed up somehow to see better. He reached out his arm, stuck in half his body, and fell. It was an accident. An accident, Inés. An accident. I'm sorry. I'm sorry. I'm sorry."

I suppose I must have started to cry. But I don't remember that.

Just as Ana was telling me what had happened to my son, Chief Inspector Silvelo finished watching the images on the security cameras. He went to inform the commander.

"It was an accident. A damned terrible accident."

Ruipérez stared back at him with the expression of a fat, slimy toad; he adopted this look whenever a situation got away from him. It tried to express superiority, even contempt, but it really meant, *Go on talking because I don't have any idea what I'm supposed to say or do.*

"This changes things, Commander."

"This doesn't change anything, Inspector," Ruipérez said at last. "For the moment, none of this should come to public notice. Who else knows about it?"

"Nobody else," Silvelo lied. "Just the detective who saw the images, Ana, and me."

"Well, it better stay that way. We'll decide when we want to make it public."

Just as he left the office, Silvelo got a call. It was Pedro, the director of the lab. He was looking for Ana, but he couldn't find her.

"She's not here. She's with the family of one of the kids. Can I help you?"

"Yes, please. Come by when you can. We've got a match."

As soon as Silvelo got to the lab, Pedro showed it to him—a fingerprint.

"Sorry, but I don't understand."

"We've found several good prints in the house where the two boys were discovered."

Prints from the crime scene felt like a break; however, he reminded the scientist about the fundamental problem of how to show that they were recent. Any good defense attorney would toss this evidence right out: *My client was there long before the boys disappeared, so you can't convict him of anything. Goodbye.*

What was needed was to situate those prints in the period of time during which the boys were there. That was the only way to demonstrate the guilt of whomever the prints belonged to.

Pedro remembered having read something about a new technique for dating prints. He went searching among the piles of scientific journals under his desk and found the article. Two researchers from the National Institute of Standards and Technology of the United States had been working on the use of palmitic acid. They found that this acid, present in fingertips, degrades at a constant rate. Therefore, it was possible to know when a given print was left on a surface.

"And presto!" he said. "All you need is a mass spectrometer, and you can determine the age of the print. It's like carbon 14 but for fingerprints. As you can imagine, here"—he pointed around the police lab with a resigned expression—"we don't have any such thing. A mass spectrometer? Ha. That'll be the day. So what I had to do was ask for a favor. Outside the police force, of course. A friend at a private lab analyzed the sample. You can thank the butterscotch croissants." Silvelo looked at him blankly. "So voilà."

"So?" Silvelo echoed.

"What do you mean, 'So'? This is the first time this technique has been used in Spain. And one of the first times in the world, I might add." The lab director failed to mention—and this was an important nuance—that so far, no judge had accepted this kind of analysis as evidence. "This technique will revolutionize forensic science. Up till now, fingerprints put an individual at the scene of a crime, but not in the moment of the crime. Now we can show that the suspect was there right when the crime took place. It's almost a miracle," he said, his excitement evident. "Don't you see?"

Yes. He saw. But he wanted the results. He was tired of waiting. But the man was incorrigible. And you had to have patience and wait for him to work through his reasoning. If you cut him off, he might never tell you.

"So onward." Here it came at last. "It turns out that one of the prints we found next to the boys was left the same day those teenagers spotted the bodies. So it has to be the kidnapper."

"Bingo!" At last some good news.

"And there's more. I've got another little present for you. I ran the print through the CODIS, and there's a match. Here it is. Let me introduce you to The Taker."

47

RICHI

That day it was sunny, so Richi was content. He liked the sun. It was warm and made him happy.

When it was sunny, his father let him out of the house, and he could go take care of his treasure. When it was cloudy, he had to stay inside. The clouds were not his friends. Richi got nervous when there were clouds in the sky. They made him feel bad. They hurt.

He checked the hands. One, two, three, four, five. Five fingers on the right hand. Five fingers on the left. Everything was still okay. He just had to be careful not to squeeze them very hard. Because sometimes that happened. If you squeezed too hard, things broke. The first time someone told him he was a killer—and that was the first thing he remembered in his life, his first conscious memory as a human being—Richi had just broken his sister's doll. And she screamed and screamed, "Murderer, murderer, murderer," until the sun went away and the clouds came out; then it was Richi who screamed and screamed and screamed.

"Broken dolls can be fixed," his mother had said that day while she rocked him back and forth in her arms. But "Murderer, you're a murderer," his sister would still say when nobody else could hear. The word stuck in Richi's brain. *Murderer.*

Broken dolls can be fixed. But a broken bird can't. That was the first time Richi had blood on his hands. The bird was so pretty that Richi wanted to love it a lot. He loved it so much that it exploded in his hand. He went running to tell Mama, with the blood dripping down his forearm. "Mama, Mama, fix the bird. It broke, Mama. Fix it, please."

"Don't cry, we can fix it."

"Really, Mama, really?"

A broken bird can't be fixed, though he believed then that it could. "I'll fix it, honey, of course I will, but we have to take it away, to the bird hospital, for it to get well, because here we don't have any special Band-Aids for birds. Understand, Ricardo? Tell it goodbye, and later I'll take it to the hospital to be cured."

"See, I'm not a murderer," he told his sister some days later, when she called him that ugly word again. "I'm not a murderer. Mama saved the bird. It's in the bird hospital. So don't call me that. I don't like it."

But the hamster couldn't be fixed. However much Richi cried and begged his mother. There was no hospital for hamsters. "Why not? Why not? Why not? Take it to the bird hospital, Mama, take it to the bird hospital. They know how to cure it with the magic Band-Aids." And his mother just cried and said no, it couldn't be done, a broken hamster couldn't be fixed.

Just like the sun couldn't. The clouds came to stay for a long, long time in Richi's head.

Murderer.

48

ANA

"Ricardo Vera. Thirty-five. No known occupation. Lives with his father."

"Very close to where they found the two boys."

Finally, some good news. They had caught The Taker. It seemed that they had caught The Taker.

"I've sent some officers to watch the house. The suspect is inside," Silvelo went on.

"Should we give the arrest order now? I don't want to risk losing more time. The sooner we get a confession out of him, the sooner they'll let Nori go."

"So let's do it."

Chief Inspector Jesús Silvelo picked up the phone and ordered the arrest of the man whose print had been found. Within an hour, he got word that the suspect was in the interrogation room.

"Hello, Ricardo. Have you been treated well? Would you like something to drink?"

"A little water, please."

Nobody had taken off his handcuffs, but they weren't chained to the metal anchor on the table, which would have restricted all his movements. He seemed calm and relaxed, as if a weight had been lifted from him. Ana sat across the table, facing him. Silvelo remained standing behind her. If necessary, they could play good cop, bad cop.

"Do you know why you're here?" Ana asked.

"Yes, because of the boys in the house."

"You knew they were there?" Jesús leaned in, intensely looking him in the eyes.

"I took care of them."

"How did you take care of them?" Ana asked.

"I cleaned them. I gave them food and played with them."

"What did you play?"

Ricardo looked like he didn't understand the question. Play? What could you play? Lots of things.

"Did you play touching? Did you touch them?"

Once again, silence. And that look of not comprehending what was going on.

"Did they make you excited, Ricardo?" Silvelo demanded. "Did you get aroused around them? You don't get hard except with little boys, right?"

"They're just my friends. I like to have friends."

"I know, Ricardo," Ana intervened. "I know you need friends. How did you do it? How did you get them to be your friends?"

Ricardo told them that very early one morning a long time ago, he couldn't say exactly when, he found Nicolás leaning against one of the gates to the Pilar Woods. He seemed like a doll. Ricardo brought him to the house so nobody would take him away. "They always take things away from me," he said. "They always take away all my friends." He worked for days cleaning up the kitchen and the basement under the trap door. He went to see his friend almost every day. Sometimes he would escape at night, too, like the night Patricia and her boyfriend found him. For almost two years he had taken care of his friend there.

And the sweater? The sweater he was wearing?

Ana was talking about the sweater that had been on the corpse, the wool sweater holding the hair that pointed toward Nori as a suspect, the sweater Nicolás hadn't been wearing when he disappeared. Ricardo told them he'd found him dressed like that. All he did was wipe the clothes with a towel, once in a while, to clean them up. And cover the boy up with a blanket at night so he wouldn't get cold.

Charo opened the door. "Inspectors, could you come here a moment?"

"Tell us." The three officers were now standing in the middle of the hall, talking in low voices.

"I sent Barriga to the hospital with a photo of the suspect. Manu recognized him. It's the man who took him from the mall."

Instead of going back into the interrogation room, Ana Arén ran to the other end of the hall. She went up the stairs, two at a time, and into the commander's office, without knocking.

"We've got him. Javier Nori's innocent. We can let him go."

Jesús Silvelo came in behind her, also at a run, worried about what Ana might do.

"That you two want a corrupt homicidal policeman, who happens to be your friend, to be found innocent is one thing, but—"

"Commander!" Ana yelled. "Commander, with all due respect," she said, tempering the volume of her voice, "we have a confession from a suspect, we've got his prints at the scene of the crime, and we've got a survivor who has made a positive identification from a photograph. What more do you want?"

"An explanation for the sub-inspector's hair on the sweater."

"Contamination, it has to be," Ana said, even though she knew Nori hadn't had any kind of contact with the crime scene or the corpse.

"You know something, Chief Inspector?" The commander stood and came around the immense desk without taking his eyes off her. "You think you're so smart. Do you believe I would have put the Minister in front of the cameras if all I had was a piece of evidence that the defense

could reject on the grounds of possible contamination? Lookee, lookee."
He waved a sheet of paper at her.

The commander had ordered a forensic test that Ana didn't know
about. She glanced at Silvelo, who shook his head. He didn't know any
more than she did. Fucking Ruipérez had also kept him in the dark. It
turned out that as soon as Nori was arrested, Ruipérez had ordered a
hair sample taken from the sub-inspector and sent it for processing in an
external lab so there wouldn't be any leaks. He had asked for a compari-
son of Javier Nori's hair with the hair that had been found at the crime
scene. The DNA analysis showed that they were from the same person,
no doubt, but the layers didn't coincide. The layer from the sweater was
much older. Perhaps from the time when Nicolás disappeared.

"See? Here it is." Ruipérez pointed to a graph on the paper.

Yes, there it was. Irrefutable scientific evidence. Two of Nori's hairs,
one current and one from at least six months earlier. Ana had to admit
that maybe her sub had some kind of relation to The Taker. To Ricardo
Vera, the man they had just arrested. She still hadn't gotten used to
that. *Ricardo Vera. Ricardo Vera,* she had to repeat to herself. Now they
had him. Yes, it was true: they had him. They had caught The Taker,
whom she'd spent two years searching for. At last, he had a face and a
name. But Ana didn't feel that indescribable high, the *eureka!* feeling
that opens your body at its seams out of pure joy. The *there it is* moment
that can make you cry out of relief from the stress and accumulated
emotions. Something didn't fit. Inside. The pieces of the puzzle still
hadn't gone *click* inside Ana's head.

She went back to the interrogation room.

"Ricardo, what about Manu? The other boy who was with Nicolás.
How did Manu get there?"

"I wanted a friend for Nicolás so he wouldn't be alone at night."

As simple as that. He went to the closest place where he could find
children—the mall. He saw Manu from the hallway with the emergency
exit, waved to him, and out they went hand in hand. "Do you like *Paw*

Patrol too? And Superman?" he asked the boy. And they went on talking about cartoons until they got to the house.

Then Manu started to complain. He wanted to leave. He wanted to go back to his mother. It was nighttime, and Ricardo had to go home, so he gave Manu one of the anxiety pills that the doctor had been making him take for years. Ricardo gave the boy pills every day so he wouldn't scream, so he'd spend hours half-asleep. But one night, there were noises above, and Ricardo was afraid he'd be caught. So he took off running. That was his mistake.

That was the end of the questioning, because Ricardo's father appeared with a lawyer. "Any questions you have for my client," the attorney told them, "must be asked in my presence. But first, I need to talk with him. Alone. That will take a while, I can assure you."

Ana slumped in her office chair in a state of complete desolation. The building was practically empty, almost all the lights out and hardly any noise. The suspect had confessed to taking Manu, and they had sufficient forensic proof. But what had happened with Nicolás? Who had left him just outside the Woods? Was he alive or dead when Ricardo found him? And why was one of Nori's old hairs found on the corpse? Ana hoped the next day's interrogation would dispel all her doubts.

In the meantime, her head was about to explode. She reached into her purse in search of ibuprofen. But her hand found something much bigger. Her laptop. With all the craziness, she'd forgotten that she was carrying it around in her purse.

She opened the computer and read Joan's instructions about deciphering the results. "You're going to find two curves," he'd written, "one green and one red. The green one measures the level of nervousness of the person, and the red measures the level of excitement, likely arousal. All you have to do is look for peaks that register more than 20 percent and determine whether those peaks coincide with the dates you're interested in—when the boys were kidnapped."

When she clicked on the tab that held the results, nothing was evident at first. There were a ton of superimposed lines. She didn't understand anything. Then she remembered the mistake she'd made when dumping in the data, bringing over not just Nori's records but also those of all the friends Joan was monitoring. The program had processed three years of keyboarding patterns of twenty-some people.

Nonetheless, when she enlarged the parts of the graphs for the dates that interested her, she could see clearly. There they were. Among the spiderweb of lines, two of them, one green and one red, stood out above the rest. They shot up precisely on two dates. Nori? It couldn't be. She made herself look.

And suddenly, she saw. There it was. Clear as day. Incontrovertible.

It was a shock she didn't expect. Not exactly a punch in the gut or a stab in the back. Not the way you expect to feel when the discovery is going to shake your life from top to bottom. This was something subtler, something that at first didn't hurt because it was simply impossible. In fact, she didn't even feel the pain until she was already cut wide open, bleeding.

Ana grabbed hold of the edge of the desk.

"What have you done, what have you done, what have you done?" she whispered, before her mind went dark. "What have you done?"

Then what exploded in her was a rage so great she couldn't let it out. It just stayed there, knotted in the pit of her stomach, pulling her down. Spitting bile.

When she recovered, she felt she'd woken from a nightmare, that it had only been a bad dream. But the evidence remained in front of her. Right there on her computer screen.

And then, in her head, a thought that had been lurking in some neuron—crouching, waiting—popped out, as if by miracle. Jumping the synapse, this thought began linking one memory to another, tying together forgotten ideas, and erasing those she'd been holding on to until that moment.

It all fit.

Chief Inspector Ana Arén's brain went *click*. At last, it went *click*.

Shaking, she managed to reach for her phone.

Please, please, please. Please answer. Please.

And yes, he answered. For the first time in several days, she didn't get his voice mail.

"Hi, we're finally done. I was just about to call," he said. But all he heard was hysterical crying. "Ana? Ana? What's the matter? Are you okay?"

"I, I . . . she," Ana stammered. Her sobs wouldn't let her go on.

"Ana, for God's sake, settle down. Settle down and tell me what's wrong. Ana, answer me. Should I call someone? Do you need help?"

"It was her," she managed to say.

"What 'her'? Who? Please, Ana, tell me what this is about."

Joan knew they were being listened to. Someone was spying on their call. Someone who would write an urgent report and send it to a higher-up who would decide whether the report needed to continue up the chain. But he didn't care. Let them listen. Let them find out. Let them interfere. Whatever. All he wanted was to get out of there and help Ana. Right then, he wanted to jump every physical and temporal barrier that separated him from her. To be there, in Madrid, and not pacing outside of a high-security bunker, no idea where he was.

"It was her. All this time, it was her. Please, Joan, come. Please, I can't stand it. She's the murderer. There is no Taker. Come. Come."

As soon as she hung up, Ana's phone received a message. From Pedro, the lab director. "There are no matches for the evidence you gave me. Unidentified DNA. But I found something much worse. I know whom the female hair we found in the boy's sweater belongs to. To try something out, I cross-checked it with other databases in the system, restricted ones. And I got a positive. A positive with one of the relatives of one of the kids. Call me before I have to tell Ruipérez about this."

49

INÉS

I'm a reporter. I know how to tell stories. I know how to tell stories very well. I have a special ability—I won't call it an art—for taking a story and turning it into something that keeps viewers glued to the screen.

But by the same token, I don't know how to invent things. Because I always have the stories at hand, in the world. I've gotten used to taking reality and making it pretty. No, on second thought, that's not exactly right, because the life we journalists report on is not a pretty one. Maybe I should say "make it interesting." Or striking. Or easy to digest. The point is that the news story has to interest the public. It has to make them want more.

As they do with anyone halfway famous, the publishing houses started to get after me. Years ago. *Write, write, write.* "We'll give you the plot. We'll give you all the ideas you want," they said. "We'll give you an editor to help." I know—what's the point in fooling oneself?—that they weren't after me because I was good at telling stories, but because they wanted to take advantage of the name recognition that television provides. To sell more books, of course. The literary market is screwed up in that way, and if you're famous, you sell more. It doesn't matter what you write.

So television gave me a certain advantage. Fame. It would be easier to promote the book, but would I know how to write it? They had no doubts. I had plenty. In television, we write for the ear. Our texts are often fragments of sentences that make sense only when you say them out loud with the right tone and intention. But a book is written to be read silently, and its words make sounds only in the reader's mind. Could I do that?

I had one other advantage, besides fame. I was used to connecting with an audience. Maybe I knew how to do that through paper too.

What I needed to do was keep on telling stories with which readers would identify. Give them pain to share and fear they could feel running up and down their spines. A way for readers, like viewers, to feel lucky that what they were seeing hadn't happened to them.

To feel relieved.

But to tell those kinds of stories, I've always needed for them to have actually happened. I need a thread to follow, I need reality, and I need some characters with a story.

And the publishers kept on chasing me without understanding. I don't know how to make up a story. *I don't know,* I told them. *I don't know.*

Until Albert started planting bombs.

Really, until we *discovered* that Albert had started planting bombs.

The first one exploded on a nearly inaccessible beach, at night. It was practically just a firecracker, a bluff of a bomb, something two kids could learn to make by watching YouTube. It got barely ten seconds on the national news, but in the local dailies, it was front-page news for a week. The two leading papers competed day after day for another detail, another clue, another suspect. Something more to sell their readers about the bomb on the beach that had turned the area upside down.

Little by little, interest declined. It was just a tiny bomb, nobody had been hurt, and there was nothing more to find out. All the details had been told, and even the most enthusiastic readers got tired of the topic. The papers moved on to something else. A strange kind of snail had colonized part of the rice fields of the Delta. This became the next journalistic fascination of the summer.

The province had a couple of peaceful weeks. Then came the second bomb. This one also went off at night, but on a cliff near a campground, so a lot of people heard it. The bomber, or bombers, had improved their work. This one was a much better imitation of the real thing. The bombers had gotten more daring.

What exploded next to the campground was not a firecracker but a fusillade. The national networks sent their mobile units, and the event provided stories for several days. But that was it. There were no clues to follow up on, no demands put forward by any group, no bad news with which to prolong the coverage. The end. Again the local media followed the story longer, especially the regional paper *La Terra Avui*, which had a very good source in the police and surprised its readers every day with some previously unknown factoid.

But that story also died after a while.

Until the next bombing. Because the third was a true bomb. It went off in broad daylight next to a very busy highway. The police said that whoever had planted it—nobody dared use the term *terrorist*—wanted visibility but wasn't trying to harm anyone.

The bomb had been placed fifty meters from the expressway, on the slope of a highway cut—a piece of land that didn't lead anywhere, one of those places that simply die off, between two worlds, when a six-lane expressway goes through and isolates them. The explosion massacred a couple of ant colonies and killed some vegetation. It also sent a good part of the hill flying into the sky. We thought perhaps the bomber was perfecting his technique. We never guessed that he was growing more daring because more visibility was what he was after.

By a stroke of bad luck, at the time of the explosion, a Russian couple who had recently moved to the realm of the Spanish sun were driving by in their new car. The first thing they'd done to the vehicle—a

Mercedes customized to the taste of the nouveau riche owners—was install a camera in front and another on each side to record everything that happened around the car from the moment the ignition went on. These cameras had become fashionable in Russia because insurance fraud was so common that almost no company would deal with any damage to a vehicle unless there was footage to show someone else was at fault.

So there were the Russians, speeding along the AP-7 in their Mercedes, when the third bomb exploded. And there were the cameras, filming the exact moment when half of the highway cut flew through the air, in living color and high definition. Producers went ape over the images, a true gift from God. Boom! There was no sound—the camera only captured video—but the sight was striking enough that you barely noticed the silence. To cap it off, the camera pointing toward the rear caught the chain reaction produced after the explosion: seventy-three cars tumbling like dominoes. It was impossible to account for the lack of serious injuries.

But the definitive success of the third bombing came via social media. That stretch of the AP-7 found its way into catastrophe tourism guides. Thousands of people per day stopped in the beachside bar that had the best views of the site, and they all took selfies to post on their Twitter and Facebook pages. The "Unabomber of Tarragona" now had his trending topic and fifteen minutes of fame, to the benefit of the international television companies.

But the real bomb, one none of us were expecting, went off three days after the last explosion.

It had never occurred to us to suspect that Albert was the one planting those bombs. And we wouldn't have believed it if the Mossos hadn't caught him red-handed, in the act of placing the fourth bomb on the pier in the port of Salou. He was arrested in full view of hundreds of tourists and their cell phones.

What had made the Mossos suspicious, we later learned, was Albert's ambition. He was a young reporter for *La Terra Avui*. At first, he'd managed to make it seem like someone was leaking him information about the bombs, how they were placed, and how they were made. And thanks to this stellar source, Albert managed to unearth more details about the Unabomber than any other reporter on the story. This initially aroused no suspicion, because who's going to be skeptical of a well-informed journalist? But Albert hadn't been on the paper very long, and it was hard to see how, within a few months, he could have snagged a source who knew so much and would risk so much to tell it.

If he'd been careful, maybe he could have gotten away with it. But in the Judicial Police of Catalunya, a bulb lit up in someone's head. "What if the guy knows so much because he's in contact with the person setting off the bombs?" They set up a surveillance operation, and within a few days, they caught him with a bomb that, this time, might have killed someone.

Why did he do it? For a headline. For a scoop. To tell something other reporters didn't know. Not only to leave the public in awe but to do the same to his rivals. At first, he wanted to impress those who competed with him for space in the paper—because more space equaled more importance. Later he couldn't resist the lure of being praised and envied by reporters from other media outlets. What had started as an innocent firecracker on a beach evolved into an addiction. He couldn't stop. Like a drug addict, Albert needed more each time. More scoops. More front pages. More renown.

He was sentenced to seventeen years in prison.

So, I thought, if a reporter placed bombs to get scoops, why couldn't I create my own story to write a book?

But, what story would that be?

50

INÉS

I was a specialist in human suffering. Don't misinterpret that. I knew how to report human suffering very well, and to tell it to evoke pity and relief. Pity for those who suffered. Relief because it wasn't happening to the viewer.

I had that special ability to find just the right words to convey the exact level of anguish to touch my viewers' hearts. Not so dramatic as to drive them away, nor so gentle as to fail to catch their attention.

But one day, I got blocked. It happened a few months after Albert's arrest.

A four-year-old boy had been lost in the woods. His parents were spending the weekend at a country house with friends. They tuned out for a minute, and Carlos disappeared. At first, they weren't too worried. *He must be around here somewhere.* That's what all parents think. Your heart rises in your throat, but your reasoning forces it back down. But you do another search around the house, and the child's still missing. You and your friends all start calling his name. You venture out, calling for him, moving farther and farther from the house that, in a cursed moment, you had found on the internet—so solitary and ideal for a weekend retreat with your friends, all couples with children, just like you.

I got there at ten at night, three hours after Carlos had gone missing and just before the police closed off the road to keep the media and curiosity seekers out. I spent the whole night with the parents and the other families. I took part in the search operation and made hot soup for the volunteers. Since they knew me from TV, the parents grabbed hold of me like I was a magic life preserver, someone who could miraculously make their son reappear.

Maybe it was exhaustion or . . . I don't know. I don't know how to explain what happened. But when, the next day, they set up a feed to the studio, I told the story like I was reporting about something mundane, like the price of butane canisters going up five cents. I couldn't put any emotion into it. I couldn't get through the screen to reach the viewers. I didn't know how to evoke what was happening to this child alone in the woods—the intensity of his fear or the cuts the brush was carving into his skin.

My boss called me, practically screaming. "What the hell's going on with you? Have you seen the shit you put out on the feed? It's the big story of the day, and you're lost in some cloud. It's a missing child, for Christ's sake. There's no better drama than that. It's your bread and butter, the kind of story that lets you shine. I'm not talking about reporting facts. I've got plenty of reporters around here who can do that. You're special because you know how to transmit the pain so the viewers feel like something is breathing down their necks. Start your engines, Inés, start your engines!"

And that's how it all began. There, in that argument with my boss, was the beginning of what really matters to *this* story.

That's where Nicolás's death began.

Because I needed Nicolás to save me.

As you all know by now, I found him in a shopping mall. You've heard a thousand times how he let go of his mother's hand and headed for the Peppa Pig rocket ship located on the ground floor. In a monumental oversight on the part of mall security, that juvenile attraction was situated in a dead zone with respect to the mall's security cameras, right next to one of the maintenance doors used by service personnel to get in and out of the bowels of the building. That's where you lost sight of him. And you didn't know any more about him until his corpse appeared a few days ago.

It wasn't easy for me to choose. Not just any child would do. It had to be a very careful choice. If not, so many months of waiting, so much work, and so much thinking and rethinking of the plan wouldn't be worth a damn.

I spent several afternoons staked out, watching. None of the children who went by seemed quite right. Those in the proper age range, between four and five, were all too dependent, too clingy with their parents. I couldn't use a child who wouldn't stop crying, who would curl up on the ground in fear. I needed action.

I was looking for a boy. With shoelaces. Shoes with laces meant old enough, independent, wanting to do things on his own. Shoes with Velcro closures meant the boy was still too little and wouldn't fit my plan.

I saw some with a lot of potential, but none of them were tuned out enough, neither them nor their parents, for me to be able to grab them. Until Nicolás appeared.

This one's different, I thought, *so take a good look.* His clothes say he's old enough. Not very tall, but he must be at least four, maybe five. Look at how he moves. Lively, intelligent.

And look—he just let go of his mother's hand. What did he see? What caught his attention?

So I thought this was my lucky day. I was afraid, of course, very much. This was the point of no return. But I knew Nicolás was perfect. I felt a spark. I knew if I didn't go for him, it would take me a long time to find another one.

That boy was going to be my salvation.

The game began.

This time, for real.

How did I do it? Easy. I'm sure at one time or another you've gotten those alerts on WhatsApp or Facebook that say that in such and such a mall they've caught a pedophile putting a wig and a dress on a boy in the bathroom to sneak him out, without raising suspicion, and luckily, because they closed all the exits, they caught the kidnapper in time. We always laugh. *Rumors. False alarms. Don't pay attention,* the police say over Twitter. Don't be afraid. Take precautions, yes, but there's nothing to fear.

But that's how I did it. There's no better way to hide something than in plain sight, right? I showed Nicolás a coin to tempt him over to the rocket. The door for getting into the ride was angled toward the wall, so if he came close enough I could push him into the service area. Then I put him to sleep with half an Orfidal under his tongue. I put a blond wig and a dress on him and lifted him onto a folding stroller. I took him out through the workers' area, behind the bathrooms, where there aren't any cameras. Nobody paid any attention, but I'd put on a wig, too, and blue-tinted shades, and loose clothes with stuffing in case anyone gave my description or any camera spotted me.

What did I want Nicolás for?

So I could write my book.

Nicolás was going to be the hero. I wanted to tell the story of a boy who gets lost in the woods and spends a few days alone outdoors. How would he act? How would he feel? What would he eat? Where would he sleep? What would he call out? When would he start crying? They say kids are natural survivors, because they're closer to our animal selves than adults. That's why I needed to watch what Nicolás did. To be able to write about it later.

I set him loose in the Pilar Woods, taking advantage of the month it was closed to the public because of a plague of caterpillars that threatened to wipe out those eight hundred hectares of pines. The authorities weren't sure whether humans helped spread the infestation, so they had closed off the Woods. Nobody could get in or out. And nobody did, because the authorities circulated a rumor that the caterpillars were poisonous. That assured me of complete privacy.

My idea was to watch Nicolás for three or four days. I would leave food and water beside him while he slept, so he wouldn't get too weak.

What did you think? That I invented *A Dense Wood* out of whole cloth? The book that broke sales records in Spain was, in fact, the story of how Nicolás survived those days in the forest, but when it was published . . . well, as you know, everybody thought it was based on Carlos, the little boy who'd spent twenty-four hours lost in the woods of the Sierra de Madrid months before.

I watched Nicolás with a drone, which allowed me to follow him and record all his reactions. I, too, lived in the Woods for those three days and nights. I brought a sleeping bag and provisions and set myself up in a tent in the middle of the forest. Each night, before erasing the images, I watched them, taking notes on the boy's every move.

At some point I had doubts, of course. When he cried or said he was afraid or called desperately for his parents. But you've got all that from the book. Half of Spain has read how Nicolás lived during those days.

How did a strand of Nori's hair get on the sweater found on the corpse? I think I can clear this question up too.

As for the sweater, I put it on him when I removed the wig and the dress, when I first left him in the woods. I didn't want him to get too cold at night.

As for the hair, there's one other part of the story I have to tell. The day I decided to take Nicolás back because I had enough material for the book, I didn't want to run any risks. I waited for night, put on a mask, and while he was asleep, I opened his mouth and slid three sleeping pills under his tongue. Then I carried him to the nearest gate, so I could take him in my car to the other side of the Woods, where it would be credible that he'd gotten lost by himself. I wanted to leave him next to a stretch of the fence with houses, so he'd be found at first light.

But as soon as I put him in the trunk, who should appear but Nori? Nori, with his damned obsession about going running as soon as he got off work, no matter the hour. He came along the path parallel to the fence around the Woods. I couldn't hide. Luckily I saw him before he saw me, so I had an advantage. I leaned against the fence and started crying with my head in my hands. I could hear him slowing down. He stopped in front of me.

"Señora, is something wrong?" I looked up. You should have seen his face. Like Our Lady of Sorrows and half a dozen heavenly angels had appeared. With wings and all. "Inés? What are you doing here? What's wrong?" he said, shyly reaching out his hand.

I kept on crying while I tried to think something up. I threw my arms around him to keep him from asking any more questions. He was a policeman, so I was worried he was going to figure it out. But my tears weren't completely feigned. There, in his arms, I cried out all my accumulated remorse for having inflicted what I did on a little boy. Until then, I wasn't truly aware of what I had done.

"I'm so lonely without Pablo," I ended up telling him. "So lonely I can't sleep. I go out walking, and I get so sad."

This was when Pablo was spending the summer at his father's house in the United States. It was the first time I'd been separated from him, so I thought my excuse would be believable. I started to tremble. From fear, from cold, from remorse.

"Is this your car?" he asked.

I thought he was accusing me, that he'd heard something in the trunk. *Shit. If we're so close to my house, why did I bring the car? Think, come on, think.*

"Driving relaxes me," I said, and sobbed. "I wanted go into the Woods through the Pozuelo gate, but as soon as I left the garage, I remembered." I was still sobbing. "The Woods are closed at night. So I left the car here and started walking along this path."

"Come on, let's get you in the car so you can warm up. It's cold out."

That was true. It was June, but the temperature had dropped a lot.

"No really, it's okay. I don't need to get in the car." Not with Nicolás in the trunk. He was completely sedated, but I still didn't want to take the risk.

So I kissed Nori. I swear I didn't know what else to do. So I kissed him. Next thing, we were having sex against the trunk of the car with the boy inside. Nicolás was only a few centimeters away. My god. You can't imagine the rush. It was the best fuck I ever had. All the tension and nerves and fear channeled into an orgasm of explosive proportions.

We never talked about it again.

When I was sure Nori was gone, I started the car and returned to my plan, even as my body trembled with fear and pleasure. Then, when I took the boy out of the trunk, that's when I must have accidentally transferred Nori's hair. I left Nicolás on the opposite side of the Woods, several kilometers away, still expecting someone to find him the next morning. I don't know whether he died that night. Maybe I fed him too many sleeping pills, given how weak he was after three days alone in the Woods. The truth is, I don't know. When I left him, he was alive.

I waited for days for someone to say something. I studied every teletype and every tweet. I searched on Google. And nothing. No news about a child found by the Woods. I despaired.

The man you arrested must have found him, that Ricardo, who seems to have psychological problems. I don't know what kind of madness led him to take the boy to the abandoned house, where he kept him all that time, and then kidnap Manu to keep his friend company.

Not a second goes by when I don't think about what I've done.

It was an accident. I didn't mean to kill that child. I just wanted to tell a story.

Don't look at me like that. I, too, have lost a son.

I'm not a monster.

EDITOR'S NOTE

Inés Grau wrote this book in prison while awaiting trial for the kidnapping and death of Nicolás Acosta. It has broken all records, with more than a million copies sold in Spain and twelve million abroad. A leading Hollywood director has bought the rights to bring the story to the big screen.

Inés is currently working on a third novel about her experiences in jail.

ACKNOWLEDGMENTS

In making Ana Arén a believable chief inspector in the National Police Corps, I had the help of three good friends—three great officers in love with their profession—who generously shared what they have lived and learned in all their years of service. Esther, Charini, and Juan have been my personal police unit, ready to answer all my questions as the novel unfolded. What division should Ana Arén be part of, if she's to be in charge of investigating the disappearances of children? Is she a chief inspector or inspector-in-chief? Where does the clothing of a murder victim go during an autopsy? What does a corpse smell like? How long does it take for worms to emerge from a body?

Berna, my husband, was my first reader, loyally and critically reading as I wrote. When I sent him the last part (for I had never told him how the story ended, so as not to ruin the suspense) he was away on a trip. He stayed up all night reading it. I'll never forget the message he sent me when he finished: "I'm proud of you."

África Silvelo and her husband, Javier Rodríguez Lázaro, were my test readers for certain parts of the story. I was worried about my treatment of Ana's family history, how it would fit in the narrative, but Javier found it fascinating. "I want more," he said.

When I finished *I Am Not a Monster*, I felt lost. Was it any good? Did the ending work? Did the story flow? Did it get stuck somewhere? After letting it sit for a while, I asked three friends to read it. Yolanda

Aguilar, Eva Tribiño, and Esther Barriga, I don't know how to thank you for the support you provided. You gave me wings. Without your caring and enthusiasm, I wouldn't have dared to fly.

But there was still one thing missing: someone to look at the mechanism, the structure, someone who could tell me whether the plot itself would work. A writer, in short. I sent the manuscript to Carmen Posadas. "Give me two weeks to read it," she answered. Then she didn't even give me time to get nervous. Ten days later, she sent me a long email that made me cry. I can never thank you enough, Carmen.

In the course of the journey that led to the book you're holding in your hands, I reencountered a good friend, Laura Santaflorentina, now turned literary agent, and her colleague Palmira Márquez. Infinite thanks to both of you for making my travel into this unknown territory so easy.

That voyage included the best references a writer could hope for, the jury of the Premio Primavera. Thanks to Carme Riera, Ana Rosa Semprún, Antonio Soler, Fernando Rodríguez-Lafuente, and Ramón Pernas for all the marvelous things you said about this book. Thanks for falling in love with this novel and for your caring and enthusiasm for the text. I'll never forget it.

The final push for *I Am Not a Monster* came from the magnificent crew at Espasa and Planeta, who have contributed all their passion and know-how. The enthusiasm of Carles Revés and Myriam Galaz dispelled all my fears. The work (up against deadlines!) of David Cebrián and his team of publicists could not have been better. And the magnificent cover by Ferran López brilliantly crowned the novel.

I extend thanks to others as well who helped me with vital information for the story.

To my friend the journalist and historian Xavier Riera, who taught me about Roman and medieval Barcelona, to provide location and atmosphere for Ana Arén's childhood home.

To Dr. Julio Mayol, Director of Medicine and Innovation at the San Carlos hospital and clinic and co-director of the Madrid-MIT M+Vision Consortium, through which I learned about the neuro-QWERTY project, which does in fact study means for early detection of Parkinson's by way of the manner in which we type on a keyboard. Thank you, Julio, for your generosity.

And to Renfe for technical information on the AVE train. Renfe's public relations director Elisa Carcelén Peña put me in touch with engineer Juan Carlos Luna, who patiently answered my questions about wheels, friction, and axles on the Spanish high-speed trains.

Thanks as well to those in whom I confided about this story before it became the book you're holding: Xavi, Silvia, Dolores, Alba, Patricia, Paloma, Pepa, Olga. And my mother and my brother, Xavi.

And always, and everywhere, a shout-out to music. I needed to feel the fear, anguish, vertigo, desperation, rage, and emptiness that destroy the characters. I wrote some of the most difficult scenes of this book while listening, on repeat, to Sílvia Pérez Cruz's prodigious version of "L'Hymne à l'amour." For many other parts of the story—and for so many other things in life—thanks to Bruce Springsteen, always.

I'd also like to thank those who made it possible for this book to appear in English, starting with my agent, Alexandra Templier, at Dos Passos; AmazonCrossing Senior Editor Elizabeth DeNoma; and translator Dick Cluster.

The final part is for you to write, dear reader. Thank you for believing in this novel. Thank you for buying literature, for reading, for giving books as gifts, for sharing them. Now *I Am Not a Monster* is in your hands.

I am not a monster.

—*Carme Chaparro*

ABOUT THE AUTHOR

Photo © 2017 Jotxo Cáceres / Groupon

Carme Chaparro is a journalist in charge of the main news editions of the Mediaset group, *Telecinco News* and *News on Cuatro*, programs for which she has covered the most important national and international events of the past two decades. Carme has combined her work in television with collaborations as a columnist for the magazines *Yo Dona*—in which she has a weekly column—*GQ*, and *Mujer Hoy*. *I Am Not a Monster* is her first novel.

ABOUT THE TRANSLATOR

Photo © 2017 Toby Sackton

Dick Cluster has been translating fiction and nonfiction from Latin America and Spain for twenty years, most recently Gabriela Alemán's *Poso Wells*, from Ecuador; Mylene Fernández-Pintado's *A Corner of the World*, from Cuba; and his own anthology *Kill the Ámpaya!: Best Latin American Baseball Fiction*. He is also a writer of history and fiction, including *The History of Havana* (with co-author Rafael Hernández) and a crime novel series featuring car mechanic and sometimes sleuth Alex Glauberman. He has been a translation mentor for the Banff International Literary Translation Centre, the Mills College MFA in Translation, and the Yiddish Book Center.